THE ORANGE WITCH

ORANGE STORM SERIES #2

NED MARCUS

ORANGE LOG PUBLISHING

Copyright © 2023 by Ned Marcus

1st edition (paperback)

ISBN 978-626-96929-0-3

All rights reserved.

No part of this book may be reproduced in any form or by any electronic or mechanical means, including information storage and retrieval systems, without written permission from the author, except for the use of brief quotations in a book review.

This book is a work of fiction. The characters, places and events are products of the author's imagination or have been used fictitiously and are not to be construed as real. Any resemblance to persons, living or dead, is entirely coincidental.

Published by Orange Log Publishing

Cover Design by Damonza

To my father

CONTENTS

Preface vii

Chapter 1	1
Chapter 2	8
Chapter 3	20
Chapter 4	27
Chapter 5	31
Chapter 6	35
Chapter 7	40
Chapter 8	46
Chapter 9	51
Chapter 10	55
Chapter 11	59
Chapter 12	67
Chapter 13	72
Chapter 14	76
Chapter 15	81
Chapter 16	87
Chapter 17	96
Chapter 18	105
Chapter 19	109
Chapter 20	114
Chapter 21	119
Chapter 22	124
Chapter 23	132
Chapter 24	137
Chapter 25	145
Chapter 26	151
Chapter 27	158
Chapter 28	166
Chapter 29	171
Chapter 30	179

Chapter 31	185
Chapter 32	194
Chapter 33	203
Chapter 34	210
Chapter 35	218
Chapter 36	222
Chapter 37	227
Chapter 38	237
Chapter 39	248
Chapter 40	253
Chapter 41	261
Chapter 42	270
Chapter 43	274
Chapter 44	279
Chapter 45	283
Chapter 46	291
Chapter 47	300
Chapter 48	304
Epilogue	317
Please Leave A Review	325
Books By Ned Marcus	327
Short Stories	329
Keep in touch!	331
About the Author	333
Acknowledgments	335

PREFACE

The Orange Witch is the second book in the Orange Storm duology, but it also follows on from the Blue Prometheus series. It could also be read as a standalone book, although some details relating to the characters would be missing.

1

A bell tolled in the ruined church as magic forced its way into the world. Inside, a door formed in the air; it could only be seen by the line of flames flickering around its edges. It opened, and a bright, fiery figure stepped through.

Lucy turned to the shimmering door, and with great care, wove the threads of energy together, sealing it tight. She had no wish to let that which lived inside the grey world of illusions escape. Alone, apart from a pair of doves that cooed from the wooden arches supporting the roof, she walked along the nave, sending a cloud of blue moths into the air. She was on Earth, but it felt different.

Why? she asked herself. *Why was I called? And why here?*

A shaft of sunlight shone down through an old stained glass window, depicting an angel. For a moment, she had the feeling that this church was a place of power. Perhaps it wasn't coincidental that she'd arrived here.

Slowly, she grounded herself, and her two magics faded. The tolling bell may have attracted unwanted attention; she needed to leave quickly. It was possible the aliens she'd seen six months earlier were here. She stepped through the broken church door and breathed the pure forest air. Opening her inner senses, she listened to the whispers of the forest. The flora and fauna of these woods came from several worlds.

But something else was amiss.

Beyond the outer edges of this exotic forest, a feeling of hopelessness ebbed and flowed. She closed her eyes, and slowly her mind sank deeper into the energetic fabric of the world.

She gasped.

Appearing as candles in the wind, she saw the souls of millions of people as flames flickering in pain. A sickness was spreading across the land.

Was this the reason she'd been called?

She opened her eyes. If the aliens were still active, they could be the cause.

Several flowers in the forest glade glowed in greeting, and a large yellow bird watched her from a branch. Britain had changed, but at least this part retained strength. There was a sense of goodness about it. She touched an orange flower, and it brightened in response. The forest resisted the sickness. Perhaps an alien graft like this was one part of the cure to the alien illness. She'd become part alien, too, though in a very different way.

The forest felt vibrations on its floor; she felt them, too. Something was moving towards her. Whispering to the plants in the True Language, they softened, and she slipped easily into the undergrowth. Something of the sentient ancient forest of Prometheus had come to Britain, and it seemed to have begun to communicate with the native trees. Their words were hard to hear. It was something to investigate later. For now, she waited, concealed in the forest.

Two men entered the glade. She sensed traces of magic

around them. It was the type the aliens used. There was no other way to tell from this distance because, on the outside, they were almost identical to humans.

Was this small magic reason enough to be called?

"The energy fluctuation came from the building," one said in the imperial language of the world she'd left behind.

They referred to the portal.

The alien men entered the ruined church. She needed ears inside and remembered the doves. Gently, she reached out to them in the True Language. They were simple animals, but they still thought in their own manner. She sent them feelings of peace and smiled when she saw their eyes watching her.

"An evil has entered your home."

It was the truth.

The male tilted his head questioningly.

She imagined the two men, imparting part of the feelings they exuded. The doves understood.

"Let me see."

The trust animals gave her often surprised Lucy, but she knew that it came, in part, from their ability to listen directly to her heart.

She saw through their eyes, blinking while she adjusted to the dove's rich colour vision. She now saw in shades of ultraviolet, too. The men were examining the wall near to where she'd entered this world.

"I need to hear, too."

The female remained in the nest with her two eggs. The male flew down to the pulpit, and through his ears, she listened to these lesser sorcerers.

"Alden, here," the stockier one said. "Something entered here."

The traces of magic leftover from the door would take

weeks to fade. Lucy felt his magic moving backwards and forward around where the door had opened. So, they were still searching for portals.

"What's wrong?" the stocky man asked.

Lucy realised that the other man was staring at her. Surely he couldn't see her? She now wished she'd asked the dove to choose a more discreet location from which to eavesdrop. Both men stared at the dove.

"That bird's strange."

"Fly!" Lucy commanded.

She was concerned for the dove's safety.

"Not home!"

It swerved in flight. She didn't want to bring danger to this innocent creature's partner or eggs. The dove landed on another of the wooden arches.

"It's just a bird."

Alden looked thoughtful. "She taught me how to steal a soul."

Lucy shivered. Two things were wrong. It was a dark form of magic; very few had the skill to take a living soul and place it inside an object, but the word 'she' disturbed her more. Lucy prayed that the 'she' the man referred to was not her old enemy, the empress of the world she'd left.

The stocky man seemed puzzled.

"Quinn, for all your skill, you've not understood the mysteries," Alden said.

"We've only got seven days. We can't waste time."

"She taught me to draw the soul from a living creature and place it in fluid," Alden said. He pulled a vial of ultraviolet fluid from his pocket. "If I put the bird's soul in this, I can read it. We can discover what happened."

Quinn shrugged. "It wouldn't last long in that."

"It'd last long enough for me to see through its eyes."

Now Lucy was worried. Not only would he kill the dove, he'd discover her. He may not pose a direct threat, but she didn't want her old enemy discovering she'd returned to Earth, if that was who they spoke of.

"Fly away!"

But it was too late. Alden had touched the mind of the bird. It fell to the ground, stunned. He hadn't sensed her presence yet, but only the most inept of sorcerers would not sense her once they entered deep enough. She felt the sorcerer tug the dove's spirit, and she shuddered at the sheer terror this small bird felt.

Lucy gasped as bright light flared inside the church. Alden screamed. Her connection with the dove was broken. Something terrible had happened.

She waited. Several minutes later, Alden staggered from the church. A bright red scar ran from his empty eye socket to his mouth; his shirt was bloody. She could smell his fear as he staggered alone along the forest path.

Lucy felt like fleeing, too.

What had these fools done?

She waited another ten minutes, but when nothing else emerged from the church, she walked towards it, ready to run at any moment.

Inside, it was as it'd been before, apart from the body on the floor. Near the alien man was the dove. Neither moved. Picking the damaged dove up in both hands, she felt a faint heartbeat. She sent healing energy into it; this was her first skill in magic.

"What happened?" she whispered.

The dove shared a vision of light, and in the light a figure looked down.

Lucy's skin tingled as she looked up. An angel watched her, power radiating from his body. She'd been right. The church had been consecrated by a priest of true power, and the evil that had been attempted within its walls had triggered its protection.

"Thank you," she said, unsure whether the angel was still there.

Lucy released the dove, which flew back to its nest.

Then another vision came to her. Three figures wrapped in black magic stood in darkness. In the middle, a woman radiated terrible power. Streams of magic poured from her. She had three souls that gave her demonic power: apart from her human face, a shrunken head grew from her neck, and a mouth in her belly chanted a dark spell. It was as she'd feared—she faced her old enemy.

"Give me strength," Lucy prayed.

She closed her eyes, not wishing to see any more, but the vision remained. Was the empress of the nine planets the source of the spiritual sickness? She knew she had to kill her. At least, banish her from this world.

"Well, well, the orange witch has returned."

Lucy started, turning to face the revived man. He spoke in the imperial language.

"That's what she calls me, but she's the true witch."

Quinn moved unsteadily on his feet. "What are you then?"

"Her enemy."

He laughed, but the effort was too much, and he fell against the pews.

"She's stronger than you."

It was true. Perhaps even her lieutenants were stronger than she was, but not this damaged man.

"Where is she?"

"I'll take you to her."

He lunged at her, and she let him pull her closer.

"You're not so tough."

She touched his heart.

"*Stop.*"

The man clutched his chest and stared at her with wide eyes before falling dead to the ground.

Lucy saw herself as a healer not a killer. She didn't want this, but as she dwelt in dark thoughts, light re-entered the church.

The bright angel stood before her. His voice vibrated with power.

"To withstand your enemy, you must first temper your soul."

This was something she already knew, although she struggled achieve it.

"Anything else?"

She dreaded his reply because she feared it could only increase the burden she carried.

"Call the third magic."

The third magic was a gift from above, rarely held by physical beings.

"How can I call this magic?"

"The knowledge is inside you, and the struggle to find it is part of the solution."

She shook her head at the terrible task before her. To face one of the darkest witches and her cohorts.

"My task is too dark."

"You're a sword of light, and needed. Find friends to help you. Have faith."

And then she was alone apart from the doves cooing in the rafters. She was thankful for the angel's words, but the thought of the task ahead felt like lead in her guts.

2

It was Saturday evening. Luke Lee stared out of the dirty classroom window at the slow-moving London traffic, momentarily forgetting his students' struggles to speak French. His life wasn't working. His wife, money, and previous career as psychologist and part-time linguist were gone. Even this job was temporary. The last teacher had left without warning, and the school was desperate. All he had was his son, William.

As a psychologist, he was aware of a nihilistic mood that had fallen over Britain. With the general election on Thursday, the new mood had given political pundits plenty to talk about. The left blamed the right, and the right blamed the left. He saw a mental contagion.

A student coughed.

He realised he hadn't spoken for several minutes. All the students were looking at him. He glanced at the clock on the wall behind them—forty minutes left. Forcing himself to look at the grammar exercise in the book, he began to speak but was interrupted by raised voices in the reception.

Forgetting his students again, he opened the classroom door and listened.

In the reception area, a man spoke with an alien accent.

"Is Dr Lee here?"

Luke chilled. He realised his naivety. He'd actually believed the news reports that everything was back to normal. It'd been six months since his shocking encounter with the aliens. The receptionist had no idea what she faced —on the outside, the aliens appeared to be human.

"You'll have to wait till nine o'clock."

Luke tried to calm himself. These men killed people who crossed them; he'd done more than that. His students were staring at him. He didn't care. What would happen to his son if anything happened to him? That one thought decided his action. He was leaving now.

"Take a break," he muttered.

Without further explanation, he walked out of the classroom, turned right, and walked to the fire exit. He pushed the horizontal bar on the door, but nothing happened. Quietly cursing, he shoved it hard, putting all his weight into it. The door flew open, slamming into the wall of the stairwell.

Footsteps approached.

Luke ran down the stairs, taking two steps at a time. He nearly slipped and had to slow down. By the time he'd reached the floor below, the alien man was already on the stairs.

"Dr Lee?"

On reaching the ground floor, Luke ran at the old exit, hitting it hard. It stiffly opened onto a narrow side street, and he ran towards the main road, praying that the man wouldn't see which way he turned.

"Come here, Dr Lee."

Luke felt a compulsion to obey, but he remembered what Amelia Blake had told him about the way they used mental suggestion to make people do what they wanted. She'd warned him against making eye contact with them, too. Still, he couldn't resist a quick glance. The man's eyes loomed in his vision, and a sense of dread paralysed him. He noticed nothing else about him.

"We know where you live."

A chill pervaded his body. Could it be true? These people lied whenever it suited them. He now struggled to move his sluggish limbs.

"You're come with me."

The alien's poor grammar snapped Luke from the hold he'd been gaining over his mind. Luke immediately sprinted towards Stockwell tube station. A minute later, he ran under the flickering fluorescent lights above the entrance to the station. It was dark, and he hoped the man hadn't seen him enter. As he glided down the escalator, Luke glanced back. A man dressed in a black suit walked onto the escalator above him. He was staring into his phone. Luke realised he remembered nothing about the man apart from the sound of his voice and his eyes. At this distance, the man's eyes were impossible to see.

The man didn't seem to be paying him any attention. Luke relaxed a little. Fumbling for his phone, he called Amelia. She was a member of MI7, the secret agency dealing with the alien incursion. If he'd made a different decision six months earlier, he'd now be part of their team, too.

There was no answer. He reached the bottom of the escalator feeling desperate and walked quickly towards the platform. He called again.

This time, she answered.

"Amelia, I have a problem—"

"Slow down, Luke. What's happened?"

He spoke between gasps. "The aliens are back—"

"We know," Amelia said quietly. "Luke, are you okay?"

He explained what had happened, then said, "They may have William."

"Are you sure they know where you live? Your address was hidden."

"They found me at the school."

"A few language schools in London have reported strangers with threatening behaviour. They may have randomly been trying to find you."

"Why?"

"Like it or not, you have connections to us. And who else speaks their language?"

"I started training a few intelligence officers—"

"They can't match your knowledge."

"Should I approach the police?" he asked, noticing a member of the British Transport Police on the stairs.

"The police have no idea about aliens in the UK. This is classified information. They don't even know we exist." She paused for a second. "I'm worried that they may have been compromised."

Luke felt his life descending into chaos again. "Help me get William!"

He walked onto the platform.

Amelia spoke to someone else, then her voice returned. "We'll send a team to your house."

She hung up.

When the train rumbled into the station, the man in the black suit appeared further down the platform. He was still staring at his screen. Luke entered and sat in the nearest seat. The man sat in the next section. Luke pretended to look at his phone, but he watched the man from the corner of his eyes. His hands were shaking, and he couldn't help but notice that the man's hands were twice as thick as his. The train stopped at Clapham North. A woman got on.

He'd taken up martial arts on a friend's suggestion, but six months karate didn't make him a fighter. He'd changed a lot, but Luke knew his limits, and although his anger made him want to challenge the man, fear, incapacity, and uncertainty stopped him. The aliens were capable of killing a man in seconds, and he knew he couldn't put up a good fight. It was also possible he was wrong. Perhaps the man wasn't an alien. Luke convinced himself it was wisest to wait; dying today wouldn't help William, and his stop was next.

The platform at Clapham Common was empty. Luke waited a few seconds after the train stopped, then left the train just before the doors closed and walked to the escalator. He didn't look back until he reached the booking hall.

The man in the black suit was following him.

Luke tried to pretend he wasn't terrified, but it wasn't true. His hands were trembling. He walked fast to the turnstiles, noticing a member of the British Transport Police watching him.

He couldn't run too soon because if the man was an alien, he'd outrun him. Although they looked human, they had a different anatomy and physiology. As Luke walked up the final flight of stairs, he hoped he could lose the man in the streets of Clapham. He broke into a run at the final steps, and the man sprinted after him. This was real. He ran into the night, still unsure who the man was, cutting down an alley, then taking a series of turns, hoping to lose him. He reached the only main road he had to cross and almost screamed in frustration. Two lanes of traffic moved steadily in each direction.

Someone shouted.

Turning, Luke saw the man in the black suit running towards him. He ran so fast it was uncanny, knocking a passerby to the ground.

Luke ran into the moving traffic, causing cars to brake as he slowly weaved his way across the road, ignoring the blasts of horns. One driver actually accelerated at him, bumping into his legs. The car still moved forward, forcing Luke to change direction and loop around it. The passenger wound down the window and threw the remains of a drink at him while the driver shouted obscenities. It was too much. Luke slapped the surprised passenger in his face as he passed. He shocked himself, too. This wasn't the person he was. Or perhaps it was. With his son threatened, his perspective had changed.

Seconds later, Luke reached the other side and sprinted down one of the smaller streets. Five minutes later, he reached the street where he lived. All was quiet, and for the first time that evening, he felt more relaxed. Too exhausted to run, he walked to his house. He stopped outside to glance back, but couldn't see anyone.

Luke hurried inside, relieved when William gurgled happily to see him. He picked his son up, only then noticing the babysitter giving him a strange look.

"Are you okay?"

Luke nodded. He knew he'd have to move home again. He didn't think the man had seen him enter; he might not even be an alien, but they knew where he worked. Finding out where he lived wouldn't take that long.

Someone banged on the door. The babysitter went to answer.

"Leave it!" he said.

"Dr Lee, what's wrong?"

He didn't want to say too much. "Someone followed me from the Tube."

"You should call the police."

"Police! Open the door!"

Luke had to restrain his babysitter from unlocking the door.

"You can't stop me leaving."

"It's not safe," Luke said.

"It's the police," she said, looking bewildered.

He needed to hear the man speak more before he could decide that. The door shuddered in its frame.

"He's kicking it!" the babysitter exclaimed.

Splinters fell to the floor, and a hole appeared in the door. Whoever was kicking was strong. Then the door burst open. The man's eyes pinned Luke to the wall behind him, and the babysitter screamed at the gun in his hand. He shot her. Luke tried to speak, but felt his throat constrict. He couldn't breathe.

"I have some questions, Dr Lee." Now the alien accent was clear.

Luke gasped as the pressure against his throat lessened. William stared at his father in shock.

"Tell me about the psychic."

He was talking about Amelia Blake, the woman who had fought the aliens by his side.

"What about her?"

"What's she done?"

The question surprised him.

"She's called something into this world," the alien said.

"What?" Luke was confused.

The man watched him carefully, perhaps to see if he was speaking the truth.

"How many of you speak our language?"

Luke shrugged. "I don't know."

The alien looked at William. "Tell me what I want to know or I'll hurt your son."

William was now crying in his arms.

"Let me put my son down."

The alien agreed, and Luke put William in the high chair the babysitter had placed next to the old vase by the front door.

"Now tell me!"

"Seven," he said, hardly remembering how many people he'd trained. He didn't add that they weren't very good.

Luke moved back, almost knocking the vase over, but the man followed, pushing his pistol in his face.

"Now, tell me—"

Police sirens sounded outside, and for a moment, the man was distracted. The fuzziness left Luke's mind. He hit the alien in his head with his favourite vase, then managed to pull the pistol away. The alien laughed.

Luke shot him.

"That won't help you, Dr Lee."

Luke backed through the door, taking William in one arm. He fired again. The man must be wearing protective clothing, although he knew they had toughened skin, too. He rushed down the stairs two steps at a time, pausing outside one of the flats to shoot the alien. A red-faced man stared at him through a crack in the door. Luke had always disliked this neighbour. He ran downstairs; the alien followed. Opening the front door, Luke fired again as he ran out.

"We'll be in touch," the alien said.

Luke shot him in his back as he walked along the ground-floor hall towards the back door. He kept firing until he ran out of bullets, and a police officer tackled him.

"My son!"

He fell on his elbows, trying not to crush William. Two police cars with lights flashing were outside his house. Several neighbours gathered to watch the scene; his red-faced neighbour soon joined them.

"Dr Lee, you're under arrest," the officer said, dragging him outside.

A second police officer pulled William away from him, while another roughly handcuffed his hands behind his back. A fourth officer, a police sergeant, watched the house.

"Stop the man leaving through the back door," Luke said. "He murdered the babysitter." He was desperate to protect William. "Give me my son."

Two of the officers entered the building; they were both armed. Minutes later, one returned.

"There's a body in Dr Lee's flat."

"What happened, Dr Lee?" the police sergeant asked Luke.

"A man broke into my flat and murdered her." Luke tried to point but couldn't move his hands. "He's getting away. Catch him!"

"We saw you shooting inside the building. We didn't see another man."

"He's getting away."

"Well, we've got you. You'll have plenty of time to tell us what happened at the police station. If there's someone else, we'll find him later."

A white car stopped on the opposite side of the road. A tall woman got out and walked towards the police sergeant.

"Officer, I'm from the social services. I have a care order for Luke Lee's son, William Lee." She showed him a piece of paper.

Luke noticed the police officer's eyes cloud over. Something strange was happening.

The police officer nodded. "Give her the child," he told the officer holding William.

"No!" Luke shouted. "I've never harmed my son."

"We have full reports on your family situation, including your missing wife, Dr Lee," the woman said. "Everything's in order."

"Nothing's in order. I'd never hurt my son. This is insane." If her accent hadn't been so good, he'd have assumed that she was one of the aliens, too. They must have called the social services and somehow entered misinformation into the system.

William looked at his father.

"Give me my son!"

"Your son is in good hands."

Luke felt sick.

"You're coming with me to the police station."

When the officer gave the baby to the woman, Luke rushed at her, but one of the police officers tripped him. He hit the ground hard. Blood flowed from his nose, and he saw stars. Some of his neighbours laughed. Feeling lightheaded, he struggled to get up with his hands behind his back.

"She's stealing my son!"

"Actions have consequences, Dr Lee," the sergeant said. "You, of all people, should know that."

"I've not done anything."

The woman looked down at him.

"I think the danger to your child is clear," she said.

"I've never hurt him!" he repeated.

For a second, she smirked. Her nostrils flared, and with the flashing blue lights of the police cars, Luke saw a small set of gills briefly flutter.

"Alien!"

The woman glared at him. "How dare you?" She walked towards her car, taking his son with her.

Luke struggled to his feet and tried to follow, but was restrained.

"He was on the news last year," his red-faced neighbour said. "Murdered dozens of people. He should be locked up."

The man was an idiot.

He shut up when a red Mini Cooper raced around the corner. The police officers stared at the speeding car, and the sergeant stepped into the road, raising his hand. He cursed when the Mini almost hit him. It stopped by the alien woman. A man and a woman got out.

MI7 had come.

Luke held his breath as he watched Amelia pull his son free.

"Help!" the alien shouted, struggling as Jack forced her arm behind her back.

The sergeant strode towards Jack. In alarm, Luke watched the alien woman reach inside her jacket with her free hand.

"Jack!" Luke shouted.

Jack drew his pistol and shot her in the back of her head. She was dead before she hit the ground, her pistol clattering onto the tarmac. The police sergeant stopped and stared at the gun. The armed officers standing behind him hesitated, seeming unsure whether to fire. Surely even the police would find it suspicious that a woman working for the social services was carrying a pistol.

Seconds later, Jack jumped into the Mini Cooper. Amelia applied her rally-driving skills, and the car accelerated down the road, took a hard right, and was gone, taking William with them. There was silence in front of his house.

Luke closed his eyes in relief. He didn't care what happened to him. William was safe.

"Who's Jack?" the sergeant asked.

Luke remained silent as he looked at the dead alien lying on the road. The crowd of neighbours stared at him in shock. One of the police officers was busy reporting the kidnapping and killing. The sergeant asked more questions, but Luke said nothing. A minute later, they shoved him roughly into the back of a police car.

3

Luke listened to the police sergeant berate him.

"You're not above the law."

The Security Service had called. After three hours in a police cell, he was free.

"The killer left by the back door."

"There're no other prints on the gun."

"They've altered their fingers."

Luke didn't know if it was true, but he knew the alien prints wouldn't be recognised as fingerprints. He left the police station. Forty minutes later, he was in Amelia's plush second-floor Pimlico flat, relaxing on the settee. William was safe asleep upstairs.

Luke watched a party political broadcast. It showed incidents of rage from around London. The scene switched to the studio, where the rising star of politics, Eva Noone, argued that the increase in despondency and depression in Britain, as well as the increase in random acts of violence, was caused by the blinkered policies of the present government, which she promised to fix.

"The people are in pain," Noone said.

Luke turned down the volume when Amelia passed him a beer.

"She's appeared from nowhere," Amelia said. "Six months ago, no one had heard of her. The media are suggesting she might have a place in the cabinet."

Luke nodded. But his mind was not on next week's general election.

"Why did you join MI7?"

"The Security Service contacted me," Amelia said. "Actually, it was Jack. The threat is increasing."

She looked serious, and although William was now safe in this fortress-like building, he was still worried.

"We have many problems the public don't know about, and my skills help."

"The killer asked about you," Luke said.

Amelia was immediately alert. "And?"

"He asked what you've called into the world. He seemed upset."

She went quiet.

"Amelia?"

"I think the orange witch is here."

He remembered how Amelia had summoned an alien witch from another universe. She'd burnt the carpet the first time Amelia had called her; the second time the witch had reached through her and killed one of the aliens.

"Has anyone seen her?" he asked.

"A single sighting of a woman with burning orange eyes in the alien zone." She paused, sipping her spiced rum. "I think the alien killer's right. I'm worried that I opened a way for her to enter."

"You don't know that."

"Not for sure, no."

"At least you're annoying them," he said.

"We try. We've killed several aliens already."

"Not arrested?"

She shook her head. "Unofficially, the government see this as a war. We've lost territory, and that's really upset senior ministers, although they're presenting it as an ecological disaster. Also, the aliens aren't easy to take alive."

He looked around her flat.

"Do all intelligence officers have such posh accommodation?"

Amelia smiled. "We have the whole building, but only a handful of intelligence officers. Originally, they'd planned to hire more."

"What happened?"

"There's official resistance to our existence, let alone expansion. We're seen as too strange and too independent."

She took another sip of rum.

"That said, MI7 has a position open for an expert in alien languages and psychology. It's yours, if you want."

He smiled. "I'm not sure I'm an expert."

"You're the best speaker of their language we have. And you know more than most about their psychology. We could do with some help."

He already knew his decision. His academic career was finished, and he was barely scraping by. London rent was high. And he feared that William was still in danger.

"I accept."

Amelia didn't seem surprised. She detailed the role he'd play, and some benefits, including a flat upstairs and a nanny for William. It took a lot of the burden from him.

"You'll need to carry a pistol."

He raised his eyebrows, surprised that intelligence officers for MI7 were permitted to carry guns.

"The danger is very real," she said.

"Do we have a license to kill?"

"Only aliens. And only if there's no other choice. Is fear of losing William the only reason you want to join?"

He shook his head. "No, but it's a big one." He knew they must be stopped. He looked directly at Amelia. "Do we know their plans?"

She shook her head. "We were hoping you could help us with that. The linguists we've got are not up to the job."

"Do you have any recordings?"

"Some." She paused while she thought. "We're assuming they still want to find a way home, and that they may want to bring something back with them. It was important to them last time. It's critical we discover how they might do this. Last time, the method was explosive."

"Another device?"

"Perhaps." She took another drink.

She was drinking more than normal and was clearly stressed.

"Luke, I may have made a mistake when I summoned the witch."

"That's not true. She saved your life, remember? Anyway, it's too late to worry about it."

"You're right, but I still worry about what I've unleashed on the world. We still have no idea what she is. Jack thinks she may belong to an alternative faction of aliens."

"Do you?"

She shrugged. "I don't think she's with the aliens we've met so far, but it's possible there's another faction."

The thought was not appealing to Luke.

"I'm worried that she'll make the situation worse," she continued. "Her power scares me. Even if she fights the aliens, the cure may be worse than the sickness."

If Luke hadn't seen magic with his own eyes, he wouldn't

have believed it, but he still found it hard to comprehend the level of threat it actually posed.

"I thought she was in another universe?"

"She was."

"Did you bring her here?"

"No, I think she found her own way. But I attracted her attention." Amelia looked at her empty glass, then changing her mind, she poured a glass of water.

"The desert's no longer a desert."

It'd been a desert when he'd last seen it. "Where did it go?"

"The northern rain had some effect."

Luke smiled.

"When the sand blew into our world, it brought new life with it. The seeds, and whatever else was in the sandstorm, have taken to our world."

"Alien?"

She nodded. "Flora and fauna. Ruth's having a field day. Mostly it's the former, but wolves have appeared."

"In north-west England?"

"I know. And the oases have turned into dense forests. Three of them."

"What's between them?" He asked.

"Grassland, but the forests seem to be growing towards each other." She paused to think. "Ruth knows more than me, but she said the wild animals are a problem."

"Why? I mean, they're just animals."

Amelia's brow wrinkled in concentration. "They're hard to kill."

"Even with modern weapons?" he asked.

She nodded. "If a new government's elected, they're going to be very surprised at what's hidden behind the wall in Cheshire."

"They don't know?"

She shook her head. "Not much."

That the animals were so hard to kill disturbed Luke a little. He was silent, remembering the blue demon that had fallen from the sky six months earlier. It had been almost impossible to defeat.

"Magic's new to me, too," Amelia said. "I'm psychic, but this is something else…" Her words faded. "You were around magic."

Luke nodded. "Do you think the portal may still be open?"

Amelia frowned. "I just don't know. I pray not because we really don't need more strange things coming through from another universe."

"I've seen the border wall on the news," he said.

"There's a border force, too," Amelia said. "Chief Inspector Gully's in charge. He spends most of his time there."

"Gully?" Luke remembered the man cowering on the top of the tower. "And he's been promoted?"

She nodded. "He's not an easy man to work with." She paused. "There's something else, too. The forests aren't friendly."

He almost laughed. "Not friendly? What does that mean? They're just forests." He quickly corrected himself. "Apart from the alien lifeforms."

"The wolves are dangerous," she said. "They're bigger than our wolves. But that's not what I meant. The northern forest is by far the worst, but they all give off a strange feeling."

"What kind of feeling?" Luke asked.

"A sense of foreboding."

Luke listened carefully. "I've been feeling that, too. Even

the news this morning said a new feeling of pessimism is sweeping the country."

"We're aware of it," she said, "but I'm not sure it's the same. The country is feeling despondent and depressed. The forests radiate fear."

4

It was late and Amelia yawned. Luke had returned to his new flat, just two storeys above hers. She wanted to go to bed, but before she slept, she was determined to speak to her spirit guides. She bolted the door. Pimlico House was built like a fortress, but she still worried about what the alien magicians and their servants might do.

Minutes later Amelia lay on her bed. Although she'd never imagined it possible, she now questioned the motives of her guides. She'd always believed they wanted the best for her. Now she wondered whether they had 'higher' objectives, and that in the larger scheme of the universe, she was a tiny cog, or perhaps just the oil that ran between the cogs.

With trepidation, she closed her eyes and altered her breathing. She'd done this many times, and a minute later, her mind left her body. A desert formed around her. The heat was intense, and the air burnt her lungs. A sandstorm blew towards her. Within it, seven figures loomed. Her stomach sank slightly. The number of guides varied, depending on circumstances, but usually it was around four. If there were seven, then it might mean that Viktor, the warrior leader, had returned. He made her feel uncomfortable.

They stood before her in a semicircle. She was right; Viktor stood in the centre wearing his black metal armour. His sword was by his side. To his left was Teal—also a warrior. She wore her brown leather armour and sword. Next to her was the sombre Ernest. Victoria, formerly her chief guide, stood to Viktor's right. Next to her stood the androgynous figure of an angel. Sam rarely appeared and was usually silent, but today he whispered to Victoria. Two other guides, ones who appeared in times of great need, stood like sentinels at either end of the semicircle.

Amelia realised she was shaking.

Victoria spoke first. *"We're only permitted to tell you so much. You need to experience events as they unfold if you're to effect a profound change."*

"Well, tell me something." She didn't like the sound of profound change. "I need help."

"The forces against you are incredibly strong," Viktor said. *"We're doing what we can in the background, but any change we can bring about is small."*

Amelia felt deflated.

"Can you tell me anything about the orange witch?" Amelia asked. "I think I've made a bad mistake by summoning her. Her power is terrible."

"Her enemy is more deadly," Teal said. *"And her enemy is yours."*

Amelia suddenly didn't want to be there in that scorching desert talking to these spirits; she'd rather be anyplace else.

"Why is she here?"

"To remove life that persists beyond its natural time—life that refuses to die," Ernest said.

Amelia shuddered.

"Is she human?"

Her guides silently watched her. Amelia forced herself to continue, wanting to get any information she could squeeze out of them.

"The life she's come to take..." she hesitated, feeling light-headed in the heat, *"you mean the aliens, right?"*

Again they didn't answer.

Ernest stepped forward through the sandstorm. *"Support her!"*

"Even if she kills?"

"Yes," Ernest said.

Amelia trembled as the sandstorm swirled around her guides and they started to fade from sight. She expected to return to her body, but for the first time since she'd begun to consult with her guides, she felt stuck. For a moment, she thought she was in quicksand, but she didn't sink, she just couldn't move. Panic began to set in.

"Victoria!"

There was no answer, yet she remained in the desert.

A solitary figure surrounded by a bright aura walked towards her. It was Sam. She watched the androgynous form of the angel approach.

"It's been a long time since we've spoken," Amelia said, remembering the few words the angel had once spoken.

Sam smiled and the chill left Amelia.

"I only speak when I have something to say that your other guides cannot," the angel said.

"Can you tell me more about the orange witch?"

The angel was silent for several seconds before speaking. *"Death brings new life."*

Amelia didn't want philosophy.

"Can you help me?"

"When you're in darkness, speak my name. I will come and give you strength."

Her anxiety began to subside. Then the angel spoke again.

"Return to your body! Luke is in peril. Find him!"

The angel vanished, and she was again in her flat in Pimlico.

"Luke!"

She sat up on her bed, feeling dizzy.

Her phone beeped. It was a text message from Luke.

"I couldn't sleep. I've gone home to pick some things up and look for clues."

She left her flat feeling a sense of dread.

5

An energetic web vibrated around Lucy. Invisible to most, she saw it clearly. It was the fundamental energy of the universe, but here in the forest, it was stronger. Perhaps that was why the sickness she'd sensed beyond the forest had little effect here. Disturbances in this web alerted her to movement around her. The breath of every animal vibrated its threads, however slightly. As did powerful intention.

Lucy looked up. Although she couldn't see the animal, she knew she was being watched. Two bright orange eyes burnt in her mind. A predator. Not having time for forest animals, she returned her attention to the hidden energetic world.

The remnants of two portals had left their signature in the forest. The older one, created by the aliens' machines, had almost vanished. The more recent one in the church was diminishing. She'd closed it, and soon it'd be hard to open without a key. She'd learnt more about the portals to other worlds during her dark journey between the universes and now knew why she could open and close them with magic alone, while her enemies, despite their power, could not.

Natural magic, the most human of all magics, was the key. But her primal magic of fire provided the raw power she needed to push open the unlocked portals. She doubted if even one sentient being per galaxy possessed this knowledge. The aliens' contempt for the softness and simplicity of natural magic, and their intelligent fear of the dangerous primal magic that lies locked deep within all life, had limited their power in this area. Lucy shuddered to think what would happen if the empress and her cohorts gained access to the multiverse, and learnt how to traverse it at will.

The predator moved.

It was stalking her. It was inconvenient because she wanted to locate portals beyond the forest in order to determine whether any were ajar, and therefore likely to be targeted by the aliens. She doubted if they could even see a portal that had been closed for any significant amount of time. The animal moved closer, pushing through the undergrowth. Lucy sensed intense pain and realised she had to communicate with it. She touched its mind; it growled.

Her eyes widened in surprise. It was a glimmer leopard. These animals only came from Prometheus. They were bigger than normal leopards and breathed fire. They also had the ability to change colour at will. With complete confidence, it walked up to Lucy. Its power was intense. But it was curious, too, perhaps recognising her as a kindred spirit.

Lucy's eyes glowed as she spoke. *"What's your name?"*

An image of a dart appeared in her mind, accompanied by a soft sound.

"Darta?"

She snarled her approval, some of the tension leaving

the big cat. Lucy smiled when Darta admired her eyes. They stood facing each other. The panther was almost Lucy's height, and her skin glowed with bright spots that appeared and disappeared. She pushed her head against Lucy's chest.

"Show me your life."

Images and emotions rushed through her mind. She saw the jungle where she'd had been born. She saw Darta playing with her siblings on the day she'd been captured, then she saw her captors kill her mother and felt her hatred. The cruel training that followed made Lucy feel sick.

"I've come to kill them!" Lucy whispered.

Darta made a small cry and pushed her head harder against Lucy, and as she did so, her spots glowed brighter. Lucy stroked her neck, sharing images and emotions of her life in that same jungle. Lucy knew the animal's true nature; she saw many of the things she'd done. Creatures such as this didn't know embarrassment; she just showed Lucy the important events in her life. Some were bloody. Darta had adopted her, and for good or for bad, they'd bonded. And she knew what that meant for an animal like this. A glimmer leopard was special, even on the planet of Blue Prometheus.

Lucy had many questions, but she had to carefully frame them using sense impressions and feelings that the panther would understand. She imagined the forest around them. Darta listened carefully; this was her domain. Then Lucy imagined the edge of the forest and looked beyond it. After several attempts, Darta showed her grassland and another forest to the west. Glimmer leopards, for all their ferocity, were sensitive, too. Darta had noticed an open portal there but kept away from it. Lucy kept pushing, and she showed a boundary wall. The authorities must have built a wall to contain what was inside; she didn't blame them.

"And?" she pushed.

There was something the leopard didn't want to reveal, which was unusual with this sort of animal. They seldom kept secrets, but Lucy knew she'd been abused as a cub.

"Show me."

A third forest flickered briefly in her mind, then it disappeared. Lucy felt a sense of dread. She understood Darta's reluctance. She sensed dark magic.

"Have you been there?"

Darta's mind turned to hunting, and when Lucy tried to push, she growled. Lucy stopped, not wanting to distress the animal. However, she already knew she had to visit the northern forest. Darta overheard her thought and became agitated. An image of a man appeared in her mind. He seemed to live alone in the west wood. Darta was trying to distract her, and it was working. She was curious about the man.

"Who is he?"

She didn't expect a name and didn't get one, but she did see a collage of images. Darta had spent time with this man, and the more she watched, the more she understood. The man appeared to be a mercenary. He'd worked for her enemy but was now alone. Darta felt loyalty to him. Encouraged by her interest, the panther shared images of their hunting trips together—except that the prey was human. The man was a paid killer. That didn't bode well for his character, but if she were to succeed, she needed someone capable of killing. She decided to meet him, too, but first she wanted to visit the mysterious northern woods.

6

Luke couldn't sleep. Lying in bed, he remembered he'd left some of William's toys at his old flat. He needed to pick them up, as well as some of his son's clothes. It was three in the morning, and nobody would see him enter. He got up. Perhaps he could find some clues that could help him learn more about the aliens. Something the police had missed.

Having finally persuaded himself that it was a good idea, Luke left Pimlico House. He wore a jacket that he'd found in his new wardrobe. It fitted well. It was as if they'd expected him to join. Under his jacket, he wore a holster with pistol. He'd learnt to shoot during the last alien attack, but doubted he'd need to use it in the early hours of the morning.

He called a taxi. When he arrived, the road outside his old home was quiet. Opening the front door of the building, he walked up the four flights of stairs to his old flat. Police tape covered the entrance; the broken door hung loosely on one hinge. He carefully removed some of the tape and stepped inside. He turned on the lights.

The floor was strewn with objects. Luke frowned. It was as if someone had searched the flat since he'd last visited. He walked through the other rooms. Each one was a mess, except for the bathroom, which appeared untouched. He gathered some of William's toys.

"I thought you'd come back."

Luke turned. His red-faced neighbour stood in the doorway.

"I've called the police."

"What?"

Luke tried to understand what the man was talking about. The last time he'd seen him, he'd been cowering behind the garden wall during the shooting of the alien.

"She told me you'd arranged to have your son kidnapped."

"Who?"

"Your ex-wife. She was here a few hours ago. Told me that the police are after you. How did you escape?"

"I didn't escape. What did this woman look like?"

The man gave a cold laugh. "Don't know your own wife?"

Luke chilled. He couldn't be talking about Molly.

"What did she look like?" he repeated.

"Tall blonde."

Molly had dark hair. The aliens had been here. It made sense from the mess in his flat. Now he wondered about the wisdom of returning.

"She asked me to keep an eye on it. Asked me to tell her if you came back."

"You idiot! She's not my wife. She's part of a criminal gang."

"Then it's just as well that I called the police first."

Luke realised he'd already wasted too much time.

"Get out of my flat!"

The man grinned. He was enjoying this. Didn't he have anything better to do? Perhaps he really thought he was performing a public service, but Luke didn't want another fight.

"Get out!"

The man had squeezed through the tape and walked towards Luke.

"I'm going to perform a citizen's arrest."

Luke pulled out his pistol.

His neighbour's eyes widened.

"Out!" he shouted.

"The police are coming." The man was already backing away.

Luke searched for anything the aliens may have dropped or taken on their second visit. Ten minutes later, he'd almost given up. They'd left nothing.

"We need to speak to you."

Two police constables stood on the other side of the doorway. They were both armed.

"Put your gun on the ground."

"I'm allowed to carry it," Luke said.

No explanation satisfied them, and he put the pistol on the floor. His neighbour watched from the stairs leading up to the next floor. Two minutes later, the police were examining his ID.

"Is this real?" one asked.

"Call your police station and ask," Luke said.

"I will."

After a short conversation, the constable returned his ID and handed back his pistol.

"I'm sorry. I didn't know who you were."

The other officer looked a little disappointed.

"Do you need any help here?"

Luke shook his head.

The police left the flat. Luke heard them tell his neighbour not to call them again. And then they were gone. He just needed to find a few more things. He soon filled the bag he'd brought. He sat on one of his favourite wooden chairs, debating whether he'd like to have it in his new place. He'd already texted Amelia to tell her where he was, just in case she needed to speak to him, and he was about to leave when he heard a voice coming from the stairs, and he sighed. Didn't his neighbour have anything better to do?

Realising he was finished, Luke stood and reached for his bag, but stopped abruptly. The alien in the black suit pushed through the tape into his living room.

"Dr Lee."

Luke took out his pistol and pointed it at him. The man grinned.

"Put that away, Dr Lee."

He stepped forward, and Luke fired. The man staggered back a pace, but then stepped forward again. Luke fired three more times before the man knocked the gun from his hand and pushed him onto the settee.

"That's a toy for children."

He took out a larger gun and slapped Luke's face with the barrel. He felt blood dripping down his cheek.

"Come with me, Dr Lee!"

Something clicked in the passage outside his flat. The man looked confused. Blood came from his mouth. He fell to the ground—a hole in the back of his head. Luke's eyes widened as a shadow moved in the darkened hallway.

Amelia Blake stepped into the room holding a pistol with a silencer as long as her forearm.

She ripped the jacket from the man's torso.

"Special alien protection."

She tossed it to him.

"We have to leave. Now!"

7
———

Darta pawed her, not liking her decision.

"I must," Lucy said.

The leopard pushed her head against her again. She realised this dangerous animal was alone; glimmer leopards were only partially solitary, and while the man had been a companion of sorts, he hadn't satisfied her needs.

Minutes later, they ran together silently through the forest, and then into the grassland beyond. Trees were growing there, too. The forests were expanding. It was already night, perhaps not the best time to enter what Darta seemed to believe was a haunted forest.

Two hours later, they were within sight of the northern forest. A bird screeched. Lucy was familiar with forest worlds, where each forest was like a tribal unit with its own character. This was the darkest she'd encountered.

"It's not normal," she said.

Darta shared a mental image of them running towards the western wood.

It wasn't fair to keep her here.

"Go to the western forest. I'll come to you soon; I want to meet the man."

Darta sat and waited.

Lucy would have to enter; the black panther—she'd lost her spots—would leave once she'd gone. The forest's energy was uneven. It seemed divided; two distinct feelings washed over her. Neither was comforting, and both were far stranger than the atmosphere around the church. That was a blend of two or more universes; this one was alien in a different way. It almost felt as if it had fallen directly from the grey shadowy world between universes. Praying it was not so, she walked right up to the edge. Dagger-like trees with curved blades growing from their trunks blocked the way. Normally, she just asked, and plants would soften their branches, allowing her to pass through. These formed a rigid ring. Howls came from within. Worried, she turned to Darta.

"*Go!*"

Darta sensed her urgency and ran towards the west forest. Seconds later, she'd disappeared into the night. Lucy returned her attention to the forest, this time her mind moved deeper into it. She heard the cracks and moans of trees and sensed magic. Scores of red burning eyes looked from the forest in the direction Darta had taken.

Night wolves.

Incanting a spell of invisibility, she faded from sight. When it worked properly, she ceased to exist in the minds of all creatures around her, but the stiff trees stubbornly barred her way with their razor blade protrusions. When she asked them to move, they mocked her with clicks as the blades snapped together.

One of the night wolves pushed out of the forest and stared in her direction. Its red eyes brightened; her heart beat hard. These had been altered by magic. Despite her skills, a pack of these things would rip her apart. More night wolves stepped from the forest; the bigger ones were the size of ponies. While most of them stared along the path Darta had taken, another night wolf turned to look at her. It growled.

She had seconds to act. If more of them took an interest in the strangeness they sensed at the edge of the forest, she'd be dead. Trying not to freeze, she again focussed her mind on nothingness. They sniffed the air and stepped towards her. She realised her mistake. They couldn't see or hear her, but she'd forgotten scent. Silently, she incanted no smell, but they still crept towards her. Altering the direction of her magic, she instead imagined the smell of the surrounding trees. She became one of them in her mind, and, it seemed, the mind of the wolves. The two wolves appeared confused. One of them barked.

A blue demon stepped from the trees. It turned towards her, searching for something. A sawing sound panthers made came from the long grass, distracting it. Darta had remained.

"Thank you," Lucy whispered. *"But go!"*

The demon and the wolves turned towards the new sound, and she feared for Darta's life. Night wolves bayed in excitement, more of them running from the forest. The two night wolves nearest to her rejoined the pack.

"Run!"

Darta rushed through the tall grass. The night wolves charged after her.

Lucy returned her attention to the forest. The dagger trees were not fooled when she pretended to be one of them. When she imagined herself as a wolf with its scent and wild anger, their branches parted a little, but it was still hard. Perhaps she needed something more forceful. Martial magic was not her skill, but she knew some tricks, a few of which had saved her life. Calling her primal fire magic, her hand turned into a fiery blade. She thrust it into the stubborn branches. They immediately opened, and she entered the forest.

Heat engulfed her. It was a tropical forest. At least the interior was easier to move through than the tight outer barrier. She knew it'd been grown intentionally, but she wasn't sure if it was the forest protecting itself or something inside, intent on keeping strangers out.

Clouds of insects rose as she moved through the vegetation. The disguise she'd adopted did nothing to stop them from biting her, and she felt their joy at the softness of her skin. In order to maintain the disguise, she had to feign the hatred and bitterness of the wolves. Too much of this would sicken her, but it was the only way to move through this hostile territory. A dog barked. Hiding behind a tree, she waited. A few minutes later, a small pack of dogs, their fur patterned with dark zigzags, trotted past, unaware of her presence.

Another strangeness of this forest was the location of the portal. Usually, she literally felt the open portals pulsing, but this time it was different. It moved, and sometimes it disappeared completely. Normally, she'd just walk directly to the nearest portal, but now she was unsure what to do. For a second, she wondered what she'd got herself into. The attitude of the trees was consistently hostile, and matching her feelings with them was becoming harder.

A dagger tree discharged one of its blade-like pieces of wood, almost stabbing her. She immediately slashed the tree with a fiery hand. That stopped it. She picked up the curved blade it'd flung at her, and with the fire that leapt from the pores on her fingertips, she burnt its root into something approximating a handle. She'd just acquired a deadly blade.

Instead of imitating the hatred of the trees, she allowed the fire to rage inside her. It was less tiring, but also dangerous. Primal magic needed feeding and created intense hunger, and she no longer had enough fat on her body to satisfy it. A second and greater danger was that the fire fed on itself and could easily burn out of control. Once, it'd scarred her body, but now she had more control. She was no longer completely human—no human could bear this burden. Strangely, the changes to her body no longer bothered her.

Looking back, she realised she'd left smoking tracks behind her, but at least there were four of them. Her magic burnt as if she were a wolf. For a moment, she didn't care about being too easy to track, but she knew that was an arrogance brought about by the power that flowed through her. Not useful if she wanted to remain concealed. At least the trees that had been most hostile now bent their branches to let her pass unhindered. Even the notoriously difficult whipping vines did no more than quiver as she passed.

Suddenly, the forest went quiet. She stopped. A subtle magical barrier blocked her way. Gently, she tested it. It stung as she pushed her hand through, but on the other side, it was cool and damp. She stepped through into a temperate forest; ferns and oaks surrounded her, and a streamlet flowed by her feet.

Something moaned.

Feeling uncomfortable, but still drawn towards the sound, she followed the small stream. Eventually, she reached a moaning marsh. Mist drifted over its surface. The sound seemed to come from the water or something in it.

Squatting by the shore, she drank. The fire burning within her turned the water into steaming vapour, instantly purifying it. She drank until she'd quenched her thirst and managed to catch a small fish, but it didn't satisfy her. When a tall spiky plant lashed out, she pulled it up and ate it, too.

The food allowed her to concentrate. The portal had gone. She was sure it'd been here. Still, her intuition told her to continue walking along the shore. Alert to danger, she walked slowly, taking the time to eat any appetising plants that strayed too close to her or attempted to block her way. When a cloud of blue flies tried to bite her, she sucked them in with a low level magical charm. Even the fire in her mouth and stomach couldn't disguise their foul taste, but she needed energy.

In some places, the water appeared shallow, and she was half-tempted to cross it, but when she listened carefully to the vibrations, she instantly knew it was a bad idea. The bottom of the marsh was only feet beneath the surface, but it was quicksand, containing life of its own. She continued until she reached a path that stretched out into the marsh. She walked along it, straining to see through the mist that hung over the water.

Something was happening further along the path. She smelt magic. Strengthening her disguise, she pushed into a bed of reeds. She wanted to watch unobserved. The vegetation stung, but she forgot her pain when something softly screamed.

8

A girl with pale blue skin backed away from a disfigured demon. The demon was short, but something else was odd. Lucy found it difficult to focus her eyes on its body. Its skin seemed to shift and shimmer. Watching carefully, she started to suspect an illusion. It seemed to have wrapped itself with energy, creating the appearance of a demon. She tried but failed to penetrate its disguise. Although she couldn't see through its disguise, she could see the nature of the disguise. Her nose wrinkled in disgust. It'd collected jars of stolen souls and hung them around its body. The souls writhed inside the jars. It was using their life energy to power its magic. She had a good idea what it planned to collect from this blue-skinned girl.

Lucy already knew what she had to do. Pulling out her blade, she stepped closer and stabbed it in its back. Anything working with this sort of black magic was beyond saving. Leaving the knife stuck in it, she turned her hands into fire blades and cut the entities from its body. It screamed as they popped and vanished. Then it fell to the ground.

Curious, she watched as the disguise faded. A man lay dead on the ground. His empty eye socket and the bright red scar across his face identified him as Alden—the alien from the church. His corpse still grasped a vial of liquid.

The girl stood unsteadily, seemingly unsure what she was looking at. She was short, only reaching Lucy's chest, and definitely not human. But she was undeniably beautiful. Lucy had met a variety of non-humans and guessed that the blue watery girl was a water elemental—a nymph.

A voice spoke in her mind. It wasn't the girl.

"Why does a dragon wander my marsh disguised as a dog?"

Lucy turned to face another water elemental. She was taller than the first, almost reaching Lucy's shoulders. She radiated magic.

"Actually, I'm a wolf," she said, slightly aggrieved that her disguise was so easy to see through.

The woman's laugh sounded like water bubbling in a brook. *"Wolves don't walk on two legs."*

Lucy let her disguise drop, but unable to fully control her primal magic, she blazed in the form of the fiery witch.

The young nymph recoiled, but the older one watched her through a pair of eyes that looked like turquoise stones, beautiful but blank, apart from a light that glittered deep within.

"What are you?"

"Dragon," Lucy answered immediately. She was part dragon, at least.

The nymph shook her head. *"No, you're something more."*

Lucy studied the subtle weaving of magic around the woman. She was incredibly beautiful but dangerous, with the same smooth watery blue skin as the younger one. Power radiated from her in patterns, both attracting and repulsing her. It was impossible to determine her age.

The young nymph said something.

"She thanks you for saving her life," the woman said.

Then the girl slipped into the water and disappeared.

"Who are you?" Lucy asked.

"The queen of this realm."

Lucy sensed danger and felt the need to choose her words carefully.

"At first, I thought you were a fire elemental," the queen said. *"I nearly killed you for trespass. But you killed the ally of my enemy. That's worth thanks."*

The queen continued to study her, and Lucy felt as if she could literally see through her.

"You're part human, too. Very interesting."

As the queen spoke, several nymphs pushed their heads above the surface to watch Lucy.

"Why are you here?"

"To kill an alien sorceress. She spreads sickness through the land—."

The queen's eyes brightened dangerously.

"I know."

"And I need to close the portals," Lucy said. *"They give power to my enemy."*

The queen regarded her quietly, her turquoise eyes shining. The queen spoke to her nymphs, but Lucy heard nothing more than the sound of gurgling water. It was rare that she couldn't eavesdrop on a telepathic conversation.

"We will help you," the queen said.

"Why?"

This was too easy, and Lucy was nervous about enlisting the help of elementals. You needed to understand their terms.

"Demons encroach on my realm. Your enemy," she glanced at the corpse, *"has joined with mine to destroy me. They've*

made a big mistake. And now I've met you, my method for closing the portal has arrived. You will preserve life in my realm."

Lucy wondered what this queen wasn't saying. But with a magical creature like this, searching for deception was almost impossible.

"Where's the portal? I can usually sense them, but this time it's masked," Lucy said.

"It's hidden in the underground palace of Tavth." The queen's eyes brightened as she spoke.

"Tavth?"

"A demon that calls itself king." The queen paused, considering her words. *"Your alien enemy is playing with things it shouldn't. When the door between worlds opened, my realm flowed into this world; I moved with the water and my nymphs. But other things slipped in, too."*

"If I close the door, you won't be able to return," Lucy said.

"We lived here once before," the queen said, *"in a time before humans or dragons. Our mistake was leaving in the first place. The problem is not being here, it's the things that slipped through with us."*

Lucy wondered what would happen if she removed the queen's enemies. She noticed that more of the nymphs were now watching her from the marsh.

"To enter his palace, you must disguise yourself again," the queen said.

"I know."

"Not as a night wolf. He doesn't allow them inside; you must become a painted dog."

Lucy had seen the dogs in the forest; in some ways, they seemed easier to copy than the night wolves.

The queen described his palace and occupants. It had two entrances, and they were guarded. The main entrance seemed more difficult, being protected by a species of blue demon. The second passed through a ruined chapel.

"*There's an alien sorcerer with the demons,*" the queen said. "*The one you killed was a novice, but the one with Tavth has considerable power.*" The blue nymph looked at her. "*Perhaps more than you.*"

Lucy suspected it was one of her enemy's lieutenants.

The queen held out a glass vial. It contained a pale blue liquid.

"*A gift. It may help you live.*"

"*What is it?*" Lucy asked.

"*Running water from my realm.*"

The water inside slowly swirled around the vial.

"*It has two properties. Drink it and it will alter your body; you'll become like a water nymph, flowing into any body of water nearby. The effects only last for a short time.*"

"*And the second property?*"

"*It heals sickness. This stream leads back to the demons' domain,*" the queen said, pointing to a small stream nearby.

Her form altered, and she flowed into the lake as a streamlet of blue. The other nymphs had vanished.

9

It was early on Sunday morning, and Amelia couldn't sleep. She thought about the man she'd killed; he was an alien, but still a man. She'd changed so much. As a nurse, she was used to death; now she dealt in it. It was the only feasible option. Her mind turned to her fears that the aliens were infiltrating British society. Intelligence reports suggested they mixed with the rich and powerful, including politicians. She looked at the clock. In a few hours, a driver would take them to the alien zone up north.

Sitting up in bed, she turned on the TV. More coverage of Thursday's general election. She was about to change channels when Eva Noone, one of the new candidates for Parliament, appeared. She was wearing a hat that looked like a hummingbird hovering over an exotic desert flower. The media swooned over these new style politicians who made their presence felt on social media in a way that traditional British politicians didn't. Apart from their use of social media, and their wit, which they displayed on TV every day, their unmistakable sartorial style made them stand out amongst other candidates. Hats had started to come back into fashion.

Eva Noone, in particular, made Amelia uncomfortable —nauseous would be a better description. She'd not had this feeling since being trapped in the tower in the middle of Shakerley Mere. The woman had come into public consciousness at about the same time. It was strange, too, that Eva Noone had stood for and won the East Cheshire seat made vacant after the murder of Leander Amis, the previous home secretary. Part of her constituency was now located inside the alien zone. Eva Noone was not only expected to retain her seat in the House of Commons, her name was also being put forward for a position in the cabinet.

Amelia turned the TV off.

Was she simply reacting to the woman's politics? She wasn't sure. A few new candidates for the opposition had a similar effect. Fearful that her feelings were more than simple feelings, she wondered whether the aliens had infiltrated British politics? Were these newcomers aliens? When she'd mentioned the possibility of alien interference in British politics, no one had seemed concerned.

She couldn't ask her guides. They'd made that clear, but that didn't mean she couldn't explore herself. Psychically prying on people was unethical, but she believed she had strong enough reasons to allow for some spying. After all, she was a member of MI7. She thought it through. There was a real danger, especially if Eva Noone was really more than she seemed, but Amelia was an experienced astral traveller. She was confident in her ability to get out fast, if she had to.

Closing her eyes, she calmed herself and altered her

breathing. Slowly, she left the physical world behind and moved her consciousness beyond her body. The image of Eva Noone appeared in her mind and served as a compass. She moved quickly to another place. The astral home of Eva Noone rose before her. A little surprised by its grandeur, the astral homes of most people were modest houses, Amelia moved closer. It was a dark, shiny mansion surrounded by manicured lawns. A sense of foreboding washed over her, and she considered leaving, but it wouldn't do any harm to look a little more closely.

Amelia climbed over the wall into the garden. It was technically trespassing, but she'd walked close by the astral homes of people before. It shouldn't be dangerous. She decided to walk around the outside of the house to get a better feel for it. A curtain in an upstairs window drew back.

Amelia stopped.

Someone stared at her. A shiver ran down her spine. That had never happened before. Most people were unaware of their astral homes; they just existed in people's dreams, places people unconsciously withdrew to in times of stress. The curtain fell back in place; she then realised that all the curtains were drawn. At the very least, Eva Noone was an accomplished psychic, and perhaps more.

Amelia considered leaving at once, but the garden was peaceful. Then she noticed a small dog watching her from the porch.

"Hello."

The dog growled and grew in size. Its aura darkened, and its eyes turned red. It crept towards her, and she backed towards the wall. Then it charged, and she turned and fled, leaping over the wall. It followed on the other side. The garden turned into a patch of wildly growing black flowers that hissed at her. The hiss then turned to a high-pitched scream. Something flew from the garden, slapping her in her head.

Amelia woke in a cold sweat.

10

Lucy pushed through the energetic barrier at the edge of the queen's realm. The heat of the demon world rolled over her like a wave. She breathed deeply, orienting herself to the hostile environment. As her body adjusted, she considered her meeting with the queen. It'd been too easy. It was likely the queen hadn't told her everything, and whatever she'd left out could be important.

An insect bit her. She swiped it away and concentrated on her appearance. Disguising herself as a painted dog was harder than she'd imagined, and she wished she'd paid more attention to their bodily proportions and complex colouring when she'd seen them earlier. She chose the easier option, resuming her disguise as a night wolf. Instantly, the malevolence and nausea natural to them returned. She ran towards barks in the distance. The armoured vegetation let her pass, but reluctantly; she felt its resentment to life.

Time felt slower as a wolf, but eventually she reached a lichen-covered mound rising from the forest floor. She watched from the edge of a clearing in the forest. It appeared to be the remains of the half-buried mansion the queen had described. Groups of blue demons gathered around the main entrance to the underground palace, playing gambling games with stones. Heaps of painted dogs slept on the dome above them. The night wolves were in the trees.

This wasn't dangerous; it was suicidal. She crept backwards and began her search for the second entrance. Now she'd seen the painted dogs more clearly, she created a mental image of the bat-eared creatures with their exotically painted fur, and slowly her appearance changed. The nausea left her but was replaced by anger and even greater resentment. She doubted that the painted dogs were more favoured than the wolves; it was more likely the latter were kept away from the palace because of their ferocity and the small amount of magic that infused them.

She walked through thick vegetation, angrily, burning it away with fiery hands, before realising she'd absorbed the resentful nature of the painted dogs more deeply than she'd intended. She didn't care, wanting only to get out of this place.

According to the queen, the second entrance was no more than a hundred yards from the main entrance; she simply had to walk in a circle around it—hopefully meeting nothing on the way. Ten minutes later, she stopped. A ruined tower rose from the ground. To the right, the sloping roof of the buried chapel was just visible beneath a green covering of vegetation. From the top of the tower, a pair of painted dogs stared down and growled.

There was no way back now; this was the test of her magic. One side of the tower had collapsed, leaving a rough stairway of rubble. Lucy ran straight towards the pair of painted dogs barking. They backed away, growling. They were scared and about to attack, but she needed to know more.

"What's wrong?"

Smells filled her mind.

I smell wrong. Lucy felt annoyed; it was the second time she'd made the same mistake.

They were frightened, and that triggered her fear. Before they could bark, fire poured involuntarily from her mouth. One died instantly. The other whimpered by her feet; it was badly injured. She'd acted instinctively. Calming herself, she touched the dying dog, easing its pain. Then, closing her eyes, she sank into its canine mind. As she'd hoped, its mind was connected to the pack, and their desires washed around her. She'd entered their dreams. Within the dream, they turned to watch her. Some approached her, pushing their snouts against her, sniffing and probing, almost playful. For a few seconds, she saw them as they could be.

Then she withdrew. The painted dog watched her.

"I'm sorry," she said.

"I feel peace." Then the dog died.

From the few seconds she'd spent inside its mind, she knew that the life of a painted dog was unremittingly hard. Only their close bond, and the few moments play that they sometimes found, sustained them.

Reaching the bottom of the stairs, she walked into the interior of the ruined chapel. Two shafts of light came from the broken roof above, partially illuminating the dozens of painted dogs lying on the ground. Several watched her pass, then one approached her. It was a white-muzzled dog, and she allowed it to nuzzle her. A pair of painted dogs pushed against her legs. She suspected she'd not completely copied the energy of the dogs, and that something of her old self remained—something that was missing from their world.

She walked towards the altar, her mind still deep within the dreaming mind of the painted dogs. A door to her right was closed. She opened it with her human hand and slipped through; a few of the dogs tilted their heads as they stared at her. She didn't wait for further reactions, and quickly shut the door behind her.

A long wooden-panelled corridor stretched out before her. Maintaining her disguise, she walked along it. Soon the little light there was faded. Unable to see, she sensed her way by listening to the earth and stones around her. It was a long time since she'd had to do this. The wooden panelling on the walls had burst in places, allowing sandy earth to pile inside. As she felt her way along. The collapsed passageway became more constricted, and for the first time since she'd entered, she felt the pulsing portal. It was somewhere above her. The passage widened. Broken tables lay around a large chamber. In front of her was a wall of earth. It looked like part of the building had collapsed under the weight of the earth above. To her right, what had once been a grand staircase, swept up. She began to climb.

Shafts of blue, orange, and red light cast patterns on the stairs, but it was the sounds that unnerved her. Screeches, snaps, snarls, and demonic laughter came from a room at the top of the stairs. Something screamed, followed by howls of laughter. She almost faltered in her resolve to enter this hell, but the portal was in a room somewhere just beyond the top of the stairs. She started when something inside the room shrieked. Then, slowing her breathing to calm herself, she crept towards the demon court.

11

Something moved in the darkness at the top of the stairs. Lucy's heart beat rapidly, and for several minutes, she didn't move. The dirt on the stairs indicated they were hardly used, but something was there. It smelt like a wolf.

Dropping the disguise of a painted dog, she shifted her thoughts and feelings to match those of a night wolf, but began to doubt herself. Perhaps she'd been wrong. Nothing had moved for minutes. Perhaps the smell came from the room beyond. Stepping forward again, she'd almost reached the top when it moved again. An old wolf watched her from the top of the stairs. She smelt blood, realising that her magic had caused a more profound change than she'd thought—she'd attained a wolf's sense of smell. It was bleeding from its hind leg. Strengthening her disguise, she reached towards it with her mind, sensing hatred, but curiosity, too.

"Why are you here?" she asked.

"I could ask the same," it answered. She moved closer, and it sniffed her. *"You're a strange wolf."*

"So I've been told."

It sniggered.

"And you're not a good guard dog," she said, not completely understanding its lack of reaction.

"I'm dead."

It was then Lucy noticed the chain.

She was tempted to ask it why it spoke so well. It seemed more intelligent than it should be; she suspected magic, but she didn't want to give herself away. Another scream came from the room beyond the door.

"Unless you want to die with me, I suggest you go back the way you came."

Lucy had an idea. *"I need to know the layout of the throne room."*

"Why?"

"I want to close the portal."

The night wolf stared at her. She sensed confusion.

"I fight Tavth. I want to make you an offer."

The wolf sniffed her again. *"You're not what you seem."*

"That might help you."

"I'm going to die very soon, so say what you have to."

She'd made her decision.

"I can snap your chains. You can die fighting."

It looked away; it didn't believe her.

"I mean it."

She touched his hind leg, immediately becoming closer to the wolf, sealing the wound with healing energy. His eyes widened in surprise.

"What are you?" he asked.

"We have no time." She whispered, worried that whatever was in the room next door could overhear thoughts, too.

Footsteps approached the door.

"Why do this?" he asked.

"I've already said. I want to close the portal. If you fight by my side, I may be able to do it."

"Then we die together."

The doorknob began to turn as Lucy grasped the chains, and with a powerful blast of fire, broke them in half. The wolf was free.

"The portal is in the centre of the room, for what good it will do you. Fight with me instead!"

"I have to close it," she said. She could already feel her fire rising.

The door opened, and turquoise light poured onto the top of the stairs. A blue demon looked at them from an adjoining room. It looked confused. She could almost see it think, and before the night wolf could move, she sent two jets of fire into its chest. The wolf finished it off.

A demon in the throne room issued an order to the dead creature next to them. Lucy ripped a bone horn from its side. She had a vague idea of using it to cause a distraction. When a second demon came to look, they rushed into the throne room. Lucy's fire almost cut it in half.

"Impressive," the wolf said.

The demon king sat on a tattered velvet upholstered armchair, watching two female demons with curved horns and perfect blue skin dancing in front of it. The king's horns were straight. Dozens of demons were drinking, hooting, and laughing. Lucy's gaze drifted to the man next to him. She chilled. An alien sorcerer looked back at her, showing no surprise. The pressure of magic coming from him almost overwhelmed her.

The night wolf attacked a demon guard standing by the throne. The king turned to it. But then, a blue demon pointed at her and uttered some obscene-sounding curse. The dancers slowly stopped dancing, and the demon musicians turned to watch the intruders.

"What are unchained wolves doing in my throne room?" King Tavth's voice boomed.

Searching for the portal, Lucy almost faltered when she saw what was in the middle of the room. The portal was a giant shimmering turtle. It was alive, malevolent, and it watched her.

"Why didn't you tell me?" she whispered.

The distant queen heard.

"It may have affected your resolve," the queen whispered.

"How can I deal with a living portal?"

"I don't know," the queen said. Her voice becoming faint.

"You don't know?" Lucy repeated.

She felt like blasting the faerie queen with fire. Desperately, she ran towards the turtle. This was not what she'd expected.

"No one knows how to control it."

Then the queen of the nymphs was gone.

"Great," Lucy muttered.

She wondered what other things the faerie queen had conveniently forgotten to tell her. She sent a stream of fire into a demon that got in her way.

In a semicircle behind the turtle, a choir of shorter black and blue demons chanted spells of spiritual malaise. So the sickness was coming from several places. And the portal that was the turtle seemed to amplify it. Behind them, glints of light came from the upper parts of broken windows, and water flowed from the forest into a gully that ran along the ground. She was beneath the grassy mound in the woods. The giant turtle possessed its own magic, too, snapping as she approached. This was getting complicated.

"I'm a friend."

It spat a globule of corrosive substance, only just missing her as she leapt out of the way.

"Take the dogs alive!" Tavth roared. *"I want to know the meaning of this!"*

She had seconds to sort this out. The old wolf was giving her time. He was near the row of thrones and surrounded by three demons; one of them was bleeding badly. He fought fiercely. The turtle snapped at her again, and she made sure to keep her distance. Without a spare moment, she pushed straight into its cold mind. It immediately tried to cast her out.

"What?" The alien sorcerer stood; he'd sensed what she was doing.

As she stared at the turtle's shell, she had a strange feeling of vertigo; the turtle's back glimmered, and she saw glimpses of other worlds. One was peaceful and green. The turtle's shell was the portal. Slapping its head away with a fiery hand, she stepped right up to the creature. Touching it, she sensed the crack along its back. Through that gap lay a familiar green forest from another world. She was drawn to the peacefulness of the world, but her mission here was unfinished.

Two large demons, one blue, the other orange, grabbed hold of her. The demon king's laughter reverberated around the throne room. Two more demons dragged the badly injured night wolf to her side.

"Sorry," she said.

"It was fun," the wolf said. *"And you're no night wolf."*

"She's not," the alien sorcerer said, invading their minds with his speech.

It was a long time since anyone had been able to do that to Lucy. She desperately tried to maintain her disguise, sinking her thoughts deeper into her mind. As long as they didn't know what she was, she retained the smallest chance. Sparks of magic flew from the demon and man stinging her like a swarm of hornets. She breathed fire, burning them.

"What is she?" Tavth said.

"Half human, and half something else," the sorcerer said.

The king seemed surprised, but Lucy's thoughts were on the portal. She had to find a way to operate it; she could probably do it from where she was, if she could think of how to do it.

"Can you transport yourself through your own portal?" she whispered in the deepest level of True Language she could manage.

The snapping turtle looked at her.

"Would I be here if I could?"

Her stomach dropped. She couldn't die now, with her mission still unfinished. If she died, the empress would twist the world, turning it into her personal playground. She planned a last blast of fire. That was reserved for the sorcerer. Then she'd be depleted unless she got away from the morose band of demons and their depressing chant.

"Save your final blast of fire for me, half-dragon," the turtle whispered in her mind. She glanced at the sorcerer and the king. Neither seemed to have heard.

"Why?" she asked.

"To break the bonds that hold my shell shut and open a way for me to go."

Lucy's eyes widened. What she'd thought were lines decorating the turtle's shell were fine bonds that held it shut.

"I just need to turn around," she said, struggling with the blue demon that now held her.

"It's no use," the night wolf said.

"The wolf's right," Tavth said.

The blue demon holding her screeched and staggered; steam rose from it. The turtle had spat a burning substance onto its back. She pushed it away and ran to the turtle, her fire already rising.

"Stop her!" the sorcerer shouted.

"There's nothing she can do, Mr Alistair Walker," the king said.

She burnt the bonds on the back of the turtle, and its shell snapped wide open. The segments of the shell seemed to project an open portal before it, sending a shock wave into the demonic choir chanting by the broken windows. It crushed the first three rows of the choir and knocked Lucy to the ground. The turtle leapt through the portal. For a second, Lucy saw that green world again. And then the door slammed shut; the living portal was gone. A howl rose from Tavth and his demonic followers.

The choir was in disarray, and the amplifying effect of the portal had disappeared. Lucy breathed deeply in relief —some of her energy returning. Although still weak, she sent a jet of fire at the orange demon still holding her wolf ally. It was a poor attempt, but the demon was surprised enough to let go.

"Follow me!" she said as she ran across the room.

The wolf ran to her side, but the demons blocked the only entrance and exit to the throne room. Lucy backed into a wall. She felt a small stream of water was running down her back. Her eyes darted around her, looking for another option. Seeing none, she turned to face the sorcerer and demonic horde.

"We're trapped," the wolf said, *"but I never expected my death to be such fun."*

"I have a plan."

The wolf looked at her questioningly. She took out the vial of blue liquid.

"Drink a drop and you'll flow into the water that falls from the forest."

The night wolf backed away. "I prefer to die fighting."

"I need an ally to help me escape."

"How can I help if I'm flowing water?"

"You'll change back."

The demons advanced; this time they were intent on murder, and Lucy knew that if it came to a fight right then, both she and the wolf lacked the strength to survive.

"You can save the pack."

She had no idea if it was true. She took the first drop of blue liquid and offered the second. The wolf hesitated, but a dart in his side convinced him. He took the second drop.

"Nothing's happening," he said.

Then Lucy felt her body changing; the queen hadn't lied about that. She flowed into the water. The night wolf gave a mournful moan.

"Swim upstream!" she said.

Then her world turned completely blue.

12

Lucy swam along the streamlet towards the trees. She sensed the changed form of the wolf following her. Then her body began to solidify. She crawled out of the water and lay on the bank, gasping for breath. She was human again. Her hunger and tiredness had gone.

The night wolf scrambled out of the stream next to her, vomiting water from his stomach. Anger radiated from him.

"Better to die than that," the wolf said.

"You're alive," Lucy replied, returning to her wolf disguise.

"I'm no longer wolf."

Lucy studied the night wolf.

"You're a wolf," she said. *"And the dart's gone."*

"I'm softer," he growled.

"The water of the nymphs," she said. *"It's healed you of demon sickness."*

"What you call sickness, I call strength."

The wolf was right, in part. The experience of becoming a flowing form left her feeling more peaceful. At least, she was alive, but she worried that her urgency to escape had seeped out with the watery magic. She shook the water from her own body, surprised to find she still held the bone horn; perhaps she'd find a use for it.

"*We have to leave before they begin searching for us,*" she said, trying to convince herself that it was true.

She looked around the forest. The green palace was about twenty yards away, but she didn't see anyone coming after them yet. Still, they needed to act quickly.

The wolf didn't move.

"*If you stay, Tavth will kill you.*"

"Better for me," he growled.

"*There's no time for this.*"

She turned and ran deeper into the forest. As she moved, her old energy returned. The wolf followed. After a few moments running, the sound of painted dogs baying reached her ears, causing her adrenaline to spike. From what she could tell, they were still near the green mound.

"*They're waiting for their king,*" the wolf said. "*Then they'll hunt us.*"

"*Then we need to leave the forest,*" she said.

"*My pack's here. If we leave, we weaken.*"

"*You mean Tavth's magic will weaken; your pack will strengthen.*"

The wolf was quiet as they ran through the trees.

"*Perhaps. I feel strength returning.*"

The sound of painted dogs racing through the trees, accompanied by the shouts of demons, was growing louder behind them. Her heartbeat raced, and she welcomed her feeling of fear.

"Without their demon masters, the dogs are nothing," the wolf said.

They ran faster, her adrenaline flowing freely, giving her

the sense of urgency she needed to survive. Fire flew from her, spouting from the pores in her skin.

"What's the plan?" the wolf asked.

"First, find the pack."

Her fear had turned to anger, which radiated from her as heat. She followed the wolf deeper into the forest; he glanced back at her.

"Better," he said.

He seemed to have recovered his former energy, too. She tried to maintain the appearance of a night wolf, but looking down she saw lines of orange fire spreading across her body. Some wolves appeared the same, but she was no longer copying them; her primal magic was taking over. One danger of the primal energy that now flowed through her was that it could lower the level of consciousness unless balanced with the more human natural magic. Her primal magic was making her more animal, but for now she needed its energy.

A horn sounded behind them.

The wolf bared his teeth. *"The king's horn."*

Her fear returned, driving her forward and distracting her from her surroundings. Her only thought was to escape. She ran straight into a blue demon, almost choking on the putrid smell.

"Out of my way, dog!" it shouted.

It seemed her disguise was working again. The demon grabbed her by her throat and threw her away. She ran back to it and touched it, telling its heart to stop, but that just made it angry. Perhaps she'd touched the wrong place; she knew nothing about demon physiology. She tried again, this time adding fire. It staggered back, grasping its chest, and fell into a tree, staring at her in surprise. Then she had an idea. She copied the demon's outer form. The two blue demons stared at each other before the real one fainted.

With the demon dealt with, Lucy followed the wolf into a small clearing by a stream. About fifty night wolves lay on the ground. As soon as they saw her and the wolf, they stood. Some growled at her.

"They're not happy to see one of your kind," the wolf said.

"Would they be happy to see what I really am?"

"Unlikely, though I'm not sure what you really are."

"Will they obey me?"

"You're a lower-class demon," he said. *"If you had orange stripes on your face, they may."*

She rubbed her face, and slowly fiery orange lines appeared. They made no difference to the mood of the wolves.

"A little help would be handy right now," she said.

"We hunt!" he said to the pack of night wolves.

They waited.

She raised the bone horn she'd stolen in the demon king's palace and blew it. The wolves howled.

"Tavth will hear," the wolf muttered.

She shrugged. There was nothing she could do. *"I need to ride from the forest."*

She could hear the painted dogs howling become more frenzied as they realised where she was. The sounds of pursuit grew louder as the dogs and demons neared.

"Ride me."

Tavth appeared through the trees fifty yards away. The sorcerer Walker ran with him. Unfortunately, her enemies were not out-of-shape leaders so common in the human world. Glancing down at herself, she mostly still appeared as a blue and orange demon, but she was already failing in some areas. Bursts of fire escaped from her back and the top of her head. Raising the horn to her lips again, she blew. The wolves around her responded with bays and howls, not seeming to notice that she wasn't their real master. With some trepidation, she mounted the old wolf, jumping and pulling herself up. Howling like a demon, she led the pack through the forest.

"To the west forest," she said.

The wolves took routes through the forest that only they knew. The old wolf was strong and fast and led the pack with ease. Even the fire that sometimes burst from her pores didn't seem to bother him. His own skin was cracked and fire seeped from the gaps. He was more magic than she'd first thought, and she hoped she was right that leaving the forest would not harm them. She felt the wolf's fire, but she now burnt inside and out, and no longer cared about such things; she knew the person she'd once been would have been shocked.

"What's your name?" she asked.

"Tallis," the wolf said.

They left the forest and raced onto the grasslands, Lucy's red hair flowing behind her as she led the wolves through the night.

13

Luke sat in his expensive Pimlico flat but took no satisfaction from it. It was just after midnight on Sunday morning. He had orders to go up north and was waiting for the driver to arrive. No one had told him the reason, but he knew it wouldn't be good.

While he waited, he played the audio recording again. His knowledge of the alien language was increasing, but despite playing it several times, he only just got the gist. Some things stood out, though. Dates and times were amongst the first things he'd learnt, and he heard two references to Friday. One part of the recording referred to Sunday morning. Now. He played that part several times. A code was given in English. He hadn't recognised it at first; the alien mispronounced the English badly. There was another word that sounded English. Something like zoo.

He stared at his computer for several minutes. The time mentioned in the audio had just passed.

"Zoo, zoo, zoo," he repeated as he thought.

"Zoom?"

He opened the app and typed in the code. Seconds later,

he was in a Zoom meeting. He started recording the meeting on his phone. Praying he wouldn't be noticed, he held his breath. It did no good. Someone spoke to him in the alien language. He agreed without understanding to what.

A man laughed.

So far, so good. He waited and the conversation continued. None of the participants had turned their video on, which was very good. He listened to the alien Zoom session, recognising the words crystal and machine. Putting the two together reminded him of the strange apparatus that had destroyed a row of houses six months earlier in Battersea.

A man asked a question. The other speakers went quiet. He asked again. Hoping the man wasn't speaking to him, Luke tried to translate. It was something about quality. But of what?

"Crystals!" the man said forcefully.

He recognised that word. So they were speaking about a crystal machine, and something was happening on Friday.

The intercom buzzed.

"Good quality," Luke said. He was painfully aware that his alien accent was not the best, especially his pronunciation of new vocabulary.

Several other participants spoke at once, then one of them switched to English.

"Who are you?"

The intercom buzzed again.

Luke felt nauseous. He thought about the food he'd eaten in the past five or six hours, but he couldn't think of anything strange. He definitely felt light-headed and was about to close the app when his vision dimmed. A small head floated in front of him. He backed away, but it followed. Its breath stank of rotten meat.

"I know you."

It was speaking to him. Luke became dizzy with fear, his legs giving way under him. He fell back onto his chair. Something buzzed in the background, but he couldn't respond. He just wanted to keep this thing away from him.

He felt hands touch him.

"Luke?"

Amelia stood next to him; she was shining with white light, a bright sword in her hand.

"Fight it!" she said.

He tried to push the thing away, and Amelia's sword flashed before his eyes. Then everything went dark.

"Luke?"

He opened his eyes. He was lying on the carpet in his living room.

"What happened?" he asked weakly.

"You were attacked." She looked at him closely. "I only just arrived in time. I entered your mind. They nearly killed you."

He realised that the buzzing had been her trying to get into the flat. Luke sat up slowly, groaning with the effort. He pressed a hand to his head, hoping it would stop the throbbing.

"I was eavesdropping on their Zoom meeting, and they found out I wasn't one of them. What did they do?"

"A psychic attack," she said. "They're stronger than before."

Luke felt truly shaken. This was something he hadn't expected. Slowly, another memory came back to him and he looked at Amelia in a new light.

"You had a sword."

She nodded. "I wasn't sure if you'd see me. I surprised them."

"Is this normal for them?"

"You made a connection. If this happens again, break the connection immediately. Slam the computer shut."

"Will that be enough?"

"If you shut it before they enter your mind, yes. If they've already entered but not taken control, it may weaken their connection."

The buzzer rang again.

"We have to go to the alien zone," she said.

Luke's stomach sank. If the aliens could do this in London, what could they do in territory they controlled?

14

Lucy dropped all pretence of disguise as she mentally joined the pack. The wolves were excited.

"*We hunt,*" she whispered, slipping into a cold sweat despite the fire within.

"*Why did I say that?*"

Tallis chuckled in her mind. "*You're closer to us than you think.*"

He was right. She was unsure whether it was a good idea. Yes, she was hungry, but what if there was nothing to hunt? What if life in the western wood was peaceful?

"*What have I unleashed?*"

"*We hunt,*" Tallis said. "*You couldn't have stopped us anyway; it's better this way.*"

"*You speak the True Language well for a wolf.*"

This was something she'd been wondering since she'd met them.

"*Magic changed us. The disgusting liquid you dropped in my mouth changed me, too. I'll never fit in the pack again.*"

"*A leader is always slightly apart.*"

They ran quietly and with intent through the dark grass-

The Orange Witch

land. None of the wolves knew anything about the western forest—only that it existed. She knew only a little more. It was the closest of the three forests to the border wall. It had more human patrols than the northern or southern forests, and the human assassin lived there. The forest loomed closer in the darkness, and she separated her energy from that of the pack.

Her primal and natural magic mixed—these were sometimes known as the lower and middle magics. This was what great magicians of other worlds called the tempering of the soul. To complete this process, she had to invoke the third or higher magic. She admitted her fear to herself. The third magic, if used incorrectly, or used by a magician without the correct conditioning, would kill instantly. Although her training had been extensive, she didn't know if it'd been enough.

She listened to the dark forest ahead.

"*Someone's there,*" she whispered. "At the edge of the forest."

"*We know,*" Tallis said. "*We smell him. A human. More are within the trees.*"

She listened to the thoughts and emotions of the humans in the forest. Two stood out. There was something alien about one of them; the other just seemed wrong. She'd have to study them up close.

"*Can I stop the pack from attacking?*" she asked.

"*No,*" Tallis said. "*If you have friends there, then stand close to them. The pack will spare those.*"

Now they were much closer. They'd been seen, and Lucy knew that fire was visible as it dripped from her and the pack. She, too, had the urge to hunt. A shot came from the forest, and a bullet grazed her. She gasped in shock, immediately healing the wound with fire. They'd targeted her.

"Not friends," Tallis said.

She slipped back into the pack mind and literally saw orange. Her blood lust increased. Incanting the spell of invisibility, she flickered and faded from human view.

A wolf yelped when a bullet hit it.

"They're dangerous," she said.

"So are we," Tallis replied.

She nodded; it was true. These night wolves had been infused with magic. Bullets sprayed the area, but despite magic, some wolves dropped. They rushed towards the trees, and then they were in the forest. Her inner fire blazed, toughening her skin, but although her fire may heal a single wound, a hail of bullets would kill.

The wolves ripped apart a handful of guards on the perimeter of the forest, and she leapt from Tallis's back and ran with the pack. Within the forest, she was as fast as a wolf. After killing the first group of guards, they silently stalked those deeper in the forest. The soldiers were quiet, but she saw them. Her eyesight was as good as any nocturnal animal.

The wolves were almost in position.

"What's wrong?" Tallis asked.

The wolf was observant.

"Small magic."

"Do humans—"

"No," she interrupted. *"But you saw the sorcerer with Tavth."*

Tallis growled quietly. *"Hated."*

"For good reason," she said. *"But this one is weaker."*

The night wolves stopped several yards from a second human group. They waited for Tallis to make a move. She probed the mind of the lesser sorcerer, curious to know why they'd targeted her. He was more soldier than sorcerer, but he'd practiced magic.

"Why shoot her?" she whispered the thought softly in his mind, hoping for a reaction.

The man was smugly confident and had no idea what she was doing. In a rush of emotion, he answered the question she'd suggested, thinking it his own thought.

"Kill the witch!"

So they knew she was here. Alistair Walker must have guessed. Like her, the more powerful sorcerers could speak a distance without the need for technology.

"They've been specially instructed to assassinate me."

"How do they know about you?" Tallis asked.

"Walker."

Some of the wolves were growling.

"We attack," Tallis said.

The first guard died without a sound. The second managed a cry. Then it was chaos. She could no longer see Tallis; he fought further to her right. Dozens of wolves ran among the guards, ripping and shredding their bodies. Their shocking appearance, with lines of fire running along their bodies, was disturbing, even to her. Soon, most of the men and several wolves lay dead between the trees. But the lesser sorcerer still fought. She moved closer. Two wolves lay dead by his feet; a lone wolf attacked.

Lucy stepped into the clearing.

"You," the sorcerer said, looking at her.

The third wolf hesitated, perhaps unsure what she'd do. The sorcerer's gun lay on the forest floor near one of the dead wolves, but he couldn't reach it. Instead, he prepared his rudimentary magic, but before the man could act, Tallis rushed from the trees, ripping one of his arms from his body. The other wolf finished him off.

She pocketed the pistol.

"The others?" she asked Tallis.

The wolf was silent for several seconds. She knew he was speaking to the pack mind. Then he spoke.

"Running."

They were no longer important. Her attention was now drawn to the portal pulsing in the centre of the forest. Then a red light flashed in her mind. *"Walker,"* she said. Tallis growled. He was moving quickly through the grassland towards the portal.

15

Lucy ran fast through the forest; the trees made way for her as she passed. This wasn't the faerie forest she'd just left, but it wasn't a normal English forest either. It lent her its senses, allowing her to choose the best paths. She soon reached the portal. It lay in the centre of a clearing, near a cracked orange log. A feeling of dread emanated from it.

Wanting to know how close Walker was, she extended her senses in six directions at once—a magical skill that had taken her years of practice. He'd reached the edge of the forest. For a normal man, it'd take hours to hack his way through the undergrowth. She suspected that he could reach her within twenty minutes.

She walked straight to the portal. The air around it was thick and shiny. Time seemed to slow the closer she got. Its pulsing energy made her queasy, and somehow it seemed attached to the orange log. She had an impression of tendrils squeezing through and feeling their way into this world.

Wondering what to do next, she studied the blue-green

phosphorescent fungi growing from the log. The portal was ajar, and the fungi seemed to thrive on the energy rushing through from another world. She studied the fluctuating web of energy and its strands of many colours.

As an experiment, she magically pushed the door. It closed a bit, but the fungi didn't like it and wailed at a frequency most humans couldn't hear. Sometimes, her increased awareness of the world was a disadvantage, but she could do nothing to stop the sound. Instead, she focussed on her job. She wasn't sure why Walker rushed towards her. Did he know she was there? It didn't matter. She didn't want him accessing this strange portal, one that was open. It was the energetic life that pushed its way into the world that had opened the way, but she feared Walker may find some way to use this portal if she didn't close it.

She'd encountered sentient fungi before. Often their minds were formed from strands of energy that looped backwards and forwards around them, like an invisible lattice. She tried to push again, but lines of energy still radiated from it. Slender protuberances were growing through the portal, blocking it. She also caught glimpses of shadows moving on the other side.

A bird squawked in the forest.

Something was approaching. She just needed a little more time to study the portal and the life around it. Imagining that she was part of it, she touched it with her mind. All life understood the True Language, although often on an unconscious level.

It noticed her.

"What do you want?" she asked, wanting to understand its relationship to the portal.

She was suddenly filled with powerful, overwhelming energy and had to disconnect. Several seconds passed before she realised she'd fallen backwards and was lying on the forest floor. Crawling back to the fungi again, she tried to manipulate the threads of energy passing through it. One lashed out, throwing her several feet away. Bright blue fungal projections grew rapidly from it; some of them grew to almost her height.

The bird's squawking became louder; the sorcerer was close, but she had no choice but to continue. Her brows furrowed as she contemplated the swirling patterns of energy that she saw with senses that, several years earlier, she hadn't even realised could exist. A clear idea came to her, but it was dangerous. With no time to think, she plunged her hands through the portal, squeezing her fingers through the crack into the space between worlds. She saw the lines of energy more clearly. Something moved along one of them. It stopped to watch. Not wanting to deal with whatever it was, she worked faster.

Lucy pulled back several strands of energy, then teased out a single strand and placed it before them. It was a basic tripwire. Anyone touching it would release a wave of magic —enough to slam the door shut. She was tempted to try it herself, but she wasn't sure what the consequences would be. Sitting back, she examined her work. A magic user who saw as she did would see the trap, if they were looking. But her enemy's magic was different from hers. Their magical world was more black and white, not the clearly defined colours she could see.

She felt Walker's magic approaching through the trees and recited the invisibility spell as she ran silently towards the far side of the clearing and dived into a patch of tall ferns. Walker entered the clearing. He glanced around, not appearing to notice he was being observed. That was typical. The imperial sorcerers disdained the natural world.

Despite their power, they considered the environment around them unimportant. That was their loss.

Walker stood at over six foot tall. He was a powerful man—some would think him handsome. She knew it to be, in part, a side effect of magic. She'd sometimes had to deal with the magnetic attraction magic created, too. It was one reason she no longer mixed with people as she once had. It was like perspiring a love potion that attracted men and women alike. Lucy remained unaffected by that aspect of his magic, but she smelt its cloying effect all too clearly.

He stopped directly in front of the portal and examined it. Lucy wondered if he'd seen the trap she'd set, and she took out the pistol she'd acquired from the alien, just in case. Magic was fine, but sometimes bullets were faster. She'd rather not be forced to shoot him, though. He probably wore protective clothing, and the upper classes of his world had genetically toughened skin, making them hard to kill.

Walker reached into the portal, and she held her breath.

He sprang the trap.

It imploded with a loud bang, and Lucy was dragged into the clearing. Walker was pulled partially into the hole. His back was smoking. Three coloured snakes rose around Walker. Lucy looked in shock. It seemed that the tendrils of energy had transformed themselves into serpents. The sorcerer frantically pulled his arm from the portal. She feared she'd made it worse, as magic from the portal ripped ferns up by their roots and sucked them into it. The magic also dragged her over the rough ground towards it, but then the pull lessened. She stopped several yards from Walker and the snakes. Unfortunately, the portal had only partially closed.

He glared at her and staggered to his feet. The fire on his back had gone out.

"You're not the power you think you are."

She'd never thought it, but she wasn't defenceless either.

"Neither are you!"

The bright serpents were growing.

"What are you staring at?" he said.

She realised he couldn't see them. Shifting her position, she shuffled to one side so as to place the serpents between herself and him, still unsure what to do with them. Then she called them, her magic stroking their serpent heads, but one turned and bit her.

She fell onto her back as a rush of dark energy entered her system. It acted like poison. Desperately, she called her inner fire. Walker frowned, not understanding what was happening. As her fire cleansed her body of the dark energy, all Lucy could manage to do was gasp from the pain. She breathed out in relief as her fire burnt the last of it and the pain lessened. She sat up, but still felt dizzy.

He evidently considered her of little importance as he studied the portal. He couldn't see the shrunken snakes that hissed at him, and again, she silently thanked his arrogance and refusal to study anything as low as natural magic. She struggled to her feet. Disappointed that the coloured serpents of energy didn't attack him, she remembered the horn in her belt. Putting it to her mouth, she blew, calling the night wolves to the hunt. As she did so, she imagined the scent of magic the man exuded. She had no idea whether they'd answer her call, but she knew they'd recognise his scent instantly. And they hated him.

He cursed her, and she braced herself as he projected a magic wave that slowly rolled towards her. The serpents buried themselves in the earth as it passed over them. She was not so fortunate, and the wave flattened her against the ground again. She was trapped.

Walker grinned. This time he walked directly towards her. He didn't see the serpents reemerge from the ground.

Two bright snakes of energy bit his ankles.

Screaming, he staggered back, and the pressure of the magical blanket he'd thrown over her lessened. She sat up just as the serpents retracted into the portal.

Sweat dripped from his forehead, and he gasped in pain. Walker struggled to pull out his pistol. Hers was already in her hand, and she shot him. His pistol flew across the clearing. The man was hurt and bloodied, but she knew it was because of the snakes, not her bullet. Howls came from the forest, and she breathed out in relief.

"The wolves will hunt you," she said.

A look of fear passed over his face as the wolves bayed. They were getting closer. She knew he had the power to kill dozens of them, but he was weakened and depleted of magic, and there were so many.

Lucy grinned.

He cursed her again and then rushed into the forest at an unnatural speed. She watched him go. The trick he had with speed was impressive. She wanted to learn it. She knew she'd have to deal with him eventually. But now, she had one more task. She crawled towards the portal. It was still slightly ajar. At least she had time. Slowly, like a magical snake charmer, she returned the snakes into their basket. Again she pushed it, and the portal popped shut. Magical energy still seeped from it, but it was now no more than an unpleasant draught.

16

Luke stared out of the window of the limousine as it silently raced up the M6. They'd already reached Cheshire, where the feeling changed, becoming more rural.

He glanced at Amelia. "Any more visions or dreams?"

She shook her head.

Luke had only known her for six months, but felt as if it'd been for years. While he respected her abilities, he didn't understand them. They left the motorway.

"Is Eva Noone really an alien?" he asked.

The thought chilled him.

"All I know is that she practices black magic, and the aliens do, too."

"So, she's probably an alien, and if she's not, she's dangerous, especially if she gets into government."

Amelia nodded.

It was a reality he'd never known, but he lacked the time to think it through in the depth he wished. All he knew was that in four days' time, something big would happen, but no one knew what. A grey concrete wall rose above them. Spotlights lit it. He was surprised to see grass growing from it in some places. He'd read one of Ruth's reports on the rapid growth of vegetation here. The chauffeured car stopped, and armed men checked their papers. Then the gate opened, and they drove down into the underground car park beneath the newly built complex—a human outpost on the edge of an alien zone. Ruth Hardy greeted them. She was the team's zoologist and botanist.

"Bad news," she said.

He wasn't sure it could get worse.

"There's been an attack on our forces in the western zone."

She led them to a lift.

"What's happened?"

They stepped out of the lift.

"That's the topic of the meeting." She glanced at her watch. "We're late."

Luke still couldn't believe Gully had been given command. He'd shown signs of mental instability six months earlier.

Ruth led them into a large, windowless meeting room. Chief Inspector Gully glowered at them as they took the seats next to Jack Ross. Jack was Ruth's fiancé. He'd served in the Special Boat Service and MI5 before joining MI7. Several men and women wore the blue uniform of the Special Border Force, as well as two in civilian clothes.

Gully turned to a man in uniform.

"Proceed, Sergeant Bly?"

"Tonight, our forces came under attack. Five men died."

"How were they killed?" Luke asked.

"A pack of giant wolves ripped them apart."

"I thought the western zone was free of wolves," Jack said.

"It was," Bly said. "But tonight, a large number of wolves crossed from the northern forest."

Luke remembered what he'd read about the three zones. The northern one was the strangest. Amelia believed magic was being employed to keep people away. No one in the Special Border Force even entertained her theories. Alien was as weird as it got for them.

"Why didn't they shoot them?" Jack asked.

Bly looked embarrassed. "We did, but they're hard to kill."

Luke knew Jack had already requested a military unit to be brought there to clear the forests of potential aliens and the aggressive invasive species. Jack's report had clearly stated that he believed the border force would not be able to counter the life forms that had occupied the three forest zones. Those in charge disagreed.

"Anything else?" Luke asked. "Any reports of aliens?"

As bad as the wolves sounded, Luke couldn't see why soldiers with modern weapons couldn't deal with them, and he assumed they simply weren't trained. He agreed with Jack's assessment.

"Everything seems alien out there. We have recent video footage of what looks like a fire-breathing woman riding a wolf," Sergeant Bly said. "Her skin was cracked and leaking a molten substance. Some of the wolves had the same appearance."

"How's that possible?" Luke asked.

Nobody answered. He glanced at Amelia's worried expression. He wondered if it was possible that she'd really summoned the orange witch. That was one part of the story he'd not taken seriously.

"How many men did you send?" Luke asked.

"Twenty," Bly answered.

Chief Inspector Gully's eyes narrowed as he leant back in his chair. "We're going to retake control of each zone one by one."

"Take control from who? The wolves or the fire-breathing woman?" Luke asked.

"If that's what she is, then yes. I'm reclaiming our country, and I'll kill or capture whoever or whatever is killing our men," Gully said, "alien witch or not."

He must have read Amelia's old reports about summoning the orange witch. Luke had been with her when it had happened. He'd never forget it. "Is there any evidence that this woman is one of the aliens?" he asked.

"What else would she be?" Gully growled.

"I mean, is she one of the group we fought at Shakerley?"

"She's an alien," Gully said. "That's clear."

"But is she the same sort of alien as the rest?" Luke asked.

"What does that matter?" Gully barked. "They're all the same. They've invaded our country, and we'll send them to hell." He glared around the room, challenging anyone to dispute his claims.

Wilful misunderstanding was a weakness from Luke's point of view.

"I'm sending in patrols to the western forest tonight. Our aim is to capture or kill the witch and exterminate the wolves. By tomorrow morning, the western forest will be ours."

"I want to capture a wolf alive for research," Ruth said.

Gully shook his head. "They're killing my men. Fifty-five armed personnel will leave in half an hour. I'll be leading the operation." Gully looked towards MI7. "You're to observe."

The meeting ended.

Luke glanced at his watch. It was four in the morning. Half an hour later, he joined the others at the edge of the airfield. A wire fence separated it from the tall grass pushing against the base. Ruth had told him it was a constant battle to keep the aggressive plants back.

"He's right about sending a night patrol, at least," Jack said. "We've hardly sent out any night patrols. We may gain a new perspective."

They climbed into one of the five Warrior armoured vehicles. Minutes later, they raced through the gates, leaving a dark trail of crushed grass behind. Luke hit his head on the roof as they bounced hard. MI7 sat together. Squashed next to them were three border force guards. A commander, driver, and gunner manned the vehicle. No one spoke. The only good thing about the forty-five minute journey was that they didn't have to walk. By the time they'd got to the edge of the western forest, Luke felt stiff and bruised.

Corporal Waites commanded their section of the border force. The drivers remained with the vehicles on the edge of the forest. Luke formed part of the line of nine men and women who pushed their way into the forest. The moon disappeared, giving the forest had an eerie feeling. His pistol only gave him so much confidence.

"I thought you cut a path through this yesterday," Waites said.

"I did," Jack replied.

"Looks like you didn't do a good job."

Jack looked at him sourly.

Corporal Waites must be new to the alien zone. Even Luke knew the answer.

"It grew back," Jack said.

"In a day?"

"Yes. Didn't you read the reports?"

The corporal looked away.

"Do you want me to lead?"

Waites shook his head. "Your job is to observe."

The guards continued to cut their way along the path Jack had previously made.

"Is it normal for plants to grow so fast?" Luke said.

Ruth shook her head. "Outside of the special zone, I've never seen anything like it."

They walked in a single line. In front of Luke was the lance corporal in charge of the Warrior, another guard and the corporal; they wore night-vision goggles. They were followed by himself, Ruth and Amelia. Jack, another guard, and the Warrior's gunner were at the rear. Something crawled onto Luke's neck; he brushed it off. More insects flew into his face. Others were suffering, too.

"What's that smell?" one of the men asked.

"Rotting corpses," a man said. "I've smelt them before."

Luke pushed his way into a small clearing. He held his machete in one hand, his pistol in the other. Something lay in the centre, and something else was moving around it.

A guard shone a torch on it. Luke blinked, not understanding what he was seeing.

"What?" he asked quietly.

They spread out, surrounding the thing on the ground. It was the size of a man and was covered in moving black spots. One guard prodded it with his foot, then leapt back as a black cloud lifted into the air. Seconds later, they ran from the glade, chased by a cloud of giant biting flies. Luke fumbled to holster his gun so he could swat the things from his face.

"Is it a body?" Amelia asked, spitting out a fly.

They watched Ruth pursuing some of the black flies

near the thing on the ground. Finally, she captured two, putting them in a small bag and waving it triumphantly at them.

"What is it?" Luke asked.

"It's some sort of corpse plant," Ruth said.

"A what?" the corporal asked.

"Amorphophallus titanum," Ruth said. "They smell like rotting flesh to attract flies to pollinate them. I've never seen one that shape before."

Luke felt as if dozens of needles had been poked into him. She held up another plastic bag, proudly displaying brown mush and some crawling insects.

"Just keep that thing tightly shut," the corporal said.

They resumed their march through the forest, which had formed its own magnetic field—all electronic navigation devices were useless. Only the night-vision goggles seemed to work.

"How did you find your way through this?" the corporal asked.

"Memory and instinct," Jack said.

The corporal raised his eyebrows. "Memory? Here?"

"Some of the trees are distinct." Jack glanced at Ruth, who grinned.

"Perhaps to botanists. Not to me," the man grumbled.

Gunfire sounded, and they heard shouts. The sound was close. They changed direction and cut through the stubborn and thorny undergrowth, forcing their way towards it.

A wolf howled.

It was closer than Luke liked.

Ten minutes later, they came across a small clearing. This time, the dark motionless shapes lying on the ground were real corpses. Body parts were scattered about the clearing. Luke trod very carefully.

"Look," Ruth said.

She'd found an injured night wolf. It growled, but its life was slipping away. They stared at the line of orange fire that cut across its torso.

"Is that a wound?" Amelia asked.

No one answered. It was impossible to answer.

The animal died, smoke rising from its body.

"They're coming back," a guard said, nervously pointing into the trees.

Scores of glowing red eyes shone in the darkness.

"I think we should back away," Ruth said.

Luke agreed.

"Won't they chase us?" Corporal Waites asked.

"If we run," Ruth said.

Jack pointed at a fallen tree.

"Behind that."

Luke scrambled over the rotten trunk. The trees here were giants; the trunk was almost five feet thick. When he saw the wolves, he realised they may actually be as hard to kill as the sergeant had said. They had lines of fire running along their bodies, and tongues of flame leapt from their mouths. Luke almost froze when a large wolf with grizzled fur raced towards him. He fired his pistol twice, but it made little difference. As it leapt over the log, Luke dropped his gun and pulled out his machete, stabbing it in its gut. It cried, but twisted round, ripping into the arm of Luke's thick jacket. Then the wolf collapsed on top of him. Luke struggled to push the thing off him. Its fur was thick with grease, and it stank. Blood ran from a bullet hole in its head.

"Thank you," Luke said.

Jack nodded and fired at the next wolf. They killed a few, but one guard was dead, and another two had lost fingers.

The wolves backed off, waiting in the trees. Then one of the guards scrambled over to his dead comrade.

"Come back!" Jack shouted as the man began to pull his comrade's body towards the log.

A wolf leapt from the trees and bit through the man's neck. Jack shot bursts of automatic fire, and it staggered into the trees to die. A loud bang, like a clap of thunder, came from deep in the forest.

"What now?" Luke muttered.

It was one problem after another. He reloaded his pistol. Jack had offered him one of the assault rifles—there were several spare—but he hadn't trained with them and felt uncomfortable using one. He realised that six months ago, the thought of using a pistol would have upset him.

A distant horn blew. The night wolves withdrew into the trees.

"That's better," Luke said.

Amelia shook her head.

"Something's coming," she said, pointing into the trees.

Luke saw nothing, but a minute later, his heart skipped. A flash of green light shot from the trees, slicing through the lance corporal. The team stared at the dead man in shock. His body had been cut in two.

"Did anyone see anything?" Corporal Waites asked.

"A flash of light," Luke said. "It disappeared into the forest."

"It was a running man," Amelia said quietly.

"That's impossible," the corporal said.

The men stood in silence.

"I can see what other people can't," Amelia said.

17

Lucy ran through the forest despite her tiredness. It was dawn, and although she hadn't slept, she had to hunt. Fire leaked from her body; if she didn't act, it would literally pull her apart. She'd drawn too much primal magic—it demanded payment.

But in spite of her hunger, she felt conflicted. She spoke to animals and knew their feelings, which sometimes made killing them difficult, even when it meant saving herself.

"Hunt," Darta whispered in her mind.

Glancing to her right, she saw the panther running through the trees. They ran silently, with Lucy extending her senses into the forest. Their minds bonded for the hunt. Through the panther, she smelt the scents of the forest, and through her natural magic, Darta felt the vibrations animals made on the earth.

"Good," Darta said as she explored Lucy's extended senses.

They became aware of the animal at the same time. Darta knew this type of creature. An image of a large boar-like animal, not originally from Earth, entered her mind. They ran towards it.

While Darta couldn't verbalise as well as the strangely altered Tallis could, her emotions, desires, and simple thoughts were clear to Lucy. And hers to Darta. The panther saw her inner conflict.

"Why?"

The concept was hard for Darta to understand, but Lucy tried to explain.

"I speak to all animals, therefore I stopped eating them."

She let the alien thought enter the panther's consciousness before continuing.

"When I gained the primal magic, I needed to stop it pulling my body apart, and I reverted to eating meat."

"You've found your animal vitality," Darta said. *"It's good."*

"Yes." She understood the power it gave her, but she still had doubts.

"It's strength," Darta said.

Lucy couldn't deny that. An image of herself as seen by Darta appeared in her mind. She was a fiery creature running through the forest. Bays from deeper in the forest told them the wolves were hunting, too. Then an image flashed in her mind. Their quarry moved closer. Through Darta, she smelt the animal. The scent intensified, almost overpowering Lucy. Darta scolded her for her lapse of attention. She was right.

"All right, Darta. I'll focus."

Flowing with the panther's mind, she sensed the animal change path; they altered theirs, too. It'd been panicked by the sounds of the night wolves. The animal turned again. It rushed directly towards them.

Lucy waited to one side of the path; Darta crouched on the other. They hit the beast from two directions at once, taking it straight down. Darta's teeth and claws, and Lucy's intense bursts of fire, killed it in seconds.

Darta looked up and snarled. The wolves had heard and were coming to investigate. They were less than a hundred yards away.

"Eat!" Lucy said.

She and Darta both possessed inner fire, and they roasted the meat as they ate. By the time Lucy saw the first wolf through the trees, they'd eaten half the animal. She still wanted more.

"Leave!" Darta said.

Although Lucy knew she may be able to convince the wolves to leave them in peace, in reality, it was unlikely unless Tallis was there. The wolves were hungry; even the old wolf wouldn't have full control of them in a situation like this. Darta was right.

Using fire from her fingertips, she cut off a leg. As the wolves crept towards them, they slipped into the trees. After running for a few minutes, feeling nothing but relief that her burning hunger had now gone, she realised she'd been following Darta without a thought.

"Where're we going?"

An image appeared in her mind. Near the edge of the forest, a man was attempting to start a fire. It was the assassin. They approached his camp. Lucy hadn't decided how to deal with him yet; that would depend on him. From Darta's memories, she'd seen something of his nature. Difficult seemed too mild a word to describe the man she'd seen murder in cold blood, but she needed her weapons to be sharp. Her enemy had no qualms about killing.

Darta heard some of her thoughts and shared an image of Lucy blazing as the orange witch when she met the man.

She was sure that would make a strong impression on the assassin, but the energy cost was higher than she wished.

"Respects strength," Darta said.

She was sure he did. Perhaps a more minor display would help.

They stopped at the edge of the clearing. The panther began to move, but Lucy lay her hand on her shoulder, dropping the meat next to her.

"Let me do this."

"He's dangerous."

She shrugged. *"Everything's dangerous in this forest. Wait for me to call you."*

Darta gently snarled her agreement.

Calling her inner fire from her fire belly, the special dragon organ deeply connected to her primal magic, she slipped from the trees. The man had his back to her. Lines of fire now laced her body, and she was pleased with the special T-shirt and shorts she'd made from dragon scales, which she always wore under her regular clothes. It was extremely inconvenient to end up naked every time she used primal fire magic. She moved silently, and he didn't hear her approach.

"Hello."

He started, reaching for his gun.

"Who are you?"

Then he noticed the lines of fire spreading across her skin.

"What are you?"

As a natural empath, she felt his aggression, hostility, and fear clearly.

"My name's Lucy."

He stared at the streaks of fire on her neck and face.

"What?"

She shrugged. "A person, just like you."

He shook his head. "No, you're not."

"The forest has many different lifeforms," she said.

"That's true. And you're one of them? A native of the forest?"

"In part."

It had a small amount of truth. She'd learnt some of her skills in an ancient sentient forest not so different from this one.

"Put the gun down," she said.

He stepped closer, still pointing his pistol at her.

"Why should I?"

He was too nervous. This wasn't good.

One part of natural magic was the ability to speak to the environment. When asked nicely, it would respond with sound. She sang a silent note and a plant behind him exploded a small seed pod, making a popping sound. It distracted him for a fraction of a second—more than enough time for her. The fire had already reached her fingertips. When his muscles tensed, her magic rushed from her. She slapped his wrist, flames bursting from her fingers. The magic resounded through the forest like a small thunderclap. She'd overdone it a little. He lay on the ground, his gun was next to him. When he reached for it, she stepped closer, breathing fire.

Startled, he crawled back, grabbing a machete that from his bag. She was impressed by his persistence.

"I don't know what you are, but get away from me," he shouted.

"I want to talk not fight. If I did, you'd already be dead."

"Darta."

The man's eyes widened as the black panther walked

from the forest straight up to Lucy, dropping the bloody leg on the ground and rubbing her large head against her.

"She's betrayed me."

Lucy was becoming annoyed.

"She's done nothing of the sort. She led me to you because I want to speak to you." Lucy pointed at the leg. "Cook the meat, and we can eat. We'll talk after."

The man glanced at the pile of firewood.

"The wood's damp."

She walked over to it, bent down, and touched it. It only took the smallest burst of fire for it to ignite.

"What's your name?" she asked.

"Angel."

He looked at the meat. "It's fresh."

"We just killed it," she said.

Angel glanced between the panther and her. She saw him look at the blood on her clothes. He put the meat on a spit he'd made, then placed it over the fire.

"It'll attract predators."

"Perhaps."

They sat in silence as the meat slowly roasted. He stared at the fire while she stroked Darta's neck and shoulders. The giant panther made a rumbling sound. Feeling a little bored waiting for the meat to cook, she leant forwards and gave it another intense blast of fire.

"You can eat the outer parts now," she said.

"The inside's not cooked," Angel said.

"I'll eat that; I like it rare."

He raised his eyebrows but didn't argue, quickly cutting off large chunks of cooked meat. She cut some of the still bloody sections off, tossing a couple to Darta, and keeping two for herself. Out of the corner of her eyes, she saw him watching her eat, noting his surprise as she roasted each mouthful.

"Who are you?" he asked.

"Your ex-employers called me the orange witch."

"What?"

"The aliens you worked for. You remember the tower in the lake, right?"

"I don't work for them now."

The night wolves barked in the forest, but they were eighty or ninety yards away. She suspected they'd smelt the roasting meat. She finished her portion.

"You killed for the aliens."

Angel tensed. "What do you want from me?"

"Your help."

He raised his eyebrows. "With what?"

"To kill your ex-employers."

He stared coldly at her. "At least you're direct. But it won't help much. They're hard to kill, even with your tricks."

"They're more than tricks, but I know it won't be easy. That's why I need help."

"Why would I help you?"

Remembering Darta's instinctive feeling that he feared the animals of the forest, she glanced at the trees.

"Do you want to spend every day avoiding wolves?"

"I have a gun."

She laughed. "Be serious."

"What do you offer?"

"Food, for one." She pointed at the remains still cooking in the fire. "A chance to kill an enemy that would kill you if they could."

He looked at her with his chin thrust out. "If they could."

"A better working environment. I need to operate from London."

She could tell he was thinking, and while she didn't think it a better environment, she guessed he might.

He shrugged. "I don't care."

That was her fear, but she couldn't indulge his dark fantasies either. She glanced at the wolves. They were much closer now. Their eyes were visible through the trees. Angel had noticed them, too, and Darta was becoming restless. She didn't like the smell of the wolves at all. Lucy ran her hand along the panther's shoulder.

"There's another reason," she said.

He looked at her, raising his eyebrows.

"It's fun."

He almost grinned, but his eyes returned to the creeping animals.

She saw Tallis watching her.

"Tallis, support a friend!"

"We're more curious than hungry," he said.

"Not that," she said.

She imagined Angel jumping up and down in fear. They listened. Then she made a mental image of Angel yelping like a pup.

The old wolf grinned. Several other wolves barked in excitement. It seemed that wolves had a sense of humour.

"You're playing a dangerous game," Darta whispered.

"Perhaps, but I need Angel to decide quickly."

She hoped she'd touched the pack's inner cub-like playfulness and achieved the right balance between that and aggression. Some of them were running in circles, barking.

"What are they doing?" Angel asked.

"They're hungry."

"Darta, come," she whispered.

Lucy and Darta walked away, into the forest behind them, staying clear of the wolves. One wolf ran around

Angel, barking. Another tried to bite his ankles, making him jump.

"Funny," Darta said.

She'd eased the tension, but only for a moment. All it would take was for Angel to shoot one of them, and their anger would return.

"Joining us?"

He grunted, but backed away from the pack before turning and walking after them at a brisk pace. When they reached the edge of the forest, she turned to Angel.

"Can you fly a helicopter?"

"Yes. Why?"

"I want to steal one."

18

Luke looked into the alien forest, wondering what else might come from it.

"Amelia?"

She shook her head.

"Something's coming," Ruth said.

"Are you a psychic, too?" Corporal Waites asked sarcastically.

"Listen to the birds," she said.

"What?" The corporal screwed his face as he looked into the forest.

"The birds!" Ruth repeated.

Luke nodded. "Warning calls. It's time to leave."

"I give the orders," the corporal said.

"Not to us," Jack replied. "Not on matters like this."

The vegetation was moving from side to side. Something was clearly coming through the forest, and it was moving fast.

"The wolves have returned," Ruth said.

They rushed from the trees. Luke froze as the giant wolves rushed around them.

"Don't shoot!" Ruth said.

"Why not?" the corporal asked, raising his gun.

Jack pushed it down. "They're hunting whatever cut your man in half."

The corporal slowly lowered his gun. They waited while the pack rushed past them. And then it was gone, following the path of whatever had cut the guard in half. "What made them do that?" Ruth asked.

No one answered.

"Let's get out of here," Luke said. "I don't think we can learn much more tonight."

He desperately wanted to get to bed before dawn, which was only an hour away. For once, the corporal agreed, and seconds later they ran back down the path they'd cut. Luke was surprised that the vegetation was already growing back.

"The alien metabolism is incredibly fast," Ruth said.

By the time they reached the edge of the forest and stepped out, it was dawn, and the grassland was becoming visible. Luke's forehead creased as he saw one of the armoured vehicles had gone; the other three stood abandoned by the edge of the forest.

"Where are the drivers?" Amelia asked.

The six of them searched each of the three vehicles.

"Empty," Luke said.

"Look," Amelia said, her head motioning to the forest.

Scarlet eyes watched them.

"Not again," Luke said.

"I don't think they're wolves," Ruth said.

Luke didn't care; he just wanted to get out of there.

"Inside," Jack said, pointing to the nearest armoured vehicle.

Jack drove, and the gunner tensely monitored the surrounding grassland. Corporal Waites joined the rest of

MI7 in the back of the vehicle. By the time they'd reached the base, the sun had risen.

"That was like hell," Amelia said. "And you say it's the easiest of the three forests."

Jack grunted a yes as they entered the base.

Chief Inspector Gully strode towards them. He didn't look happy.

"You abandoned your station!"

"So did you," Amelia said.

"Chief Inspector, we're not members of the Special Border Force," Luke said. "We're intelligence officers working for MI7, and we have been ordered to collect information."

Gully's eyes appeared to protrude unnaturally, and for a moment, he was stuck for words. Then he turned and marched back inside.

"Why the anger?" Ruth asked.

"To divert attention from his incompetence," Jack said.

The mood in the base was bad. The news only got worse. Only one of the other armoured vehicles returned, and only three guards arrived with it. Not only had the border force failed to avenge the first massacre, they'd become the victims of a second one. Sixty-one guards had been killed.

"Gully will be fired," Luke said when they sat alone in the media room.

"He should be," Jack said, "but he has some hold over the decision makers in London."

"Why?"

Jack shrugged.

They were quiet for a moment, and then they remembered why they were meeting. A camera had been found near one of the soldiers killed in the first attack. It contained the video that Sergeant Bly had mentioned. None of them had seen it yet.

"Let's play it," Luke said.

They played the video on the large screen on the wall.

"I can't see anything," Amelia said.

"It was in the middle of the night," Jack said.

They watched for the next minute, straining to see anything at all. Then there was movement. Lights seemed to move in front of them.

"What are we looking at?" Amelia asked, peering closely.

"Fire," Luke said. He could see small bursts. "It's moving."

A spotlight cut through the dark night.

"What?" Luke gasped.

For several seconds, they stared at a woman with blazing orange hair and eyes that glowed. She rode a giant black wolf.

The screen went blank.

Amelia covered her face with her hands. "What have I done?"

Jack and Ruth looked at her, confused.

"The orange witch is here," Luke said.

19

Lucy ran silently through the tall grass with Angel and Darta by her side. Morning had arrived, but the height of the grass hid them from prying eyes.

"How did you know they have a helicopter?" Angel asked.

"Darta's my eyes, nose, and ears."

He was silent, perhaps uneasy about the way she could communicate with the panther.

"Have you seen it?" she asked.

He gave a short nod. "A Eurocopter."

He wasn't a conversationist, but it was probably for the best. She doubted they had many interests in common. A few hours later, they reached the small airfield attached to the base. It was surrounded by a metal fence.

"How can we get inside?" she asked.

"Cut our way through."

They crept closer, stopping where the long grass ended, about ten yards from the fence, which was higher than she thought. The vegetation was flattened there; it looked like guards regularly drove vehicles around the perimeter fence.

"We may have to wait until it gets dark," Angel said.

She needed to sleep, but she didn't want to wait.

"Let's do it now. I have some tricks that may make it harder for them to see us. They should be tired after last night."

"You look exhausted," Angel said.

"I'll sleep on the way to London."

If the alien she'd killed in the old church had been right, she had until Friday.

"Now."

She used her invisibility spell. As with most natural magic, it was silent. They crept to the high-wire fence and studied the airfield. There was too much activity near the small hangar.

"I can cut through," he said, "and it's possible they won't see me. But when we run for the helicopter, we'll be seen right away."

He was probably right. The grass on the airfield was kept short, and her spell only had so much effect. Strictly speaking, it wasn't a spell but a suggestion that there was nothing to see. It wasn't foolproof. Some people were impervious to the trick.

"I'll think of something; you cut," she said.

She needed a distraction, and while Angel was cutting, she studied the guards smoking outside the hangar. There were no patrols around the perimeter fence, and she was grateful for their laxness. Sitting still, she brushed the minds of the men with hers, listening to their hopes, wishes, and aspirations, as well as to their fears. It always helped to know your enemy, and although she didn't like it, fears were the easiest emotions to manipulate.

They feared the creatures of the three forests. Her eyes opened wide. They also feared their commander. She wondered why. But the fear of the forest creatures was easier for her to use; she knew more about them.

"I'm almost through," Angel said.

"Darta will go first. I have a job for her. But I need to work undisturbed for longer."

He nodded and continued to work.

While he worked, she formed a mental representation of herself, fire-breathing panthers, and blue demons. All were purely mental images that she hoped to project into the minds of everyone nearby. Creating a mental replica of herself was the easiest; copies of Darta took a few minutes. The demons were harder and less clearly defined than she'd like, but they'd have to do. The next step was easier. She sent subtle suggestions into the guards' minds, suggestions of wraithlike figures wandering around the farthest points of the airfield.

So far, so good. The guards nervously looked towards the grassland, unconscious of what she'd done. One man appeared scared, pointing at the perimeter, but others seemed less concerned.

The next step was the hardest. Her magic burned as she created visual illusions, choosing real objects to hang her magic upon. A dead tree on the far side of the airfield became a burning orange witch, with multiple branches waving in the air like arms. A collection of barrels stacked against the hangar became a pack of blue demons whispering in the wind.

Angel signalled he was ready.

Pushing her head against Darta's, she whispered her plan. Darta ran straight through the hole and into the airfield. Lucy released the suggestion of a pack of fire-breathing panthers running towards a second group who had just rushed from the main building of the base. Her plan was in place. The magic glowed around her creations, and shouts came from the men. She climbed through the hole in the fence. Angel had already gone through.

"What have you done?"

"No talking," she whispered. "I have to maintain the magic." She pointed to the solitary helicopter sitting in the centre of the field.

He nodded, and they ran towards it, almost bent over double, hoping not to be seen. All the time she chanted the spell to maintain her creations. They reached the helicopter undetected.

"Open it and get ready," she said. "I need to adjust a few things."

Angel's eyes widened as he saw the giant image of the orange witch with a dozen fiery arms whipping in the wind. The guards opened fire, making limbs fall from her wooden body. They appeared to burn on the ground.

They climbed inside the helicopter.

She called Darta back, but the panther was too excited.

"Darta!"

The panther attacked a man. He screamed.

"Come back."

"Fun," the panther whispered.

"No, Darta, come here. We're leaving now!"

Reluctantly, Darta left the injured man and ran towards her, leaving the rest of the pack—all lifeless images—facing the guards. It was as much as she could do. They'd eventually wonder why the animals weren't attacking.

Darta bounded into her arms.

"In the back," she whispered.

The black panther jumped onto the seat behind her.

"I'm going to start the engine," Angel said.

"One second," Lucy said. "I want to make some noise to cover the sound of the rotor blades."

She looked at her final creation: the gang of blue demons she'd built around the barrels. Quietly, she sang. Her voice projected into the choir of blue demons as a wail. More guards ran from the base, immediately opening fire on the demons. Angel started the helicopter; the rotor blades began to turn. Lucy wasn't sure what was inside those barrels, but when they fell apart under automatic weapons fire, one of them exploded. She shut the door. Another barrel exploded. It was only then that some guards pointed at the helicopter, but it was too late. It lifted from the ground.

The second group of men had realised there was something wrong with the panthers surrounding them, and she let go of that magic projection. Slowly they faded, becoming wraithlike outlines, and finally vanishing. The giant orange witch lay splintered on the ground. The blue demons had disappeared, too, but the hangar had caught fire, and that was a bigger distraction anyway.

"It's fully fuelled," Angel said as they flew from the airfield.

"To London," she said.

Darta leapt from the back onto Lucy's lap.

"You're too big for that," she said.

The leopard nuzzled her; she'd grown her spots again.

As they left the blazing airfield behind, Lucy realised she'd depleted her energy.

"I need to eat. A lot."

Angel's eyes widened. "It takes a lot to surprise me, but you do it almost every time you speak."

Lucy grinned. She pushed Darta's face away from her.

"Not until you've cleaned up," she whispered.

20

Luke rushed from his room beneath the surface—his sleep cut short by the alarm. The ground floor was chaotic with people running, and shouts and gunfire came from the airfield. The rest of his team was already there.

"What's happening?"

"We're under attack," Jack said.

The minute he stepped onto the airfield, Luke's eyes were drawn to the huge orange witch waving eight or nine fiery arms and lashing out at border guards as they fired at her.

"That's not normal," Ruth said.

Jack gave a short laugh. "Nothing is here."

Luke thought about the orange witch. This giant burning apparition wasn't the woman he'd seen in the video. It didn't even look human, not even an alien form of human. He began to walk closer when snarls came from his left. What he saw was surreal: twenty black panthers with fire dripping from their bodies chased a group of guards.

Without a second thought, he drew his pistol and ran towards them with Jack and the sergeant. They fired. A panther took a man down, mauling him. Other panthers obscured his view. He shot, but bullets didn't bother them. The panther that had taken the man down suddenly retreated. Luke half-expected the others to join it, but they didn't. All traces of fire disappeared from their bodies. The fire was replaced by a faint blue light. The panthers watched them but didn't move.

"We're wasting ammunition!" Jack shouted.

"Cease fire!" the sergeant ordered.

"I'm going closer," Ruth called, raising her hand.

Luke and Jack hurried to join her. Luke held his breath as she walked right up to them, but the animals didn't seem to even notice her.

"Ruth!" Jack said, with worry in his voice.

Ignoring him, Ruth bent down, her head a few feet from theirs, then she reached out, and her hand passed through the nearest one.

"They're not real," she said.

The one she'd touched vanished—others were fading, too.

Amelia and Sergeant Bly joined them.

Luke moved his own hand through one, and it, too, disappeared.

"If they're not real, how was a man injured?" he asked.

"Good question," Bly said.

A loud crack came from the giant version of the orange witch. She started to disintegrate.

"Wasn't there a tree there?" Amelia asked.

The sergeant nodded.

They were illusions, or mostly illusions, Luke realised. But how were they being created?

Shouts came from the building behind him as a group of guards ran out. Gully was with them. His eyes widened as the last panther disappeared. Luke watched him carefully; he was genuinely shocked. Then a high-pitched sound came from near the hangar to their right. Luke had to blink several times to be sure of what he saw. A group of blue demons were wailing, but like the ethereal panthers, they weren't moving.

Gully went pale.

"It's war!"

The chief inspector issued orders, and men moved towards the demons.

"It's magic," Amelia said quietly to Luke.

"But who's creating it?" Luke said softly. He noticed a movement in the middle of the airfield, then he understood. "It's also a clever distraction." He pointed to the middle of the airfield. "Someone's stealing the helicopter."

The rotor blades were turning.

"We're too late to stop it now," Jack said, whipping out his pair of binoculars. His face took a grim expression.

"What?" Luke asked.

Jack's eyes had hardened. "Angel's returned."

Luke clearly remembered the cold-blooded killer who had kidnapped his wife, dragging her into the van behind his house. He chilled. Jack passed Luke the binoculars. A woman stared back at him and then turned and climbed into the helicopter. Her eyes were bright, burning orange. Angel sat in the pilot's seat.

"It's the orange witch. It looks like she's working with the assassin."

The wailing of the blue demons intensified. Luke strained to see what was really there. He didn't believe they were really demons.

"Something's behind them," he said. "I can't quite see what it is."

Ruth stared through her binoculars. "Barrels of something."

A second later, the blue demons began exploding, one by one, setting fire to the hangar.

"Stop firing!" Jack shouted.

They stopped when the final blue demon exploded.

"Look!" Luke yelled.

The helicopter rose into the sky. Gully screamed and ran towards it, firing his pistol. A couple of his men joined him, but the helicopter was already disappearing into the distance.

Ten minutes later, in the underground meeting room, Chief Inspector Gully addressed senior guards and administrators, MI7, and, via a video link with London, the controller of MI5. Luke studied Gully as he'd study a client in his old clinical psychology practice. Gully wasn't a happy man.

"This is war!" Gully shouted. Sweat dripped from his forehead.

"Who attacked you?" The calm face of the controller filled the screen.

"The orange witch."

Luke watched the reactions in the room. Only the members of MI7 were taking this seriously. The others looked confused.

"So you're saying this orange witch is real?" the controller asked.

"Yes," Gully said.

"Any proof?"

"We have a video of her riding a giant wolf."

"Riding a wolf?" The controller paused while he stared at Gully. "How do we know that was real?"

"It's on video."

"So are the panthers, and they disappeared into thin air."

"They're real projections," Gully said.

The controller frowned, then continued. "The stolen helicopter is heading towards London. We'll arrange a welcoming committee. They won't escape this time."

21

Amelia sat, squashed into the back of a rickety helicopter, as it flew over the English countryside. She turned to Luke, trying to take her mind off the rattling helicopter.

"The controller will soon be eating his words," she said quietly. "Does he really think catching them will be easy?"

"Agreed," Luke said. "They don't understand what they're dealing with. They don't believe in magic. I used to be the same."

She closed her eyes, trying to ease the headache starting to creep along the sides of her head. She thought about the assassin. Amelia hated to admit it, but in a fight, Angel was almost as good as Jack. Nothing about this was easy. Once upon a time, she'd foolishly thought she could handle stress. That was only because she'd never had to deal with pure, relentless stress before. Her thoughts returned to the controller and his smug confidence. He annoyed her; the more experience she had of people in authority, the more she saw how little they knew. And some were plain stupid.

Jack and Ruth were talking quietly to each other; Gully

was in his own world, murmuring something. She noticed Luke watching him.

"Has he lost it?" she whispered.

"I've suggested he be removed from his position," Luke said quietly, "but no one listened."

His forehead furrowed.

"What?" she asked.

"A lot of strange things have happened in the past six months."

"Magic and the appearance of aliens in Britain," she said.

"What exactly is magic?"

"It's taken you a long time to ask."

She thought about the answer. It wasn't straightforward, and her beliefs seemed to change daily, but perhaps what she'd seen from the witch was really something she already knew existed—only it was developed to a much higher degree. In one sense, she didn't believe in magic. Not as most people thought of it. For her, magic was really a name for the manipulation of unseen energy, as yet undiscovered by humanity.

"Magic, as I understand it, is the physics and psychology of parts of the world that are hidden to us; magic is the manipulation of energy not yet recognised by science." She paused. "Actually, it's more than that because some forms of energy may never be."

"Why's that?"

"Because we don't have machines to measure all of those energies, we only have people."

"So we're the receiving machines?"

"Yes, but a machine analogy isn't very good. It limits more than it helps. We can do things that machines can never do."

"For example?"

"I've just told you. We can move spirit because we are spirit. Machines are matter; we're both."

"So spirit is energy and manipulation of spirit is magic?"

"Something like that, perhaps. I think it's more complex. The magic the orange witch uses is beyond me." She looked at him. "Are you still trying to fit this into a scientific framework?"

"Yes."

"Good luck with that. When science accepts spirit as real, it'll leap forward."

Luke thought quietly about this for several seconds. "From what I've learnt since I first met you, I think that may be true," he said.

She grinned. "Talking of magic, I want to journey. This time, don't interrupt," she said, remembering the time he'd shaken her out of a previous meeting.

"Is that safe?" he asked, looking concerned.

"Probably not, but not much of what we do is safe."

"True."

When she saw he was lost in thought, she sat back, as much as the vibrating helicopter allowed, and glanced at her watch. They had about thirty-five minutes left. More than enough time, she hoped.

First, she thought about what she wanted to say to her guides. She knew they'd refuse to answer direct questions, and she knew they didn't want her relying on them; they wanted her to develop more independence. It was a painful thought, but she was aware that relying on her guides could become a crutch. Yet this situation was so serious that she needed to try. She was worried about the strange sickness sweeping the country. It had spread to France and Belgium, too. She was also conflicted about the witch. How could someone on the side of good be working with a cold-blooded killer? And the panther? That was hard to understand. Enough. She'd just speak to them.

Closing her eyes, she felt her mind sink and then she dropped onto a desolate moor; a cold wind blew. She shivered as she looked for her guides. She was alone.

"Victoria?"

A flash of light came from the grey sky, and three figures materialised in front of her. Victoria stood in the middle, dressed in a brilliant white nurse's uniform—one from some distant age. A white aura shone around her. Sam, the angel, stood to her left; Ernest, dressed as a doctor and clad in orange light, stood to the right. All three of them hummed a beautiful melody. Despite the sound, Amelia shivered as she watched the faint forms of hundreds of ill-looking people, seemingly unaware of her, flocking around her guides. Some of the people smiled in relief when the melody soothed their pain. But those further away cried in distress.

"What's happening?" Amelia asked.

Unusually, the angel spoke first. *"A spiritual sickness spreads across the land. Help heal it."*

Before she could ask how, Sam ascended into the sky, joining a choir of angels. Together they sang the most beautiful song. A bright aura emanated from them, warming her. Many of the sick people raised their heads in awe. Amelia's attention turned to the remaining two guides. Victoria still hummed the tune the angels sang; she shone in her brilliant white nurse's uniform. Her melody refreshed Amelia. Then she faded, adding her light to Ernest's orange aura.

"Ernest?"

He wore something on his head, and she strained to see what it was. Leaning forward, she reached for it but started when it chimed. He wore a clock as a hat, but in place of numbers were burning suns. The clock chimed five times, and he disappeared. Flames rushed towards her, and she backed away, unsure what was happening. The melody had gone and had been replaced by a sickening chant. Two intense eyes shone before her. She shuddered. Whatever it was, it was evil. She gasped, almost choking on the toxic odour coming from its three mouths, each of which continued its chant.

Amelia woke with a start as the helicopter lurched to a stop. They'd landed.

"We have work to do!" Chief Inspector Gully said, glaring at her.

Amelia looked out of the window and blinked. She didn't know what she was seeing; she'd returned to her body too suddenly and still felt disoriented. A giraffe lowered its head and looked at her.

"Where am I?"

22

Lucy sat in the back of the helicopter, speaking silently to Darta. They told stories of their shared alien forest home. Darta purred with contentment in her mind. It was a strange experience, even for Lucy. Angel flew without a comment. She sensed his mood and was tempted to ignore it, but she knew it was necessary to bring him into the team. Whispering quietly to Darta, she slipped back into the copilot's seat.

"It's time you learnt more about me and why what I'm doing is important," she said.

"I'm not being paid to chat."

Lucy laughed. "You're not being paid at all." She thought about the best approach; she had no intention of giving up. "Then I'll show you instead. You like moving pictures, right?"

Angel rolled his eyes, then tried to ignore her, but she wouldn't let him. She touched his mind with her magic. He resisted at first, but when Darta joined them, he relaxed a little.

"What are you doing?"

"It's called the True Language."

"Telepathy?"

"Yes, but richer."

She shared images of the ancient forest of Blue Prometheus, showing Angel some of her early struggles, and the many creatures she met there. She showed him their alien enemy and what they were capable of doing to a planet.

Angel's eyes widened.

"You did that?"

She continued, and Darta shared her story. Angel stiffened at the cruelty of the alien humans towards her. He shared Darta's anger. Spontaneously, images of abuse poured from Angel. His childhood had been troubled. Darta nuzzled the back of his neck.

"I wasn't sure before," he said.

Lucy noticed his eyes moisten.

"But what you've shown me is important. I'll help you fight this scum that's invaded our world."

Angel went quiet, and Lucy gave him the space he needed for the rest of the flight. She slept for the first part of the journey, and quietly spoke to Darta for the rest. When the city spread out beneath them, he turned to her again.

"Where do you want to land?"

Lucy was reluctant to be pulled from her cosy conversation with Darta, but she returned her mind to her work despite the panther's continued purring in her in mind. She'd have to explore her connection with her new friend in more detail later. The purring in her mind was definitely not normal. Looking down at London, she thought about locations, and her previous long-distance connection with Amelia Blake. Her sense of location had been vague, but she remembered telling the psychic the enemy was somewhere near a train station.

"Clapham Junction"

The assassin raised his eyebrows. "That's the busiest train station in the country."

"Nearby then."

It seemed a good place to start. "I remember something about a house near there."

"I almost died when it exploded." He glanced at her. "There's not much left."

"The portal may be open. I think it's the best place to start."

"Battersea Park's closest. We'll have to move fast. It won't take long for the police to arrive. They'll be monitoring us now. We should find somewhere to lay low for a few days."

She shook her head. "I want to find the portals first. I have ways of avoiding police detection if necessary."

She hoped so, but her methods worked best in quiet places. They flew low over the Thames, then veering to the south bank, they flew over Battersea Park. Police moved beneath them. Angel swung the helicopter away.

"Clapham Common then."

Lucy sat up. "No." She'd sensed something much stronger. "That way." She pointed to the left.

"Back across the river?"

"Yes. The portal here's quiet. It may be closed; there's another. It's active."

Too active, she thought. It seemed as if it was being used, and her stomach sank at the thought. It wasn't a good sign.

"No, that way."

Angel changed direction. They now flew over central London.

"We need to find somewhere to land quickly."

A few minutes later, Lucy felt the portal beneath her.

"This is it. Where are we?" She didn't recognise the buildings below.

"The Angel, Islington." He grinned at her.

"That's it. Circle back."

"We can't land there."

"There must be a park or something."

She'd not been to London for so long that she hardly remembered. Then it came to her.

"Regent's Park," she said.

"And then? It's the middle of the day; we'll be seen by hundreds of people. You know we'll be followed?"

"I know, but I'll be going somewhere they can't follow. I'm more concerned about you and Darta. Perhaps I can lead them away."

"And risk getting caught."

She shrugged. "That's a risk, but I have abilities you don't." She listened to the sound coming from the portal. The image of a long watery snake swimming in darkness came to her mind.

"Is there any water around here?"

"The boating lake in Regent's Park."

She slowly shook her head. "It's long. Maybe a river."

"Regent's Canal," Angel said.

"It's also dark."

"The Angel," he said with a rare grin.

"What?"

She wasn't sure if he was joking, but she assumed not, although she'd noticed a certain amount of dark humour.

"There's a tunnel under Islington."

She felt her fire ignite. "That's it."

Angel swung the helicopter round, and they descended towards the park. It was just after noon and crowded. At least there were no police vehicles visible, but she knew it wouldn't take long. Every unit in London would be looking for them. They landed on a patch of grass on the outer edges of the park; the point nearest the canal.

As soon as they opened the door, Darta smelt the animals in the nearby zoo. Lucy had to tap the panther's shoulder to get her attention.

"Not yet," she whispered.

Food would have to wait.

"Keep your head low," Angel said as they ran from the still turning rotor blades.

Heads turned toward the helicopter, but it was Darta who attracted the most attention, with dozens of people videoing her. They ran towards the outer perimeter, but before they'd moved a hundred yards, three police cars, with lights flashing, drove towards them.

"That was fast," she said.

"They've sent police to every open area," Angel said. "That's what I'd have done. There'll be more on the way now they know we're here."

One of the police cars raced over the grass, but was forced to slow down to avoid picnickers. Angel turned and shot the windscreen out. The car stopped. Other police officers ran after them, trying to use the trees as cover.

"If you know any tricks, now would be a good time," Angel said.

"I'll try camouflage."

"With what?"

"Mental suggestion."

She used the spell of invisibility, but this time it didn't work; they'd already been seen. Luckily, all three of them were fitter and faster than the police. They rushed towards the outer wall.

"Can you climb it?" Angel asked.

"Yes. Don't wait for me," she said, assuming the high wall wouldn't be a problem for him. She leapt at the wall and scrambled over; Angel did the same. Darta leapt over, bounding down and silently landing on the ground.

"I don't think they expected that," she said, sensing that his respect for her had increased.

"You're right." He gave a rare grin. "Do you know the way to the canal?"

"I can feel the water, but I don't know the fastest way."

"Then follow me," he said. "I sometimes used to come fishing here when I was a boy. It's about a mile to the canal, and about another mile to the tunnel."

A taxi stopped at a set of traffic lights.

"We're taking it," she said.

"He might not agree."

"I don't care."

Angel nodded. He walked up to the door, but it was locked. Lucy stood in front of the car, blocking the way. The driver pressed the horn and inched forward, touching Lucy's legs, but her fire was alight, and she wouldn't be moved.

"Do you need a hand?" she asked.

Angel shook his head. He took out his pistol and pointed it at the man. When he didn't move, Angel shot the rear passenger window out, stuck the pistol inside and pointed it at the driver.

"Open the doors."

The driver complied.

His eyes widened when Lucy sat next to him. Fire dripped from cracks on her forehead; she assumed it was the stress. She could feel the portal pulsing. It wasn't far. It was also the strangest one she'd encountered, certainly the most complex energetically.

"No animals!" the taxi driver said when Darta jumped in.

Lucy almost laughed.

Angel shut the door.

"Drive!" she said.

But the man had frozen in his seat.

Lucy whispered to Darta, and the panther pushed her head against the driver's and growled.

"Don't let it hurt me," he pleaded.

"Just drive. We don't want to go far," she said.

The man finally moved the taxi forward. "Where to?"

"Islington Tunnel," she said.

"They're coming," Angel said.

"You can't get away with this," the driver said. He glanced in the rear-view mirror. "They'll catch you. You stole the panther from the zoo, didn't you?"

Lucy slapped him with fire-laden fingers.

He cried out.

"You'll never find out whether the police catch us if you don't drive this piece of scrap any faster."

Lucy was now concerned. If he didn't drive any faster, she'd be forced to injure an innocent man, which she didn't want to do, but the police were only a few cars behind them. Again, she spoke to Darta.

"My cat's hungry."

Darta nipped the man. That was enough. He accelerated and raced his taxi through the streets. A few minutes later, they stopped and got out. The taxi burnt rubber as it sped away.

Angel led the way to the canal. Four police cars approached from one direction, two from another.

"We've been caught," Angel said.

"Not if we can reach the tunnel."

They left the road and ran for about a minute along the side of the canal.

"There's no towpath through the tunnel," Angel said.

"It doesn't matter."

They ignored the police calls over loudhailers from them to surrender. Soon, they stood by the tunnel entrance. The line of police was running along the side of the canal towards them.

"I'm coming with you."

She shook her head. "You said you knew somewhere."

"A series of derelict barges further down the canal," Angel said.

"Good. Take Darta and hide. This may take some time."

"How will I know—"

"Darta will know," she interrupted.

The police were getting too close. She touched Darta, who dived into the water and swam across the canal. Angel followed, keeping his pistol above his head as he swam the short distance. Seconds later, they were gone.

Lucy watched the expressions on the faces of the police. They didn't understand why she was waiting for them.

"You're under arrest!"

She dived into the canal and swam into Islington Tunnel.

23

Amelia blinked, but the giraffe still stared at her.

"We've landed in the giraffe enclosure at London Zoo," Luke said, grinning at her expression.

"What?" Now she was completely awake. "Why would we do that?"

Then she noticed the crowds watching them.

"The witch landed in Regent's Park."

Amelia became alert.

"But it was getting too crowded. This was the first empty space we saw."

"I thought I was having a lucid dream."

She climbed out of the helicopter.

"I spoke to my guides," she whispered. "I need to speak to you later."

Luke nodded.

"Get in the car," Gully demanded.

Seconds later, they squashed into one of the police cars sent to pick them up.

"Where to?" Amelia asked.

"Islington Tunnel," the police driver said.

"Why there?"

"They landed in the park, ran to the tunnel, then disappeared."

"And?" Jack asked.

"We're searching. The man and panther swam across the canal and disappeared into Islington. The woman swam into the tunnel!"

He seemed amused, but no one shared his humour. Amelia was sure the witch wouldn't do anything without a reason.

"How long's the tunnel?" Jack asked.

"Almost nine-hundred metres." He shook his head. "Not a smart move. She can't get out; we have men at both ends, and boats and divers on the way. We've got her."

The constable appeared confident, but Amelia withheld her judgement. They soon arrived at the western entrance to the tunnel. Trees grew on either side, their branches overhanging the entrance. Amelia peered inside. It was dark and there was no towpath.

"Why do you think she swam into the tunnel?" Luke asked.

Amelia shook her head. It looked forbidding. She wouldn't have made that choice. "I don't know, but what the driver implied about her lacking intelligence isn't true."

"What then?" Ruth asked.

"Either she panicked and got confused at the last moment and made the wrong choice, or she had a reason. I think she had a reason."

"If she panicked, we'll find her up. Dead or alive," Jack said.

Jack walked over to the tunnel entrance to speak to the police. Ruth joined him.

The tunnel made Amelia feel uncomfortable, but she

wasn't sure why. She watched a police boat emerge; the pilot shouted something. A police officer on the boat held up a human hand in his gloved hand.

Luke raised his eyebrows. "Perhaps they've found her."

They joined Jack and Ruth next to the entrance. Chief Inspector Gully was there, too.

"Is it her?" Gully asked.

The police officer shook his head. "It's been here for at least a day."

Gully appeared disappointed. "What about the witch?"

"What?" the constable raised his eyebrows.

It seemed the police were unaware of the label they used.

"The woman we're searching for."

The man shook his head. "We've not found her."

"I thought you went the whole length of the tunnel?"

"We have. She's not above the surface."

"You think she's dead?" Gully asked.

"Looks that way."

Gully smiled to himself.

The police officer frowned, then rejoined his team.

"What did your guides say?" Luke asked.

"So you believe in them now," she said.

"I don't know if they're literally real, but even if they're not, they're part of your unconscious mind. Ideas from the unconscious sometimes show solutions to real-world problems."

His psychological view was one way of interpreting it, but she preferred her perspective.

"They showed me a sickness spreading across the country, and a choir of angels singing a song of beauty in order to counter it. They asked me to play my part in helping heal the sickness spreading across our country. I think they want me to sing, too."

"What does this mean?"

"Something evil is attempting to undermine the spirit of the country."

He frowned. "And?"

"I saw a demonic figure with three mouths, each one chanting a dark spell."

"And that's sickening the country?" Luke asked.

She nodded. "At least, it's one part of the problem."

"And the correct response is to sing something beautiful?"

"In a sense. To counter the evil with good. It's a bit vague." She wondered whether this was her guides' way of telling her to stop asking them questions. Then she told him about the clock with five suns.

"Five days left," Luke said. "The timing fits what I've translated."

When Luke went to examine the hand, Amelia moved away to sit on a portable chair set up behind a police van. Body parts didn't disturb her, but something about the tunnel did. The sounds of the police faded, and her mind drifted. Despite the ominous feeling, her thoughts turned to the dark tunnel. Why would the witch have swum inside? It didn't make sense. Part of the message from her guides was hard to understand, too. What song would stop the sickness?

She'd recently been reading about remote viewing, about people being able to sense things at a distance. Having no experience of it, she was unsure if it was possible, but as everyone else was busy, she decided to test it. She needed to know what exactly was inside the tunnel and why the witch swam into it.

Clearing her mind, Amelia imagined herself inside the tunnel. All she saw was darkness, but after a few minutes, she heard distant voices chanting, making her feel nauseous. A hazy figure appeared in her mind, standing like the conductor of an orchestra, before hundreds of other shadowy figures, but instead of music, they chanted a sickening spell. Turning her attention back to the figure leading the incantation, Amelia saw three mouths. She blinked, unsure what she was seeing. She looked again. One of the mouths had no nose or eyes accompanying it. Another had small unfocused eyes. The third mouth controlled. Then, the second set of eyes widened, turning to stare at her. With a start, Amelia realised the second set of eyes had seen her; her heart beat faster. Before she could pull away, it screamed.

24

"Amelia?"

She woke up on the ground. Luke was looking down at her with a worried expression.

"What happened?"

"Something came out of the tunnel and attacked me."

The police officer standing beside Luke gave him a confused glance, then shook his head.

"I'll deal with this," Luke said.

The officer walked off, and Ruth and Jack moved closer. They all looked concerned as she explained what had happened, but she could tell they were confused, too.

"You were attacked?" Jack asked.

"The enemy attacked me."

"The orange witch?" he asked.

She shook her head.

"A dark witch."

"There are two witches?" Ruth asked.

Amelia felt lightheaded. "It looks like it. The witch may be confronting her enemy."

"Or meeting an ally," Jack said.

Luke received a call.

He looked at Amelia. "The controller. We've both been ordered to a factory in the north of London. Jack and Ruth are to stay here."

"What?"

"Daryl Cassard's warehouse. Some sort of alien business. Are you well enough to go?"

She nodded. She no longer wanted to remain near the tunnel. An unmarked police car waited for the two of them. Once Amelia was in the car, she slowly centred herself. The thing had shocked her. Luke was talking about two intelligence officers from MI5 who would meet them there.

"Cassard's known to be involved in organised crime," he said.

She glanced at his image on Luke's phone. Her first impression was to keep away from him.

He continued. "The word is out that he's been supplying criminals with body armour that's unlike anything in the world."

"So the aliens are selling advanced technology," she said.

"Looks like it."

They drove along a drab street in north London. It was Sunday afternoon, and not a person was in sight. The plain-clothes officer dropped them off on a side street in the industrial zone near the warehouse. It started to rain.

"Typical," Amelia said.

They walked towards the warehouse. The area around it was desolate, and she had no wish to be there. She glanced at Luke's grim face. In some ways, he no longer resembled a professor, as he once had. His experiences had hardened him. She looked for the MI5 agents.

"There's one," Luke said.

She noticed a man sleeping on a seat in a covered bus shelter.

"How do you know?"

He shrugged. "I don't, but I don't think many homeless people would choose somewhere like this."

"And the other?"

He pointed at a white van parked about thirty yards away. "Maybe there."

Amelia called their controller; she confirmed that Bill was waiting for a bus. He'd enter the warehouse with them. Zach would wait outside. When they approached the bus stop, the man sat up.

"Bill?" she asked.

The man nodded. It was hard to see his face, but she guessed he was in his mid-thirties. "Follow me. I've found a more discreet place to enter."

He led them down a side street, to a place where a tree grew on the pavement. Although the branches didn't extend over the warehouse fence, they almost reached it. He quickly climbed the tree, then stepped onto the top of the metal fence before jumping over. Once on the other side, he rolled an empty metal drum to the fence.

"Amelia."

He knew her name. She was reasonably fit and climbed the tree, but reaching out was harder. Luke held one of her feet from below, and she stepped onto the fence, stumbling at the last minute, but Bill caught her as she half-fell down the other side. Luke climbed over behind her.

They moved quickly to the edge of the warehouse. Bill had already scouted around the outer fence and knew the locations of the doors. Amelia and Luke followed him to the nearest door. They waited as he studied the lock, then took out a set of tools; within thirty seconds, he'd opened the door. They listened, and Amelia opened her senses as best she dared and listened in her own way.

They followed Bill into what appeared to be a room that served as an office for warehouse workers. Dirty mugs sat on a battered desk that looked like it hadn't been cleaned since the warehouse had been built. Along the top of the metal wall next to the desk was a long internal window. Light came from the other side. Bill carefully opened the office door. They heard people speaking further inside. Bill gestured for Amelia and Luke to follow. Piles of crates stood inside the warehouse, giving them cover as they moved closer to the voices. They stopped about ten yards from a small group of men and listened.

"Three aliens," Luke whispered.

Amelia didn't have Luke's linguistic skills, but she recognised their accents. Daryl Cassard stood with three of his men; they faced three aliens. The shortest was over six feet tall. He described an item of clothing he'd taken from an open box. The tallest of the three wore a crimson cloak. She suspected magic. This wasn't the first time she'd felt nervous on a mission, but it was the first time she felt she was in real danger. Her legs shook slightly as she gripped a crate to steady herself. Despite her fear, she was determined to keep still and listen.

Luke watched from the next row of containers. She wasn't sure where the MI5 man was. Then the conversation changed. The alien in the crimson cloak spoke; his voice becoming stronger.

"I have a proposition to make."

Cassard sneered. "What sort of proposition?"

"My group needs a central London property to base our activities from. Your Knightsbridge address suits us."

Cassard and his men laughed. Then Amelia noticed a

lightening of her mood. She didn't understand why until she saw the alien's grin. He was attempting to mentally influence the men, but it was a weak attempt.

"One million upfront," the alien said.

"To buy my top property?" Cassard shook his head.

It seemed the mental suggestion hadn't worked.

"To rent. We want two floors and access to the ground floor."

Cassard narrowed his eyes and pointed at the protective clothing. "We don't know if it works yet."

"I'll give you a demonstration," the alien leader said.

He nodded to the man next to him. The man looked like he was ex-military; he had an assault rifle slung over his shoulder. One of Cassard's men reluctantly put on a shirt but stepped back in alarm when the alien darted forward, knife in hand, and stabbed him. The man cried out, falling to the floor. He then sat up. Cassard examined him and then nodded.

"It works with knives."

The attacker smiled coldly, took out a pistol, attached a silencer, and as the man stepped backwards, he shot him three times in his stomach. The man fell to the ground. Seconds later, the man sat up. He shakily tried to examine himself. The protective shirt looked like any other fashionable shirt to Amelia. Then he stood up unsteadily, began to take off the protective shirt, but changed his mind and left it on. The man in crimson laughed, and Cassard gave a tight-lipped smile. He wasn't amused, but he examined the body armour and nodded.

"It works, but the deal is only for the protective clothing. I'm not having you inside my house."

"You want to see a more powerful demonstration?" the magician asked.

The alien soldier unslung the assault rifle from his shoulder.

"Stop!" Cassard said.

"Shoot him," the man in the crimson cloak said with a malicious grin.

The attacker opened fire again, but this time he didn't stop. The men with Cassard looked at him, but he didn't react. He just stared as his man slid and rolled across the floor until the magician raised his hand and the soldier stopped. The victim lay motionless next to a pile of crates.

"I don't know whether he's alive, but you'll see that none of the bullets have penetrated his torso."

"Very funny," Cassard said sarcastically. His men had drawn their weapons. He turned to one of his men. "Check him."

The man rushed to his colleague.

"He's unconscious but alive."

"Did the bullets penetrate the clothing?" Cassard asked.

The man peered inside the shirt, then shook his head. "There's no blood."

"The body armour may be good, but your manners aren't. I don't tolerate attacks against my men."

"You wanted a demonstration," the alien magician said. "I gave you one. Do you want more?"

Cassard's men tensed, their weapons pointed at the aliens.

"You misunderstand our relationship," the alien said.

"We no longer have one," Cassard snarled.

The alien's hand flicked out, and a glimmer of green light flickered around his fingers. He was a magician; Amelia had guessed correctly. The magician touched the nearest of Cassard's men. The man fell to the floor and screamed as threads of green light spread across his body.

The lines widened into rivers of fluorescent green, his screams becoming more shrill, until finally, the man died.

Cassard looked shocked. "What did you do?"

"Pray you don't find out. My offer remains." The magician raised his hand when Cassard started to speak. "I can give you an exclusive deal. And we can provide other interesting merchandise. Forget this man. What we offer could make you very rich."

"I'm already rich."

"You'll posses more wealth than most countries if you follow me." The magician held up a piece of body armour. "This is just the beginning."

Again, Amelia felt something push against her mind. She found herself involuntarily nodding, just as Cassard was doing. A few seconds later, Cassard passed a suitcase to the shorter alien, who opened it. It was full of money.

"I'll assume it's the correct amount," the magician said. "If not, we'll return."

Daryl Cassard seemed dazed. He rubbed his forehead and looked blearily at the alien.

"Who are you?" Cassard asked.

"You can call me Mr Walker," the magician said.

Amelia watched Walker. Although he had magic, he'd had to use terror and greed to persuade this criminal lord. Mind control alone hadn't been enough. That gave her some confidence. She knew the orange witch could read minds. It was something she'd never really tried. Impulsively, she tried to probe his mind and instantly felt sick. Whatever he radiated, it was noxious; she instinctively pulled away, gasping for breath as she broke contact. Walker looked up, staring directly at the crates Amelia crouched behind.

"We've got company."

Amelia deeply regretted her naive attempt to probe the

mind of a magician. What did she know about such things? She wasn't the orange witch. She staggered against a crate as her throat constricted. It hurt badly. It was as if her muscles no longer worked for her. The magician was attacking her.

"Get her."

The alien soldier ran towards her. A shot came from her right, and he dropped to the floor. Luke was helping her. Amelia gasped as the death grip on her throat relaxed. She staggered back towards the room where they'd entered. Men followed her, and she almost screamed when she ran into Luke. He had a bag of the special clothing in left hand, his pistol in his right.

"Bill?" he whispered.

She shrugged, embarrassed that she was too scared to care. She just wanted to escape. They ran back into the dirty office, then through the unlocked exterior door.

"Quickly," Luke whispered.

They sprinted to the part of the fence they'd climbed over. Luke gave her a foot up. She swung herself over while Luke clambered up. The shorter alien ran towards them—she sensed traces of magic around him. She thanked God that Walker wasn't with him.

Luke hit the ground hard next to her, slipping and falling against the fence. It was still raining. He'd cut his arm. She helped steady him. Then a bullet hit the tree, sending a small branch to the ground. They ran across the road as bullets ricochetted off the wall of the house in front of them. Turning a corner, they sprinted along the deserted grey street.

25

Blood dripped from Luke's arm as he ran. It wasn't serious, but he wished he'd put on some of the body armour he'd stolen.

"Do you know where we're going?" Amelia asked.

"No."

He plunged his hand into the bag and passed her an item of clothing. It was a grey vest. She slipped it over her T-shirt as she ran. He managed to do the same.

"What else did you get?" She glanced at the bundle of clothing he clutched.

"A few more vests, some scarves, and a pair of gloves. I wish I'd taken more."

"No." She shook her head. "It was too close as it was."

Two streets later, they stopped and put on the remaining clothes. He couldn't see anyone following.

"Do you want the gloves?" he asked.

She shook her head. "Too big."

A shot rang out, and Amelia was flung along the pavement. She was immediately on her feet. They sprinted.

"At least it works," she gasped, rubbing her side. "But I'm

going to have a big bruise." After a few minutes running, she was breathing hard. "I need to rest."

Luke looked around uneasily. They seemed to have lost the men. Then he noticed a shadow moving behind her. Something pressed against his chest, making it difficult to breathe. She turned, pistol in hand. Then she pushed him.

"Run!"

Terror gripped Luke, and he ran with Amelia. They turned a corner and crossed the next road, and Luke gasped as the pressure on his chest eased.

"What was that?" he asked.

"Something evil," she said.

He had questions, but there was no time to ask. They kept moving. Then he heard a sound.

"Someone's coming," he said.

As they ran, Luke looked for somewhere to hide. He wasn't familiar with this part of London. They turned a corner. There was nothing. No buses, no cars, no people, no gardens to hide in, and no alleys. Only unattractive rows of red-bricked houses. Normally, this would depress him, now it scared him. They kept running. After several more minutes, he needed to rest; Amelia was close to exhaustion, too.

"Here," he said.

He leant against one of the houses, adjusted the body armour, and held his pistol ready. Amelia nodded. She stood next to him, also breathing heavily, holding her gun with both hands.

Two men ran around the corner. An alien and a human. Luke shot the alien, who fell to the ground. Cassard's man fired. The force of the bullets threw Luke into the front door of a house. Amelia opened fire, forcing the man to back off. Luke saw blood on the ground. The man wasn't wearing protective clothing, or, at least, not enough.

Amelia shouted.

The alien sat up. When he lifted his gun, Luke shot him in his head.

"Good shot," Amelia said. "But watch out for future revenge attacks."

He glanced at her.

"The alien sorcerers are vindictive.

"I don't care," Luke replied. But he knew she was right. He noticed a shocked resident staring at him from one of the upper floor windows, then he turned back as the remaining man fled the scene.

"Let him go," Amelia said.

Luke nodded.

He returned to the dead man and pulled back his jacket. He wore one of the vests underneath. Luke pulled it off.

"What are you doing?" Amelia asked.

"I don't want criminals getting their hands on this stuff."

"That's already happened," she said.

He glanced up. Another curtain pulled back from the upstairs window; it was time to go. Wrapping his scarf around his face, he left the body.

"Do you know where we are?" Amelia asked as they walked along the street.

"No idea."

"Amelia? What happened back there?"

She shuddered. "I think the shadow we saw was caused by the magician. I've read about things like this. Some magicians can project parts of themselves."

"Black magic?"

Amelia nodded.

Luke had more questions, but his desire to leave the area

was stronger. He took out his phone, first checking exactly where he was. Then he called the controller. A new person spoke to him.

"We have your location and will send a car."

The line went dead.

Ten minutes later, a police car raced past them. Soon after that, an unmarked car stopped next to them.

"Luke. Amelia."

The driver was one of the security guards from Pimlico House. They got in.

"Something's happened at the base," the driver said.

Luke's stomach sank.

"What?"

He shrugged. "They don't tell me anything, but part of the building's been sealed off, and that woman, Alice..."

"Alice Greer," Luke said. She was their controller.

"That's her. She seems to be in charge."

No one spoke for the rest of the journey. Luke closed his eyes. He'd had enough bad news. When they walked into the building, Alice Greer met them in the ground floor lobby.

"Come with me."

They followed her up the sweeping staircase to the first floor.

"Alice, what's happened?" Luke asked. The mood was sombre.

She stopped outside the director's office.

Amelia frowned. "Does Toby Upjohn want to speak to us?"

Luke had only spoken to Upjohn a few times, but he seemed to be friendly and laid back for a director of an intelligence service.

"The director's been murdered," Alice said. "I'm the new director of MI7."

"When?" Luke asked.

"About half an hour ago."

"What happened?" Luke dreaded what he might hear.

"We don't really know. The police will be here soon, but I wanted you to see the scene yourselves first. I'm hoping you can pick something up that the police may miss."

Alice looked at Amelia, and Luke guessed she was talking about Amelia's psychic senses.

"I have to warn you, it's not pleasant. Try not to touch anything." She looked at her watch. "The police will be here in fifteen minutes." She gestured at the door. "Enter by yourselves. I've seen enough."

Alice left them by the entrance to the director's suite of rooms. Luke pushed open the door.

"Oh my God," Amelia said.

Luke breathed deeply as he took in the scene. Blood drenched the large oak desk and crimson carpet. Toby Upjohn's body leant back in his chair. His eyes were gone, his stylish grey suit was in shreds, and his body was lacerated with fine but deep cuts.

"Who did this?" Luke said.

Amelia pointed at the shattered window. "It looks like they came in that way."

Luke walked around the desk and stopped.

"Amelia. Come here."

She joined him on the other side of the desk. Small red footprints ran down Upjohn's grey trousers and back to the window.

"They escaped back through the window," Amelia said in a half whisper.

"What escaped?" Luke said.

He turned to Amelia, but she had her eyes closed. He waited, wondering what her psychic sense would see.

She gasped and opened her eyes.

"Animals?" he asked.

She shook her head. "Luke, it's much worse than that."

26

Lucy swam through the darkness towards the portal. The darkness didn't bother her; she had other senses. Neither did the cold water; her inner fire kept her warm. Several things did disturb her. The first was the lack of life. There were no fish, not even small ones. Few insects, too. The portal was in a hole in the upper part of the tunnel wall on the left. It was hard to see, but easy to sense. Magic imbued it, both attracting and repulsing her. One part of the magic appeared to be designed to disguise it. She stopped swimming, remaining stationary in the water, actively probing the hole and the surrounding area with all her senses, including ones unrecognised by most humans.

She had an instinctive feeling of danger but couldn't see or hear sure anything wrong. Then something touched her. Almost screaming, she pulled away. It was cold and stuck to her, sucking on her skin. She burnt it from the fire pores in her palm. An image of a snake flashed in her mind, but she knew it wasn't an animal. Forcing herself to remain calm, she searched the area for any other movement. Something withdrew deeper into the darkness of the hole above her.

She waited in the water for half an hour, but sensed no further movement. Yet she knew it was there. She felt despair. Lucy was sensitive to her feelings and very aware of which were hers, and which were coming from outside. The despair didn't belong to her. The feeling washed around her. It belonged to someone or something else. She shivered despite her inner fire.

When police boats approached from each end of the tunnel, she swam closer to the portal. A human foot floated in the water beneath the portal. *Was something feeding on humans?* Controlling her feelings of anger and disgust, she touched the tunnel wall, imagining that something had grown from the portal and reached towards her. She lit flames from her fingertips and studied the hole, but could still see nothing.

Voices came from the tunnel—the police had seen the light from her fingers. Excitedly, they shouted, accelerating towards her from both directions. They were getting too close. Even with her invisibility spell, they'd see her if they got much closer. Attempting to control her growing sense of panic, she climbed up the tunnel wall, using small holes to help her grip.

She looked into the dark hole.

"There!" an officer shouted. "On the wall."

Lucy climbed into the hole, risking whatever was inside. It was a pitch black. She crawled deeper inside. Some fibres blocked her. She brushed them away, becoming more entangled. Soon she was stuck on a giant web. Again, she lit flames from her fingertips.

She was stuck at the edge of a cavern. Translucent fibres coloured in shades of grey and yellow criss-crossed each other to form a web that stretched from top to bottom and side to side. The pale yellow fibres formed the greater part of it, but many grey fibres were interwoven with them. They exuded very different auras. She knew that the thing that had touched her in the water was one of the serpent-like grey fibres. She shuddered in disgust.

The police were searching the tunnel below, but she was deep enough inside the cavern—they could never see her. From the surface of the canal, the hole seemed small, and with the magic that disguised it, it would be invisible to them. The sounds of the police faded. She lit the fire in her fingertips again. Something moved deeper inside the cavern. She quickly burnt the threads. The grey ones fell away, but she remained stuck to the yellow ones. Some of the loose grey threads snapped at her—one lashed her lips, leaving a bitter taste. She spat the taste away.

Lucy sulked. *Life was unfair. Why was she trapped on a web when all she wanted was to help?* Then her fire blazed as she realised that the self-pitying thoughts didn't belong to her either. They'd come from the grey web. She pulled her arms away, but pulled too hard, and became more entangled in the yellow parts threads. In the distance, four eyes watched her. The empress smirked.

"I have you."

The grey threads belonged to her enemy. When the empress's voice faded, Lucy noticed something moving along a thread towards her. The empress had sent an evil parcel. She didn't know what it contained, and she had no intention of opening it. All she knew was that it came from central London, and she had to release herself before it touched her. Lucy studied the grey web. Apart from being a trap, it was a spreader of corrosive thoughts, thoughts which would find particularly fertile ground in the minds of the bitter and resentful, but they also had the potential to pollute purer minds.

Lucy had the gut feeling that she was being watched. She looked up. Eight amber eyes glowed in the darkness. Shuddering, she again tried to cut the yellow web with her fire but failed. It moved again. Reaching out with her mind, she touched something very alien and recoiled in shock.

"What are you?" she asked.

It came closer. Fire blazed from her palms and she saw what it was. Each of its eight eyes was the size of her face. A black spider, the size of a horse, crouched in the darkness watching her.

Her nose wrinkled in disgust.

"How long have you been here?"

It didn't reply. Perhaps it was simply a giant spider, but she suspected intelligence. It had the feeling of being very old. It was clearly the spinner of the yellow web. The scent was the same. Feeling the beginnings of panic, she tried natural magic. It was soft and cut through the yellow threads. She breathed out in relief.

The giant spider darted from the darkness, injecting her with poison. Lucy gasped in pain. When its long legs stroked her, she spat fire at the nearest one, severing the lower section. Its legs retracted, but it fired more sticky threads that spattered over her. Again she cut them, but these were harder to remove, and they hurt her as they stuck onto her body. The poison had entered her blood. She was in trouble. She'd been overconfident. Apart from her arms and head, she was still stuck. The spider jerked forward. One of its legs struck her.

"Time will weaken you," it said.

So it could speak.

Lucy spat fire when another of its legs brushed against her face. It quickly retracted, giving her some satisfaction. Her fire slowly burnt the poison within her; but it would take time she may not have. She started cutting and burning her bonds one by one, and not for one second could she allow herself to close her eyes. As the hours passed, she realised how serious her situation was. Although she'd cut through most of the spider's web, her legs were still stuck to the empress's web, and if neither the spider nor the parcel killed her, the empress would send someone else to do it. The parcel was already halfway along the thickest of the grey threads. It was then she heard the police officers passing by yet again in their boats. They had no idea she was stuck between two webs above their heads. The hole would be hardly visible to them. Not that they could or would help her.

As she cut the grey threads, several raised their heads like snakes threatening her. One snapped at her and she slapped it away. A vision of the empress's disembodied head appeared before her, gnashing in rage.

Lucy laughed at it, infuriating it more.

The spider watched.

Even this cold old thing had curiosity.

"Enemy?" it whispered.

"I killed her husband," Lucy said.

The spider clicked its legs in hatred. It moved closer.

"Killed her husband," it repeated.

"I've come to kill her."

The spider clicked its legs again.

"I approve of your sentiment, but she'll kill you. She wove her web for you, and now she's caught her prize."

"You survived her," Lucy said. *"And I've survived her before."*

"She tricked me," the spider said. *"That's not happened in a long time. It won't happen a second time."*

Lucy now had doubts about the necessity of closing this portal. Even the empress would be challenged by this ancient guardian sitting at the gate. The grey web vibrated again. The parcel was three quarters of the way along the thread. She was losing time by speaking. Lucy cut frantically at the remaining grey threads.

The spider crept closer. Lucy spat fire at the cold creature, again sending it back a step. She knew to never trust a creature like this, whatever it said. She ignited both her magics at the same time. The spider scurried away, disappearing deeper into its black hole. Lucy could just make it out; it sat in the middle of a second web that spanned the open portal. She shuddered, wondering what creatures from both worlds this thing had caught.

Concentrating again, Lucy continued to blend the natural magic with the primal. The primal fire was coarser but powerful; it came from the instinctive part of her—a wild fire within. Like a blacksmith, she heated her inner furnace and melded the two magics together. It was harder, but it strengthened her.

Ultimately, she needed to call the third magic, but she wasn't yet sure how. She continued to mix the hot and cold magics. The evil parcel was only yards away as she cut the last strands. The largest of them snapped at her like a viper. She grabbed it by its neck and sealed it with fire. She let go. The thick grey thread expanded, and the empress's gift reversed its course, rushing back to its sender. The empress screamed and was gone, and with her, the grey threads fell away from the spider's web. Lucy quickly cut away the few remaining yellow threads. At last, she was free.

She breathed out a sigh of relief. Perhaps she'd been too quick to dismiss her own power. Perhaps her two magics, when melded, could defeat the empress and her cohorts. For the first time since she'd arrived, Lucy felt more optimistic she could actually defeat the empress.

The spider made a harsh, grating sound. Lucy's eyes widened in surprise—alert to any attack. But it didn't come; its body bobbed up and down, and it rasped like an old man.

"*What?*" Lucy asked.

"*You burnt the black widow's legs.*"

Lucy was confused.

"*A no-legged spider's a lover's gift.*"

She'd heard that male spiders sometimes wrapped dead insects in threads as a gift to distract potential lovers who otherwise had the habit of eating them. Again, the spider's sound grated against her ears. Lucy stared at the spider, and then she understood. It was making a joke. Nothing about it was funny, but she'd learnt something new. Spiders had a sense of humour.

27

Luke woke from his dream feeling dread. He'd dreamt the creatures that had killed Toby Upjohn were stalking him. He shivered despite the warmth of his bed. Hoping it was just a nightmare brought on by the stress, he sat up in bed and turned on the lamp. When he heard a sound outside his room, he got up.

It was still dark, and he walked quietly along the passage to William's room. The nanny MI7 had provided slept in the same room. Another sound came from inside. The nanny must be feeding him. Relaxing, he knocked on the door.

A window shattered.

Luke thrust the door open, turning on the light as he entered. He stopped in shock. The nanny lay dead on the floor, covered in fine cuts and small bloody footprints. Blood pooled around her body. Her eyes were wide open in terror.

"William!"

Luke rushed to his cot. The bloody footprints ran up the wooden legs and over William's new pillow. Luke shuddered. The creatures of his nightmare had come. He called for William, but there was silence. Luke followed the bloody footprints across the carpet, up the wall, and out of the broken window. He shivered in horror as he looked out of the window into the dark night. Telling himself that perhaps William had crawled behind some furniture, he ran around the room, desperately searching for his son, but he wasn't there.

He called security, and then he called the rest of his team. As soon as he hung up, his phone rang. When he heard the man's accent, his blood chilled.

"We have your son, Dr Lee. You must follow our instructions carefully."

"Give him back!"

The man gave a cold laugh.

"Which parts would you like? You do want him to grow into a complete man, right?"

The threat sickened him. He closed his eyes and sat heavily on the nanny's armchair.

"What do you want?"

"We want you to work for us. Think of it as a job with benefits. It's not so bad. After you've proven yourself, we'll return your son unharmed. We pay more than your agency. A lot more. And all you have to do is to say what we tell you to say and perform some small tasks. We have a lot to offer. In a way, you'll be helping your country as well as yourself; it's very reasonable. And you'll ensure your son's safety."

The rhythm of the man's speech lulled Luke into a state of relaxation. He almost began to believe it was reasonable. Someone knocked on his door, snapping him out of the trance. He suspected they were using magical suggestion. He closed his eyes. He'd do anything to get William back, but he knew the aliens would use him. Doing what they wanted was no guarantee of getting William back.

"If I give you information, you'll let my son go?"

"Of course."

"What do you want?"

"We'll send you an email, you'll open it on an MI7 computer, and then you'll click on the link."

Cooperation with evil was a slippery slope. And it was unlikely to save William. He needed more time.

"How do I know my son is alive?"

The alien paused.

"I'll contact you soon."

The phone went dead. He sat on the armchair, thinking. When he looked up, Amelia, Jack, and Ruth were in the room.

"We used the spare key when you didn't answer," Amelia said.

"The aliens have William."

"Are you sure?" Amelia asked.

"I'm sure."

Luke found it hard to speak. He forced himself. "The same things that killed Toby Upjohn came for William."

They looked at the nanny's body.

"The footprints are the same," Amelia said.

"Strange prints," Ruth said. "The rear prints look like a cat, the front ones like a monkey."

"What made them?" Jack asked.

"Black magic," Amelia said quietly. "Ensouled thought forms."

"Who sent them?" Luke asked. He needed to focus to help William.

"One of the alien magicians."

Ruth's eyebrows drew together. "The prints are impossible for any living creature, so perhaps that's it."

"Who were you just speaking to, Luke?" Jack asked.

Luke knew that honesty was best. He'd seen the results

of lies and deceit in the lives of his patients in his clinical psychology practice.

"The aliens."

The team went quiet.

Luke still stared at the carpet. "They want me to perform some small tasks."

"Such as?" Jack asked.

"To spread misinformation. And they want to send me an email with a link to click."

"So they want to infect our computer system," Jack said. "What did you say?"

"I asked how I could know if my son was alive. They said they'd call back later."

"That's good," Jack said. "We must delay them as much as possible."

"I once spoke to Superintendent Dale about negotiation," Luke said. "But I never thought I'd use it."

"We should bring him in," Jack said. "He's one of Britain's best negotiators."

"He knows about the aliens, too," Ruth added.

Luke looked at Amelia. "I think they tried to use mental suggestion to influence me."

"That's typical," she said. "It didn't work, though."

"You knocking on the door helped snap me out of it." He stared at the dead nanny, realising that this was the first time he'd really thought about her; his mind had been on his missing son. "She didn't deserve that."

"No," Jack said. "Too many things like this are happening around the aliens. They lack respect for life."

Two police officers entered the room. Jack spoke to them. Luke started when his phone rang. His friends went quiet as he answered.

"Hello?"

"*Alice,*" he mouthed. He turned on the speaker and slumped back in the chair.

"The police are already searching for your son," she said. "I'll keep you informed. So the things that murdered Toby Upjohn murdered the nanny and took your son.

"Yes," was all that Luke could say.

Alice changed the subject. "We've confirmed some of what you heard in the warehouse was true."

"Which part?"

"It seems that the people you believe to be aliens are now installed in his Knightsbridge house." Alice was silent for a few seconds.

"Anything else?" Luke asked.

"I'm sorry to ask you this now, Luke, but we need all four of you back at Regent's Canal. There's been a development."

Alice hung up.

Luke didn't care; he couldn't relax with William kidnapped, and he'd do anything to stop the aliens. Killing them would be preferable.

"We can take my bike," Jack said.

He left with Ruth.

"Want a lift?" Amelia asked.

Luke nodded.

They met in the basement carpark ten minutes later. Driving calmed Amelia, and her old rally driving self returned. She accelerated her red Mini Cooper out of the underground parking area, almost hitting a parked car. Usually it would make Luke cringe, but today, his mind was elsewhere. However, as she hurtled through the London streets, it occurred to him that he needed to remain alive long enough to rescue William.

"Do you ever drive slowly?"

"Sometimes."

She skidded to a halt at a zebra crossing. A man shouted, but she didn't seem to notice.

He told her about his nightmare.

"A warning," she said. "You may be more sensitive than you think, but it doesn't sound like a psychic attack." She thought for a few moments. "If we ever get the chance to hurl back those projections, we'd hurt the sender."

"How could we do that?"

She shook her head. "I need to think about it."

They reached Islington by quarter to six. Jack's Triumph Bonneville was parked next to a police van. It was one of three bikes he owned. Amelia raised an eyebrow when she saw it.

"He beat you," Luke said.

"He had a head start."

Luke honestly wasn't sure which of the two was the better driver, but this time, their friendly rivalry failed to lighten his mood. The canal was still sealed off. After showing their ID to a police officer, they approached Ruth, who was examining something on the ground. A ring of police officers looked at it, too.

Luke felt sick when he saw what it was. The leg had been cut off just below the knee.

"A woman's," Ruth said. "But not the witch. We found other parts of her body at the other end of the tunnel. There's part of a child's body, too."

Luke's eyes widened.

"Not William," she said. "This poor boy was about five."

Luke felt weary. The darkness of the aliens' activities depressed him. Perhaps this was one part of the alien sickness sweeping the country?

"Where's Jack?" Luke asked.

Ruth pointed to the tunnel. "He's just gone inside to take

a quick look, but he should be out soon. The police can't find the witch, or anything inside, but they reported a flickering light, and one of the officers said he saw a shadow against the tunnel wall."

"So she's still there," Amelia said.

"But where?" Luke asked.

Amelia shook her head. "I don't know, but she has magic beyond anything I've seen. Apart from our enemy."

"There are odd sounds, too," Ruth said.

"Like?" Luke asked.

"Hissing or whispering, and sometimes a faint sound of voices," Ruth said. "One of the police divers thinks the tunnel's haunted."

Luke didn't think it haunted, nor did he believe her dead. "She swam into the tunnel for a reason. We need to find it."

Twenty minutes later, Jack's boat reappeared from the tunnel. A tremor sent ripples along the canal.

"Something's in the water," Jack said, leaping from the boat.

They watched the ripples coming from the tunnel entrance. A police officer shouted, grasping the side of the boat as it rocked violently. A diver scrambled out, shouting and pointing to the dark water. Ripples moved rapidly towards them.

"What's that?" Luke asked. He was unsure what he was seeing, but clearly something moved under the water.

"Too fast for a swimmer," Jack said.

They stepped back as it passed, then followed, running along the towpath with about a dozen police officers. The police vans parked right next to the canal slowed them. By the time they'd run around the vans, whatever caused the ripples was about thirty yards ahead. The water swelled and spurted into the air. Then something burst from the surface of the canal, landing on the opposite towpath. A woman stared at them with glowing orange eyes.

"It's her," Luke said.

Clouds of steam rose from her body. She turned and ran into Islington.

28

Steam rose from Lucy as she adjusted her inner flame. She looked back at the police and the men and women in plain clothes, watching her from the opposite bank. Amelia Blake was there. Although Lucy wanted to speak to them, she couldn't submit to the authorities, nor could she waste time attempting to explain what they could neither understand nor believe. She had to remain apart; there was no other way.

She ran, opening her senses to the city. The song of her enemy still sounded in her ears. Although most people wouldn't hear it, the sickening rhythm would be felt. It was still spreading. An image of Islington High Street flashed in her mind. Something was wrong. She hesitated. Her aim was to stop the empress, not to be distracted by every evil in society. But what was she if she didn't offer help when called? Her intuition told her the need was strong. Something bad was happening in Islington, and it was possible her enemy was behind it. She ran towards the high street.

A small crowd had developed by the side of the road. They watched a tall man. His mirrored shades couldn't hide the scent of black magic washing around him. She now knew why she'd been called, and she was relieved she'd answered.

A dog whimpered.

Then she paused. On the opposite side of the street, a man stood in the shadows. There was something wrong with him, too. Not just the alien magic. She listened. He was the stronger of the pair and was chanting a spell of sickness. Unbidden, her fire burnt more brightly, but first she wanted to see exactly what the alien in shades had done to draw the crowd.

She pushed her way to the front, receiving an angry glare from a man filming the scene on his phone. The alien twisted a golden retriever's ear, making it squeal, but she saw what no one else could. He was a soul catcher.

"It's not right," a woman said.

A lot wasn't right, including the inaction of the crowd. Although the sickening chant had probably subdued them. The man filming the scene tapped her on her shoulder.

"You're in my way."

She glanced back at him, not liking his look, nor the way he thrust his phone in her face. But there was no time for childish games. He could continue to film her; she'd give him something to record.

She walked up to the alien.

"Oh, I wouldn't do anything," a man whispered. "I've called the police."

At least he'd done something, she supposed. Lucy focussed her attention on the soul catcher. With one of her senses, she saw a grey light around his hands; even for her, it was hard to see. He was using it to rip the dog's life from its body. The dog desperately tried to escape, but the man held it firmly. She spied a crystal pendant around his neck: the storage vessel for a soul, most likely.

"Stop," she said.

The man snarled, but didn't stop. The dog squealed in pain again.

She tapped his shoulder. "I said stop!"

He raised his fist to her.

"I told you to stop!" This time she spoke in Dnassian, the imperial language of his world.

She knew the crowd listened to every word.

His mouth hung open as she reached forward and ripped the crystal pendant from his neck. She wanted to study it. He turned to strike her. She knew he would and was ready. Her hand was already becoming a blade and fire poured from the fire pores in her palm and in her fingertips. Moving closer, she stabbed him in his heart. He looked up in surprise.

"Eva Noone knows you're here."

So that was the name the empress used on Earth. It seemed familiar. Then he was dead. At least he'd given her the new name of the empress. The crowd stepped away in shock. She didn't think they'd seen her fire hand, but she couldn't be sure. The video may show more. The dog licked her vigorously, thanking her repeatedly.

"Look at that dog," a woman said.

He was overexcited. She calmed him as best she could while watching the chanter opposite. He'd redirected his spells, aiming them at her. A dark and vaporous cloud moved quickly towards her. It would blight what it touched. The dog, sensing it before the people around her, desperately pawed her leg in warning.

"Wait here," she whispered to the animal.

Then she stepped into the road and waited for the cloud to reach her, noticing the sorcerer's stupid grin.

Did he think she couldn't see it?

When its outer layer touched her outstretched hand, she felt the dark nausea afflicting the land, but, although unpleasant, it wouldn't stop her. She burnt it with the fire from her palm and fingertips. The foolish grin fell from the sorcerer's face as his magic rushed back to him. The man recording her warned people she was armed. She had no idea what he thought he'd seen. It was time to leave, but the alien opposite was actively sickening the people of Britain. She couldn't leave yet.

Lucy crossed the road, followed by the golden retriever. *"Go!"* she whispered in the True Language. But he refused. He had no home. She showed him the danger, but that made him more determined. She let the dog do what he wanted.

The dark cloud surrounded its creator. The man's face twisted in bitterness. His own magic was sickening him—a common problem with black magic. She didn't know, and didn't need to know, what dark magic they'd planned by taking the dog's life. It was enough to know that it was an evil and despicable thing to do. The sorcerer glared at her as he gathered his energy tightly around him like a shroud.

She heard a police car. She had to act quickly.

"Who are you?" the man asked in broken English as she got closer.

Again, her hand was a flaming blade, but this time, the police were there.

"Drop the knife!" one shouted.

So that was what they saw. Glancing at them, she saw the guns pointing at her. Now was not the time to die. She let the flames fade.

Something hit her hard in her face, and she flew to the ground, feeling a sharp pain. The sorcerer had whipped her with a thread of magic. She lay on the ground, seeing stars. The man grinned as he approached her. He had a pendant, too. Another soul catcher. She didn't want one of his kind coming near her.

She tried to sit up, but her head swam from the blow and she fell back to the pavement. She was losing consciousness. Desperately, she fought to remain conscious. She wasn't sure what this man could do to her if she passed out. But slowly, her vision dimmed. As she fainted, the last thing she heard was the dog attacking the alien.

29

Lucy dreamt of the forest around the church. It was a lucid dream. She was awake within it and felt at peace. Then the forest faded, and she saw the web of despair stretching across Britain and over the sea into France and Belgium. Reaching out, she touched one of the fibres.

"Noone."

Her enemy heard.

"I'm coming for you."

Immediately, the attack began. She knew it would. In her dream, she laughed, which was a good defence. Noone sent fibrous snakes that snapped around her but slipped from her body as if she were greased. Lucy traced the dark strands back to Noone. She knew where she was. Had Noone really underestimated her that much? Perhaps she didn't care. Overconfidence was a fault common in the imperial ruling class. One of the things bit her, and the pain focussed her attention. Then, for a fraction of a second, a spark blazed within Lucy. The attack stopped, and Noone was gone. She wasn't sure whether this spark was the third magic or whether she'd imagined it. She was lucidly dreaming and the same rules didn't apply. They'd located her. That could be a problem, but she didn't intend remaining wherever she was for more than a day. Probably much less.

Then she felt something nudge her. At first, she thought it was in the physical world, but then she realised it was still a part of her dream. The golden retriever greeted her with a wagging tail. He waited nearby, guarding her from danger.

"I'm too dangerous to be near," she whispered. *"You must find someone else."* Finally, the dog appeared to understand.

Knowing she needed to return to full consciousness, she allowed herself to slowly feel her body. The sounds and the smell of cleaning fluids told her she was in hospital. Her wrists and ankles were shackled. She kept her eyes closed. Several people were gathered around her.

Strange. The material of the restraints was soft. She became more conscious and her headache began. Automatically, she sent her fire to heal the bruises she'd suffered. Again, she felt the soft restraints and almost laughed out loud. They were made of paper.

A nurse explained that she couldn't escape because of the restraints and that there were two armed police officers outside the door. She'd been there for several hours, at least, and wasn't sure exactly when she'd had her lucid dream.

"The doctor will be here soon," the nurse said.

Lucy chilled. Although the woman's accent was slight, she recognised it immediately. The nurse was an alien. They were moving fast. She kept listening, not wanting to alert them that she was now awake.

Amelia Blake was there. That reassured her. The others must be her Security Service friends; she picked up their names in the conversation she overheard, and from the timbre of their voices, she picked up more about their feelings.

Apart from Amelia, they were hostile to her—some more than others. Even Amelia was unsure. Lucy understood. Unfortunately, they'd soon hold an even lower opinion of her. They discussed the aliens, and they planned to infiltrate a party where they'd be present tonight. Lucy had not been to a party for a long time. She decided to take Angel with her.

Someone else entered the room.

"What have you found, doctor?" Jack asked. He held the most hostility towards her.

"You've brought in an odd collection of bodies over the past few months. And now a living patient."

"And?" Jack asked.

"When she came in, she was seriously injured, but she's recovering at an incredible rate."

Lucy was very aware of the fire flowing through her. She'd almost healed herself.

"Is her blood similar to the aliens?" the woman she'd identified as Ruth asked.

"Similar but different. If you'd told me about aliens six months ago, I wouldn't have believed you," he said. "The others have two hearts, and blood that coagulates in seconds when they're cut. Their white blood cells would destroy the most virulent cancer we know within weeks."

"Is she an alien, too?" the one called Luke asked.

Lucy listened to his voice. The man called Luke was in pain; she sensed it immediately.

"Her physiology is completely unlike the aliens, but it's unlike ours, too."

"So, a different kind of alien?" Luke asked.

"Well, certainly she's not normal."

Lucy agreed with the doctor about that.

The nurse fussed over the drip they'd attached to her arm. Lucy hoped curiosity would keep the nurse in the room. She didn't want to alert them yet.

"Can you tell us more?" Amelia asked.

Lucy listened with interest. She'd never had a medical opinion about the changes to her body.

"She only has one heart. In some ways, her physiology is closer to ours, but in others she appears more alien than the aliens."

"For example?" Luke asked.

"Her blood is as incredible as the others. She stops bleeding in seconds, and her blood attacks pathogens with a ferocity that is more aggressive than the others."

"Does she have gills?" Ruth asked.

"No. Her skin's interesting, though. It's tougher than human skin, but it's unlike theirs." He paused. "The biggest differences are in her DNA, and the extra organ we found in her abdomen."

They'd found her fire organ; it'd began growing when she first accessed her primal magic. Her fire was physical, but laden with magic.

"It's made of something incredibly tough," the doctor said. "It seems to contain fire, but we'd have to cut her open to really examine it."

Lucy was about to tell the doctor what he could do with his scalpels when he continued.

"She also has special pores in her palms and fingers."

"I've seen those," the nurse said. "What do they do?"

The doctor paused. Lucy guessed nurses didn't usually question doctors like that.

"Please tell us," Luke said.

"We think they're channels for the fire. If the others are

aliens, she's some sort of super alien. Their DNA looks like modified human DNA, albeit changed in a way we don't understand, but her DNA looks more like a blend of human and another DNA; perhaps more than one other."

So it was true. She'd gained something from the rocs, too, the intelligent avian species of her forest world. They'd told her she'd become one of them. The thought of the noisy, hot-blooded birds warmed her heart.

"How can she be a blend of three different life forms?" Ruth asked. "How is that possible?"

"We've got no idea, and we're probably wrong. But that's what it looks like. We've got months of study ahead of us."

Lucy opened her eyes, immediately recognising the speakers she'd seen from a distance.

"She's awake!" the nurse said.

Lucy knew that her eyes glowed like orange embers.

"Impossible," the nurse said, leaning closer.

Lucy breathed out a red mist. The nurse jumped back, cursing crudely.

Lucy turned to the doctor. "Food."

"I can't allow you to eat for the time being."

Lucy burnt the restraints from her wrists and ankles, knocked them to the floor, where they continued to burn, and sat up on the bed.

"What are you?" the doctor asked.

"You wouldn't believe me," she said.

"What's your name?" Jack asked.

She didn't answer. Her previous life was a distraction, and she didn't want to go there.

The doctor stared at her with wide eyes and shook his head. "You've had serious injuries. We've administered drugs—"

"I've neutralised them," she interrupted.

The nurse walked towards the door—she could not be allowed to leave the room alive.

Lucy slipped from the bed and touched the alien's heart. *"Stop."*

The alien fell to the floor.

The doctor crouched next to the woman. Then he looked at Lucy in shock. "You've killed her."

"She's an alien."

"I have to get help."

"No, you don't," Lucy said. She reached for the doctor, who leapt back.

"Get away from me!"

"I'm not going to kill you," she said, "but you can't leave the room." Wide-eyed, the doctor ran into the bathroom and locked the door.

That would do.

Looking at the others, Lucy sat back on the bed and said, "We need to speak."

"You're under arrest," Jack said.

"Fine." She looked at the pistol pointed at her. Lucy reminded herself that they knew hardly anything about the aliens. "At least let me get my clothes. Hospital clothing burns too quickly."

She took her clothes from a small locker and they had the decency to look away as she dressed.

"We found a dog guarding you on the street," Ruth said. "He was very attached to you."

Lucy looked at the woman and wondered; she seemed to like animals.

"Where is he?"

"He seems to be waiting for you outside the hospital. I have no idea how he could know you were here."

"I helped him, and he returned the favour." She glanced at the woman. "He's a good dog; he needs a home."

Ruth hesitated, obviously not expecting her to say that.

Jack glared at her. "Where's Angel?"

She wasn't surprised by his attitude. She knew the history between the two men.

"Safe, I hope."

"He's a killer."

She nodded. "Yes." It was the truth.

"A killer working with a killer," Jack said.

He was becoming repetitive. "He's good at his job. I have further need of him."

"At least you're honest," Jack said. The man appeared a little surprised.

"Time's running out," Lucy said. "We have till Friday."

"And then what?"

"They plan to open a portal. Nothing good will come through it."

"The same as before," Luke said.

"It seems like it."

"Why should we believe an assassin working with an assassin?" Jack asked.

Lucy shook her head, beginning to get annoyed by Jack's rigid view. "I've only killed a handful of aliens. This is war; you've killed men, too." She could tell Jack was a little taken aback by her reply.

"What do you know about the aliens?" Luke asked.

"Their leader is a woman called Eva Noone. She's deadly. Don't go near her."

"I knew it!" Amelia said. "She's standing for Parliament."

"Then they're infiltrating our institutions," Lucy said. "Kill her if you can."

It was time to go. Her enemy would already be coming to get her.

"I must leave."

Jack raised his pistol.

She sang a short magical note to sap his strength; it was a part of her natural magic that she seldom used. For a second, Jack weakened, and she slapped the pistol from his hand, sending it clattering under the bed.

At the sound, the door opened, and two armed police officers strode in. When they saw her, they roughly took hold of her. One whipped out his handcuffs in a smoothly practiced motion. But she was practiced, too. Her primal magic exploded, and bright orange fire flared around her, sending everyone staggering back. She touched the officers, causing them to faint, then slipped through the door.

30

It was early Monday evening, and Luke Lee stood in a queue outside Cassard's house in Knightsbridge, but his thoughts were on a new report the Security Service had passed him. It was about an upsurge in slave trafficking in London. There were indications that the aliens were involved.

The report made depressing reading. It stated that there were now fifty million slaves in the world, and it was a trend that was increasing. It was also clear that the aliens held a very different attitude towards slavery to people in Britain. His phone rang; he didn't recognise the number. He felt a heaviness in his stomach.

"We've sent the email," an alien said.

"I'm on the street, not in my office."

"You must do this soon."

"How do I know my son's alive?"

He heard his son crying.

"That could be recorded."

"Your son's too young to speak. Now, do it."

"Are the rumours of slavery true?" Luke blurted out.

He was desperate to know what they were doing. He could hardly bring himself to ask if that was to be William's fate, but he knew there were people in the world who would buy a baby with no questions asked.

"You people have strange sensibilities," the alien said. "The strongest always rise to the top; the weakest fall to the bottom."

"It's immoral," Luke said.

The alien laughed. "It's natural, and more common than you think. Now do what I've told you."

The alien hung up.

The queue moved forward. The influencers were already inside; those around him were mostly reporters. He was supposed to be a technology writer and had spent part of the afternoon reading up on bulletproof clothes. They moved forward again. He showed his press card and was in. Hundreds of people milled around the white marble pillars of a spacious reception area. The reporters enthusiastically drank the free drinks being offered. He picked a glass of cheap sparkling wine, mainly because he disliked sweet drinks. He didn't want more than a sip of anything.

In the centre of the room, there was an oval space cut in the floor surrounded by a glass barrier and tables. A crowd of men looked down. He joined them. They looked down at a group of about a dozen young women wearing bikinis, sitting around an oval swimming pool on the lower level, drinking cocktails. It was a distraction; he had to discover more about the aliens. Jack and Amelia would enter separately, sometime in the next hour.

A reporter introduced himself.

"What do you think about this stuff?"

He waved the promotional brochure Luke had studied that afternoon, along with over a dozen reviews of the literature on bullet-proof clothing.

"Impossible," he said.

He knew the science supported him. The claims made in the brochure went beyond anything developed anywhere in the world. But he also knew the claims were true. He'd tested the clothing himself, and he wore one of the bullet-proof shirts right now.

"But I'm looking forward to the demonstration." Then he grinned. "Actually, I came for the party."

The man laughed and made a joke about the woman in the red bikini. Luke smiled, but his mind was on his mission. There had been a reversal in Daryl Cassard's relationship with the aliens. The man had become too deeply involved with people even more unpleasant than himself. Luke made an excuse and mingled with the other guests.

As he walked past the bar, he heard a woman speaking a foreign language. He slowed, hoping to make out her words, but she spoke too quietly. He stopped and ordered a drink he didn't want. She glanced at him, and he smiled, trying to look like the harmless academic he'd once been.

The woman turned away.

"Any new buyers?" the man she'd been talking to asked in the alien language.

"Several," the woman said. "One's looking for children."

Luke tensed.

He took his drink without hearing what the barman said to him.

The alien shook his head. "Slaves take up space."

The woman shrugged. "It's money for us, and the warehouse has no more space. Besides, this is our property now."

Luke chilled. He wished he'd been able to smuggle a gun into the reception. But perhaps it was for the best. He may have been tempted to force an answer at gunpoint. At least they'd confirmed that Cassard was no longer in charge; they'd taken over his house and warehouse. Luke pretended to be searching the crowd for someone.

One of the many journalists pushed past, and Luke missed the rest of the conversation. By the time he'd gone, the aliens had lapsed into silence.

"Are you Russian?" Luke asked the woman. He smiled.

She looked at him with disdain, took her drink, and left. The man looked at Luke and left, too. Luke didn't care. He'd heard enough. He had to find William. He'd been told to use his own discretion when inside the house. He'd lost interest in the reception and watched the kitchen doors swing open; two waiters walked out with full trays of cocktails.

MI7 had acquired plans for the house. They'd come from an estate agent and could be outdated, but they were all he had. At the back of the kitchen, servants' stairs led up to the first floor. Since the main staircase was guarded, it seemed the best route.

Seconds later, two more waiters left the kitchen carrying trays of snacks. He knew that Jack and Amelia would be here soon, but this was his chance. There would only be kitchen staff inside. When one more person left the kitchen, Luke pushed open the kitchen doors and walked in.

A chef looked at him.

But Luke had seen the stairs at the back. He strode towards them.

"You can't go there," the chef said in a local accent.

Several kitchen workers had stopped to stare.

Luke issued an order in the alien language. The reaction was instantaneous. The man's face turned ashen. He muttered an apology, but he'd obviously not understood a word Luke had said. The kitchen workers looked away, avoiding eye contact. He guessed the aliens didn't make good employers. Luke climbed the narrow stairs to the first floor.

He stopped at the end of a dimly lit landing. It was quiet. He heard voices coming from the second floor and decided to look. The second floor was also quiet, but a door half way along the passage was open. Someone was speaking. After waiting for several minutes, no one came out. He tiptoed towards it and looked inside.

A large man sat with his back to the doorway. The back of his neck was blue and horns protruded from his head. His first thought was that this was a criminal with a penchant for extreme body modification. Even so, it was odd. Luke swallowed nervously, regretting his impulsiveness. He needed to be alive to help William, and he didn't even have a weapon. He slowly stepped backwards, but froze when a gun pushed into his back. Someone hit his head, and Luke fell against the wall, seeing stars. The alien man from downstairs looked at him. Luke shook his head, trying to clear his vision.

"What?" he asked in English.

"Who is he?" someone asked from the room.

They all spoke the alien language.

"I saw him downstairs," the man replied. "I say we just kill him."

A strange grating laughter came from the room as the man pointed his pistol at Luke.

"I've come for my son," Luke said in the alien language.

The man grinned. "I knew you understood."

He pulled Luke to his feet and shoved him towards the

stairs, forcing him to climb to the fourth floor. The man pushed him into an empty room.

"Give me my son."

The man laughed, then hit his head with his pistol. Luke felt a sharp pain before losing consciousness.

31

Lucy looked at the boats, with their lines of laundry and plastic containers scattered all over their decks.

"Not a good neighbourhood," Angel said.

The derelict canal barge he'd been staying on was the worst of the lot.

"Is this thing sinking?" She was sure the deck leant to one side.

Angel shrugged.

He was right. It didn't matter. Her stomach rumbled again. She'd eaten four portions of fish and chips, four pies, and a pizza, and still felt hungry. But it was better than nothing. At least Darta had found fish in the canal.

They left the boat and pushed through a path that led to London, as most people knew it. From the road, there was no evidence the houseboat community existed. A white van waited at the end of the path. Lucy didn't ask where he'd acquired it. Angel let Darta in the back. A man on the pavement opposite gave a double glance, but Lucy no longer cared. She was about to play the first of her hands. Angel drove into the night.

He passed her his phone. A picture showed a man leaving a house. She could read the energy of people she met in person, and pictures worked almost as well. It was distasteful.

"Who is he?"

"Daryl Cassard," Angel said.

The feeling was unwholesome.

"He may resort to violence," she said, passing the phone back.

"That's his reputation."

"Who owns the house?"

"Cassard, but I've heard another group has moved in with him."

"The aliens," she said.

Angel nodded, slowing to let a car overtake them. He was taking extra care.

She'd sensed a portal at the house. It appeared to turn on and off mechanically; she'd sensed no magic, which indicated the aliens were using technology, possibly infused with black magic, to open them. She refused to believe a common criminal could have any understanding of portals. At the moment, she was sure there was no portal operating at the Knightsbridge mansion.

She prayed she was right about their use of technology. If they'd mastered the magical ability to open and close portals at will, she'd failed, and would probably be dead soon, but it was unlikely. What she'd learnt during her journey between universes could only be gained at great cost. They preferred faster ways.

Lucy looked out of the van window. She'd lost all sense of time and place and hardly noticed the people or cars passing through the streets of London. Distracted when the black panther nuzzled her neck, she rubbed her neck in return, receiving a wet lick.

Angel glanced at the panther. "I'm not sure I can get her inside."

"She'll find a way."

Lucy had already run through several scenarios with Darta. She'd been trained to enter buildings undetected.

"What do you want to do at the reception?" Angel asked. "Gathering information may not be enough."

"I need to understand this portal." She thought for a few seconds. "And I need to know if Noone or her lieutenants are there, too." She'd sensed Noone's presence, but wasn't sure if this was her permanent base.

"What's different about this portal?" Angel asked.

"It's odd that it opens and closes so completely. Usually there's residual energy around a closed portal for several days after it's been used. Even longer sometimes."

"And you can sense it from inside?"

"The closer I get, the easier it is to sense what's happening," she said.

"What if they're better at opening and closing portals than you think?" Angel asked.

"Then we have a problem." She paused while she again considered the possibility. "I still don't think it likely."

"What if they force our hand?" Angel asked.

She'd thought of that.

"Do you want me to kill?"

She nodded. "If necessary, but information is more important."

Angel stopped at a set of traffic lights.

"Will they know you're there?"

"Walker or Nimori would sense magic immediately if I used

it." She remembered Nick Nimori from the fight she'd had with him from another universe. She'd used Amelia Blake's body as a conduit for her magic. "So would Noone, if she's there."

"Do you think she'll be there tonight?"

"You know as much as me."

It was possible that one of the sorcerers would be there, especially if they were using the event to gather money. If not one of the leaders, then a member of the crew.

Angel parked the van on the street by the side of the house. They still had a little time; she didn't want to enter too early. She stared ahead, waiting for the question she sensed forming in his mind.

"What?"

"Can you beat Noone?"

The question was direct, as Angel's usually were, but even though she'd wondered the same thing, it was not a question she expected.

"Not in a direct fight."

"Honest, at least," he said. "What about the others?"

She raised her eyebrows. "Is this quiz night?"

"My life might depend on it."

He was practical.

"I could kill any of the apprentice sorcerers."

"What about Walker or Nimori?"

"Nimori's the weakest. One to one, I think I'd defeat him. But he's still dangerous. He might occupy all my attention while others attacked."

Angel nodded. "Alistair Walker?"

"He's much more powerful than Nimori. Last time I faced him, I had the advantage of surprise."

"So all together…"

"They'd kill me," she said without hesitation. "Any two of them would probably be enough."

"Then we must be careful," Angel said.

"First, I need to understand what exactly is there. Once I know that, then I hope to kill them one by one when they're alone. Non-magical means may prove most effective."

"And that's my job," Angel said.

"Our job," Lucy replied. "I can shoot, too."

"We have four days," Angel said. "Is that enough time?"

"I don't know. If Friday comes and she's still alive, I may need to confront her face to face whatever the risk."

She'd felt the elusive third magic touch her, but still didn't understand it well enough. The angel had said it was within her, but he'd also told her to seek help. She wasn't sure whether Angel and Darta were enough.

A dog walker passed the van. His dog took a bit too much interest in it. It could smell Darta. Eventually, the man pulled the dog away.

"Perhaps Amelia Blake can help. I may be able to train her, but it would take time."

Angel looked at her sceptically. "Can you be sure if there's no sorcerer present?"

"No, I can only be sure when they're using magic or the portal.

"So we may be walking into a trap." he said.

Lucy sighed. "Maybe. If I sense magic, I want you to get out fast. Remember that you'll have Darta with you; she can sense magic, and I've told her to avoid it."

"What if there are aliens upstairs?" Angel asked.

"Kill them as fast as you can, but at any sign of magic, get out of there. You can't fight it." She paused. "That said, bullets are faster than spells when dealing with lesser sorcerers."

"How will I know which is which?"

"You know what Nimori and Walker look like, and if a

woman with two heads and a mouth in her belly attacks you, run!"

He grinned.

"Darta has good instincts."

Angel nodded.

"I can see through her eyes, but can't risk speaking directly to you unless you're sure it's safe. But we have our phones."

She glanced at the house. It was almost time.

"This is the strangest job I've done," he said.

"I believe you."

"Don't drink too much," he said. "Some unsavoury types will be there."

She'd met many unsavoury types in her life. Common criminals hardly bothered her anymore. Just the magic users.

"I burn alcohol in my mouth and stomach."

She remembered an incident where she'd once drunk too much and sent jets of flames into a group of friends. Fortunately, they'd been dragons. Darta pushed against the back of Angel's head. She was still attached to him. Darta and the assassin were a lethal team; she had no doubt that they could take out three or four times their number within seconds, including any lesser sorcerers.

"I want to walk around the house," he said. "See what's happening."

He left them in the van. Lucy listened using her inner senses; Darta joined her in mind, and she used the panther's instincts as they hunted for aliens. Both Darta and Angel had great patience; she was lucky there. After half an hour, Angel returned. He didn't speak, but waited for her to return to the physical world.

She opened her eyes.

He raised an eyebrow.

"There's magic being used, but it's very low level. If Noone or her sorcerers are there, they're fast asleep. I think we're safe to go."

They left the van's sliding side door open; Darta remained inside, waiting to be called. Spiked railings around the house created a space between the building and the pavement. There was also a narrow gap between the back of the house and the next one. A tiny alley separated the two.

Angel looked up at the spikes a few inches above his head.

"I can give you a leg-up," Lucy said.

Angel seemed sceptical. She looked around. The small street was clear.

"Now."

He stepped into her cupped hands, and she lifted him up. Even without her fire, she believed she could lift him. As soon as he had one foot on top, she called Darta. The black panther leapt straight over the railings. Angel half climbed, half slid down the brickwork on the other side.

"Can you manage the rest?" she asked.

He looked at the wall with its windows and a drainpipe running down it. "I can use the drainpipe and windows."

Darta already climbed the wall, edging her way slowly up, and Angel disappeared into the shadows between the buildings. Lucy walked around to the front. The house, as far as she could see, took up almost a quarter of that side of the street. The doorman looked at her suspiciously.

"Alone?"

She was suddenly conscious of her clothes. She'd not had time to dress properly for this type of reception. And the ticket Angel had faked may not have been top quality.

"I have friends inside."

He opened the door, and she walked through a pale blue vestibule, and then into a large reception room. Crystal chandeliers hung from the ceiling. About a hundred people milled about beneath them. To her right was a long bar with barstools. Most were occupied. In the centre, the floor was cut away in the shape of an oval, with a small wall and tables encircling it. She walked through the groups of people and stood on the edge. Looking down, she saw an illuminated pool beneath her.

Angel should be in by now, although she knew he could hang from the outside of the building for quite a long time if he had to. Spotting an empty table, she sat down and studied the people. Her seat gave her a good view of the reception room, the pool below, and most of the gallery running around three sides of the room above her. The presence of the half-naked beauties in the pool meant that most male eyes were on them, not her, which suited her perfectly.

"A drink?"

A waiter stood beside her with a tray of drinks in one hand.

"Brandy," she said. She found that brandy burnt well in her stomach and left quite a nice fragrance. Beer was too watery, which meant she had to eject as frequent blasts of steam. She downed the brandy in one, putting the glass back on the tray.

"Another?" the waiter asked.

"Give me a bottle."

Although she intended to burn off the alcoholic content, the calories were always useful. She glanced up at the gallery that seemed to be reserved for VIPs. One of the tables was surrounded by a crowd of laughing people—admirers fawning over the criminal boss Daryl Cassard, while he, in turn, appeared to be ingratiating himself with some minor celebrity.

The waiter returned with a bottle of cognac. She poured a large glass. It helped. She immediately burnt the alcohol and used the calories to extend her magical senses to encompass the entire room.

Two people possessed small magic.

One source was with the table of criminals above. She spotted the man quickly. He silently chanted the sickness spell; the chant was nonverbal, a series of prearranged thoughts on a loop, projected from his unconscious mind. Weak but effective when continued over a long period of time. She searched for the second source. It took her a few minutes to locate. A woman watched her from a table on the other side of the central space. Lucy felt rushing wind brush her. Perhaps this pair worked with the air element. Most lesser sorcerers specialised in one of the elements; it was an easier form of magic.

Lucy listened, hiding her magic as best she could, but someone skilled may still sense something out of place. Perhaps this woman did, or perhaps she unconsciously felt something. Lucy looked away. She might want to provoke a confrontation later, but not yet. First, she needed to learn more about the portal upstairs.

32

"*Darta!*"

Lucy gasped when a flashing image from Darta appeared in her mind. The magic had started unexpectedly; it was strong.

"*Careful.*"

"*I know,*" Darta whispered.

Lucy wondered whether her friend was becoming more intelligent—at least, she seemed to be becoming increasingly articulate. Lucy saw through Darta's eyes as the panther padded along a passage on the second floor towards an open doorway. Her sense of smell was excellent, and this floor interested her the most. She stopped outside the doorway. Darta's fur stood on end, and Lucy felt her own hair respond the same. The magic in the room was intense and familiar. Her stomach sank. There was something else, too.

Behind an ornamental screen, something flashed. A blue-skinned demon walked across the room to look. It spoke to someone.

"*Darta, back.*"

Reluctantly, the panther moved away.

The demon lord, Tavth, was in London.

"Fools," she inadvertently said aloud. Whatever was Noone thinking by bringing a demon to London?

"Are you okay?" a man asked.

Still connected to Darta's mind, she vaguely saw a man watching her. As he wasn't an alien and possessed no magic, she returned to the scene upstairs. Angel walked along the passage towards the panther.

"Stop him!"

There was black magic, too, the type the imperial sorcerers used. The panther blocked Angel's way, growling lightly. Lucy saw his confusion through Darta's eyes. When he pushed ahead, she growled again, swiping his leg lightly with her paw. Her claws were fully retracted. Angel nodded and retreated along the passage, stopping in front of another door. Lucy was unsure who was with the demon, but the smell of magic was overwhelming. It could be Noone or Walker.

Gasping, she dropped her glass.

The portal had just opened. At least, she now knew where they were working from. This would require thought; it wasn't the right time to poke the nest of hornets. She wanted Darta and Angel out of there.

"Get out. Now!"

"You dropped your glass," the man said.

A waiter was cleaning the fragments of glass from the floor.

"Do you mind if I join you?"

The man was already sitting opposite her. That was irritating, but she was more annoyed by the interruption.

"Are you drunk?"

She shook her head. "I need more."

"What do you want?"

"Another bottle," she said, pointing to the empty bottle of brandy in front of her.

She was in two worlds. She saw and heard him, but she was still with Darta, too.

He frowned. "You drank that by yourself?"

"Yes."

"No wonder you dropped your glass."

Upstairs, Darta and Angel were in a dark passage. Darta had smelt something else. She needed to speak to Angel. The man opposite her appeared annoyed. He'd been speaking.

"Food, too," she added.

Confused, he waved to a waiter.

She called Angel.

Thankfully, he answered.

"Get out now," she whispered, turning away from the man. "It's too dangerous, and I need you here."

"Darta?" Angel asked.

She spoke to the panther.

"She's smelt something upstairs—the fourth floor, perhaps. Let her go; she can find her own way out."

Darta rushed up the next flight of stairs.

"Come downstairs. There are two aliens here."

"What about the ones here?"

"You don't want to go anywhere near those things," she whispered.

She hung up as a waiter placed a plate of sausage rolls and another bottle of brandy on the table. Being in two places at once was hard. Darta pushed her nose against a locked door on the fourth floor. The smell of unwashed bodies was intense. People were inside, and they hadn't washed in days. Darta decided to burn her way through.

Lucy wasn't sure that was a good idea, but the panther was determined.

"What's wrong with you?" the man asked.

She helped herself to some sausage rolls.

"Sorry, I'm feeling a little disoriented."

"I'm not surprised."

He picked up the empty bottle.

"I don't believe it."

She grinned and took a swig from the fresh bottle, being careful not to burp flames.

The door collapsed inwards, and the panther paced into the room. Women and children moved back. They were terrified, and Lucy didn't blame them. Darta noticed a new smell coming from a doorway inside the room. It was also shut. Darta nudged one of the women to the doorway. She screamed.

The door opened, and the panther rushed in, knocking a man to the floor. Another alien, and Lucy had to restrain Darta from ripping his throat out. She had to see what was happening first.

"Darta, look around the room. I need to see."

The panther moved her head. Dr Lee was tied to a bed. Torture implements lay around him. He bled from one of his hands. The meaning was clear.

The alien reached for a knife.

"Kill him and leave."

She'd seen enough. The final moments of the torturer's life flashed before her eyes as Darta slashed his neck open. There was nothing she could do for the intelligence officer on the bed.

"Get out!"

Darta leapt at the window, blasting it with fire. It exploded outwards. Lucy breathed out in relief as Darta edged her way down the outer wall. She allowed her mind to return fully to her body.

The man stared at her in annoyance. He looked like a petty criminal. It wasn't his face; it was in his eyes and manner. He'd seen her as his prey, but now seemed less certain. Lucy felt more concerned that the woman at the table across the room was still staring at her. She hoped she'd not given too much away.

"What's your name?" she asked.

He said nothing.

She picked up the bottle and drank.

The man stared at the bottle in disbelief.

"You've just drunk a quarter of a bottle of expensive brandy."

"Thanks."

She started on the sausage rolls.

The party of criminals and celebrities was making its way downstairs. She sensed magic there, too. Faint traces, but with what she'd seen and sensed upstairs, it was too much. Bouncers were already clearing a way for the cream of the crooks. She took another stiff drink, covering her mouth with her hand, when a small burst of flames burped out.

"What do you do?" she asked.

"I'm in business."

She realised she didn't care and watched the room instead. The real power was upstairs. If the demon, and whatever was with it, came downstairs, she was leaving fast.

"What's your name?" the man asked.

"Kate," she lied. "You're not eating," she said as she ate another sausage roll.

He shook his head. "Watching you is enough entertainment."

She smiled. "I hope I provide good value." She leant forward and whispered, "I'm going to give you a lot more entertainment soon."

He raised his eyebrows. "Really?" he said, misunderstanding lighting his eyes. He leant forward and gave her a suggestive look. "When will the entertainment start?"

"When they demonstrate the protective clothing. Do you believe it's as good as they say?"

"No, but if it's half as good, I'm buying."

A passing waiter put a plate of chicken legs on the table, and she started eating again—one at a time, including the bones, which she burnt in her mouth.

"You're strange."

She grinned.

Two members of the Security Service walked in from the vestibule: Amelia Blake and Jack Ross. The woman with traces of magic noticed them, too. Lucy finished the bottle, feeling the fire ignite in her belly.

"Are you drunk?"

She involuntarily burped several beads of fire that slowly fell to the table.

Eyes wide with shock, the man quickly moved back. "What was that?"

She brushed them off the table, hoping they wouldn't start a fire. She had too much to do.

"Nothing."

The man looked from the singe marks on the table, back to her, seemingly reassessing the situation.

"I'm going to watch the demonstration," she said. "Want to join me?"

Lucy walked through the crowded room towards the small stage, not waiting to see whether the man followed. The VIPs had taken seats in a closed off section of the room next to the stage; she joined the rest of the crowd standing opposite them. Small magic came from a man sitting with them. The woman with traces of magic sat next to him; she whispered something to him. Lucy could deal with two lesser sorcerers, but not with what was upstairs. Not yet. Noticing movement at the back of the room, Lucy saw Angel walk through a doorway. She was pleased; she knew they'd have to make a quick exit very soon. A young woman walked onto the stage holding a microphone. She was followed by a young man.

"This groundbreaking technology has been developed by the Cassard Technology Corporation," she announced.

Angel worked his way through the crowd towards her. Her eyes widened. He'd found an assault rifle, which he carried openly. When Jack saw him, his eyes widened, too. He picked up his phone and started speaking rapidly. The police would be here soon. They had to move fast.

"As you may have noticed," the presenter continued. "The tailoring is top quality. The clothing can be created in any style or fashion."

The male sorcerer wore a white suit; the female sorcerer a dark one. Lucy guessed that both suits were bulletproof, too. The presenter continued. She turned to the young man who had followed her onto the stage, but spoke to the audience. "His shirt and jacket are impenetrable. You'd need a rocket to kill him."

She laughed.

The male sorcerer stepped onto the stage. He nodded at the presenter, then pulled out a long knife. He stabbed the man in his stomach. The man staggered back, caught by two security guards. The man straightened out his suit and bowed. They applauded. Then he drew a pistol, attached a silencer, and shot the man in his stomach. The crowd gasped. Again, he straightened his suit and bowed.

Cassard proposed a toast.

Somewhere above them in the house, the magical chant renewed. Lucy felt the spell weaving through the air, but this one was different. It projected a fear of losing out. The audience was hooked. Suddenly, everyone was talking excitedly about what they'd seen. She was impressed. Her enemy had perfected a form of sales magic. Lucy wanted to provoke Noone. What better way than by spoiling her sales magic by bursting the spell the sorcerers had cast over the audience? Nodding to Angel, she climbed onto the stage.

"Shoot them!" she said, forming an imaginary gun with her finger, pointing it at the pair of sorcerers, and then making popping sounds.

"Leave the stage immediately," the presenter said. "You're drunk."

A member of security walked towards her, but stopped when Angel climbed onto the stage with the assault rifle. Some people clapped, thinking it was part of the show.

"Shoot him!" Lucy shouted.

Angel shot the male sorcerer in his stomach, knocking him from his feet; he slid across the floor. Angel followed him, carefully aiming at the man's face.

"No!" the alien woman shouted.

Angel fired.

The man was dead.

Lucy breathed with relief when the silent chant ceased. Whatever was upstairs must have noticed. They had to leave. The alien woman drew her pistol, and some criminals had also reached for theirs.

"Gun," Lucy said.

Angel tossed her a pistol. Lucy caught it and fired

repeatedly at the alien woman's chest, sending her spinning to the floor. She wore protective clothing, but Lucy knew it stung. She didn't have time to follow the woman, who was now crawling into the crowd.

A police siren sounded outside.

"Time to go," she said.

The rest of the room watched them walk to the door.

Cassard's face turned red with rage.

"I'll kill you both!" he shouted.

Lucy shot him in his stomach. With Angel by her side, she walked out of the front door as Cassard vomited on the floor.

33

Jack shook his head.

"I can't believe the brazenness of the murder."

Amelia was by his side.

A security guard stopped them from getting any closer, but he'd seen enough. He noted the effectiveness of the bulletproof clothing. The only one dead had been shot in the head by Angel.

"Let's go," he said.

"What about Luke?" Amelia said. "He should be here."

"He must have gone somewhere. Perhaps he left early," Jack said.

"Or perhaps he ran into the criminals."

"We'll find him later."

They left the building. It was past midnight, but the moon gave enough light to see the shocked faces of the guests rushing to leave the reception.

"She's spoilt their promotion," Amelia said.

"She has," Jack said. But the sight of Angel murdering a man dominated his thoughts. "We've been ordered to track them. A firearms unit's on the way."

"To arrest them?" Amelia asked.

"Yes, but they have orders to shoot to kill if they resist arrest, which I'm confident they will."

"Don't you think that's strange?" she said.

He shook his head. "It's war, and they're the enemy. They've been publicly classified as terrorists, too. Angel's a known killer. He's proven it again tonight."

They crossed the road.

"What about the witch?" Amelia asked.

"She's just shot two people. She's dangerous. It's possible Alice knows things we don't."

"There." Amelia pointed down the road.

A white van accelerated down the street. Cassard and his security team were outside. They'd noticed the van, too.

"Are you police?" Cassard shouted across the road.

Jack ignored them.

"This is my business," Cassard said.

As Jack and Amelia got into the red Mini Cooper, two black cars stopped in front of the house. Cassard and his gang got in. Both cars accelerated after the van.

"You ride shotgun," she said.

Jack relaxed slightly, taking his pistol from the glove compartment. She was one of very few people he could accept drove as well as him. He knew she'd say better.

"You know I don't like this," Amelia said.

She raced after the black cars, which now turned a corner; two police cars followed her. The firearms unit was yet to arrive.

"I know."

"I'll follow," Amelia said, "but I'm not killing them."

Jack respected Amelia, but sometimes she just didn't understand.

"Angel's a killer with a history. I've seen him shoot

women and children. He'll kill anything that moves, given the chance."

She raced through a set of red traffic lights, overtaking the first of the black cars.

"And you just saw what the witch did."

"She didn't kill anybody."

"She's killed several times," Jack said. "At least."

"Only aliens," Amelia said.

"We don't know that. No one should be murdered in the street. We have a legal system."

"What you or the police are about to do is the same," Amelia said.

"It's completely different," Jack said. "We're defending our country."

It was that simple.

"I don't defend Angel," she said. "But I think the orange witch is protecting us all."

"Do you really believe that?"

"I don't know," she admitted. "But I think we're fighting the same enemy."

"Perhaps, but it's our job to hunt them down, not hers. We can't allow anyone to take the law into their own hands."

Amelia overtook Daryl Cassard's car on a corner, and Jack grinned at the furious criminal boss. Then he remembered the scene in the hospital.

"She murdered the nurse."

Amelia drove in silence for several seconds before answering.

"We don't know what the nurse was. Her body disappeared. I asked, but our director had no information." She paused again as she raced along a street. "I'm worried we're being manipulated."

"That's nothing new," he said. He knew for a fact that their bosses withheld information.

"But doesn't it worry you?"

Jack shrugged.

"The aliens offer riches that are literally beyond this world," she said. "Why wouldn't they use them in exchange for political influence?"

He had to admit that she had a point about the potential for the aliens to influence politicians, although he'd seen no evidence, but Angel was a cold-blooded murderer. Jack admitted to himself that he wanted him dead. He remembered Bonnie—a young mother who Angel had murdered in front of his eyes.

"Our job is to follow orders."

"Politicians are capable of greed."

"Of course they are, and if we find evidence of corruption, we can report it," he said, "but at the moment, where's the evidence?"

He'd spoken more harshly than he'd intended, but he couldn't allow his mind to become divided. He was going to kill Angel; other people could worry about the aliens.

Cassard's car tried to overtake, but Amelia swerved in front of them. Jack saw the man raise a gun as they left him behind. Jack glanced back. The red Mini Cooper was followed by two black cars; the police cars lagged much further behind.

"I hope my new car doesn't get trashed like the last one," Amelia said.

He grinned, remembering the incident when the panther had set fire to her previous Mini.

Alice called. He flipped on the loudspeaker.

"I hope you've not lost them."

When Amelia raced around a corner, Jack smelt the

burning rubber. The white van was parked next to a solitary lamppost on an Islington street.

"What was that sound?" Alice asked.

"Amelia's rally driving skills," Jack said.

"Ah, I hope she doesn't trash another car."

He laughed.

"The alien?" Alice asked.

"In sight."

"Good. I've already spoken to the police. They've informed me that gang members may outnumber the police at the moment."

"That's certain," Jack said. "How long till the firearms unit arrives?"

"Twenty minutes."

"Too long!" he said.

Alice paused. "I want you both to observe, but if you get the chance, you have permission to shoot to kill."

"Angel?" he asked.

"Both of them, Jack."

At last. Angel owed for killing villagers on their last military operation together, but most of all for Bonnie.

"We should question them," Amelia said.

"If you can catch them without getting killed," Alice said.

Amelia stopped the car behind the van.

"By the canal again," she said, putting her pistol in her jacket. "They seem to like water."

"Better for us," Jack said. "Less people."

He already had his gun out.

Cassard's car screeched around the corner.

"Let's go."

He ran down the path to the canal. Amelia was right behind him. From behind, police sirens joined the shouts of

Cassard's gang. It was darker by the canal, and already well past midnight, but the moon cast enough light to see. For a second, Jack felt he'd been plunged back into a wilder and more primitive time, allowing his hunting instincts to come alive. This was his chance.

"Down there," Amelia said.

Angel and the witch had stopped. He could just see them in the darkness. Angel raised his gun as seven criminals ran along the towpath towards them.

"Are we observing?" Amelia asked.

Jack didn't answer immediately but moved forward towards a large rock placed by the side of the canal. Cassard threatened Jack, but it was all talk. The man shut up when he saw their guns.

"They're all yours," Jack said.

"Are you going to let a bunch of criminals push you around?" Amelia asked.

He grinned. "I'm going to watch Angel kill them, and then I'm going to kill him. It's a perfect opportunity. With luck, they'll draw him out."

"Is your opinion of the criminals so low?"

"I'm sure they can kill, but Angel's better," Jack said quietly. "I don't mind Angel using up his ammunition on them either."

"You don't care about their murder?"

He shook his head. "They're lowlife. Killing them's doing society a favour." Jack pointed. "Angel has cover. They're in the open. All they have is hot air and threats, neither of which will work against someone like Angel."

"The police are here," Amelia said.

Jack frowned.

The police stopped about fifty yards behind them.

"They won't do anything," he said. "They'll wait for the firearms unit. I want to move closer."

They stopped behind the remains of a wall about seven yards behind the gang. Some criminals looked at them but said nothing.

"Drop your weapons!" Cassard shouted.

Angel stood with the assault rifle in his hands. He was speaking to the witch.

"I don't think he's listening," Jack said.

The woman with Cassard threatened the witch.

"They're not very good at this, are they?" Amelia said.

"They rely too much on strength," Jack said.

Then the orange witch stepped forward. She spoke in the alien language.

"I wish we had Luke here," Amelia said.

Jack completely agreed. It was possible that the criminals held him. Now he regretted letting the criminals attack Angel. He'd let his emotion take control of his actions. He wasn't above using hard questioning techniques on them after, but now he had to hope one or two of them would survive to tell him about Luke.

The woman replied in the same language.

"She's an alien, too," Amelia said.

"Down," Jack whispered.

They crouched behind the wall.

Moving very fast, Angel shot the alien woman in the head. Her body dropped into the canal. The criminals opened fire. Seconds later, Cassard and seven members of his gang lay dead on the ground. A few others cowered behind rocks. Again, Jack regretted his burst of emotion. Angel and the witch had disappeared.

34

"I'm going after them!" Jack said, stepping over the bodies.

Seconds later, he was lying on his belly as the police opened fire from behind.

"Idiots!"

Jack shouted until they stopped.

"It's Gully," Amelia said.

He shook his head. "What's he doing here?"

Gully was shouting orders. He shone a torch at Jack.

"Keep out of my operation."

The man was irate. So was Jack.

"My orders are to observe the targets, not your incompetence. Tell your men we're pursuing them," Jack said.

He sprinted along the towpath. Amelia followed. Several minutes later, he saw them ahead of him.

"I've got them."

Then the witch dived into the canal; Angel kept running. Jack chose to chase Angel. Four minutes later, Angel had disappeared near a row of canal barges—floating slums, hidden from the surrounding community.

He called Alice.

"I'm sending Ruth and Red Five. I'll instruct the police to wait for you to locate him. Are you sure he's on one of the barges?"

"That's where he disappeared."

"He could have swum the canal or gone up to the road," Alice said.

"He could," Jack replied. "But I think he's on one of the boats."

"Get him!" Alice hung up.

Red Five was part of MI5; a team of four men. He'd worked with them before. Good guys—most of them ex-military. Thirty minutes later, Gregg, the leader of Red Five, and the rest of the group, as well as Ruth and Amelia, were in position. The houseboats floated about thirty yards away.

Jack pulled Ruth gently towards him. "We're a couple."

He opened some of the cheap cider he'd insisted she bring in order to blend in with the environment. He spilt some down the front of his old coat as he poured half away.

"You smell lovely," she said, pulling a face.

He grinned.

"I'll walk with Gregg," Amelia said.

Two members of MI5 waited on the road, in case Angel tried to escape that way; another member of the team wandered into the darkness on the other side of the canal.

It was the first time Jack had been able to spend any time with Ruth for a few days.

"Keep your mind on your job," she said, pretending to take a swig of cider.

"I am, but we have to make this look real."

He stopped to kiss her when a couple walked past, but despite what Ruth said, his mind was on the operation. Jack could hear Gregg behind him. He played his part, laughing and joking with Amelia, and apparently drinking, although Jack knew he wouldn't touch a drop. Not while on an operation. After a few minutes, they'd walked past six houseboats. Gregg and Amelia stopped at the third.

"Let's stop here," Jack said.

No one seemed to notice the couple sitting on the ground near the canal. They'd chosen a place with a clear view along the stretch of water. They watched the houseboats.

"They're like floating shacks," Ruth said.

He agreed. Several of them were rusted cargo boats with dilapidated wooden huts built on the decks. The second boat was so low in the water that it looked as if it was going to sink. He doubted whether they'd moved from their moorings in decades, and washing lines, old bicycles, wires, and metal junk competed for space on the decks.

"What do you think's happened to Luke?" Ruth asked.

"He might be a prisoner at Cassard's house. I know he wanted to search the house for William. Now Cassard's dead, we have an opportunity to investigate."

"Will Alice let us? And what about the aliens?"

"I'm not leaving him there, if that's where he is."

"You don't think he's dead?" she asked, her voice going very quiet.

He shook his head. "But if he is, someone's going to pay."

"In a way, we're on the same side as the witch," Ruth said.

"We don't know if she's on our side." He was adamant. "I understand now that she's fighting the aliens, but we don't know enough about her motives. How do we know what she said in the hospital was true? You've gone soft towards her because of the dog."

He thought about the golden retriever Ruth had insisted

on adopting. It had picked Ruth out of a crowd of people outside of the hospital and greeted her. He wasn't quite sure how that had happened.

"He's a lovely dog."

Jack agreed, but it didn't change how he felt about the witch.

"I don't think she's as bad as Angel, but she's killed, and she needs to be caught and tried. I don't plan to shoot her; not unless she makes me. But Angel is something else."

An hour passed, and Jack wondered whether he'd been right. It was possible that Angel had kept walking. Perhaps he wasn't here at all. As time passed, he began to feel bored. It'd be dawn soon. He actually considered drinking some of the cider, but the smell from stale cider he'd spilt on his coat put him off.

"There," Ruth said quietly. She pointed at the boat that looked as if it was sinking.

A shadow moved along the deck. Then he heard a faint splash.

"The panther's in the water," she whispered.

"Let's move in," he said.

He spoke to the other teams over the radio. They wandered closer. Then the panther leapt back onto the deck; it seemed to be eating a fish. The police were already on the way. Unfortunately, Chief Inspector Gully would lead the operation. Unless Angel started shooting, Jack may have lost his chance. The MI5 and MI7 intelligence officers moved closer; all were armed.

"Did you call the police, Jack?" Angel's voice was clear from the boat.

"Damn. He's seen us," Jack said under his breath.

"I don't know how," Gregg said.

"We need you to surrender, Angel," Jack said.

"You'd rather kill me," Angel said.

He didn't sound particularly bothered, and Jack wondered if he'd started taking drugs again as he had when he'd murdered innocent civilians during their special operation in the mountains. He could hardly believe that Angel had once been a friend.

"Unfortunately, I have to follow the rules."

Angel laughed. "You should have joined me, Jack. This time I'm on the right side."

"She's killed a lot of people," Jack said.

"Yes, but only aliens."

Jack ignored that. He wasn't sure if it was true, anyway. "Is she with you?"

Angel laughed, then lapsed into silence.

Jack crept onto the nearest boat, the newest of the row. A light went on below the deck.

"Whoever you are, get off my boat or I'll call the police," a man said.

Ignoring the man, he crept towards the old boat next to Angel's. The hatch swung open, and a man rushed up carrying a crowbar. He stopped at the sight of Jack's gun.

"Lock yourself inside," Jack said. "There's going to be trouble."

The man dropped down, slamming the hatch shut. A bolt shot home.

Gregg joined him. Together, they jumped to the next boat.

"He's not running?" Gregg said.

"Perhaps he wants to make a last stand."

"That doesn't sound good. Not when he's armed with automatic weapons and we have pistols."

"One assault rifle. His ammo may be low."

"Maybe," Gregg said.

"Where are the aliens?" Amelia shouted from the shore.

Jack silently thanked her for the distraction, taking the opportunity to crawl closer.

"In hell for all I care," Angel said.

"Is the witch there?" Amelia asked.

"You'll never catch her."

Eventually, the police marksmen arrived. One of them joined them on the boat. A police negotiator came with them. Gully stayed on the shore.

"My name's Sergeant Watt," the negotiator began. "I'm here to talk about any problems you have."

Angel laughed.

"I know you understand that we can't let you leave, but I want to assure you that you'll be treated with dignity."

"Dignity?"

"You'll be taken to somewhere more comfortable than where you are now."

Jack wondered who had sent the negotiator. He was sure it wasn't Alice; she seemed to want a faster resolution. As he listened, he admired the man's skills. Nothing he said was false, but with his tone and careful choice of words, he managed to sound as if he were talking to a misguided friend. Still, Jack didn't think it would work with a man like Angel.

"He's prepared to die," Gregg said suddenly.

Jack nodded. "He doesn't care."

"I'll ask my men to lower their weapons if you agree to put your gun down and come out with your hands on your head," Sergeant Watt said. "I promise you we won't shoot."

There was silence for the next few minutes. Watt waved away Gully's suggestion to shoot the man. Jack wondered why Gully was so angry, although, for once, he agreed with his suggestion.

"It looks like your chief inspector wants him dead," Jack said.

The police shooter nodded. "He hates him."

"Where's the panther?" Sergeant Watt asked Angel.

"Let her go."

"It's a dangerous animal."

"There!" Ruth whispered.

"Ruth, you shouldn't be here," Jack said, unhappy to see his fiancée crouching behind him.

She pointed. He saw its shadow. It stood alert.

"I can kill it," the nearest marksmen said.

"Not yet," Sergeant Watt said.

"It's listening to something," Ruth said.

"I can't hear anything," Gregg said.

"Panthers have good hearing," Ruth replied.

"I can see him," the marksman said.

The panther appeared to nuzzle Angel. He turned to it, putting his hands on its shoulders.

"Now?" the shooter asked.

Watt shook his head. "Wait."

The black panther dived into the water and was gone. Gully ordered men to track it.

"You won't catch her," Angel said from the darkness between two dilapidated huts on the deck of the rusty boat. "But I'm prepared to surrender." His gun clattered to the deck.

"Come out slowly with your hands on your head," Watt said.

Watt turned to the irate Gully and smiled smugly.

"I assure you of your safety."

Jack watched in shock as Angel Provost walked off the old barge. Several armed police rushed towards him, knocking him roughly to the ground. He couldn't understand it. This was nothing like Angel.

"He's unarmed!" one shouted.

"I can't believe it was that easy," Amelia said.

"It sometimes works that way," Watt said before leaving the boat.

Angel was in handcuffs. Two police officers led him to a van.

"Why this way?" Jack asked as he walked past.

He was genuinely puzzled. He'd never imagined that Angel would just give up.

"She asked me."

The police pushed him into the van, and then he was gone.

35

Luke woke to searing pain in the stump of his finger. A man holding a bloody scalpel looked down at him and smiled.

"Good morning." He spoke the alien language.

Luke's memories returned. He was a prisoner in Cassard's house. He pulled away but was strapped to the bed. The man leant closer; his breath stank. Luke managed to turn his head to see a curtained window. It was dark outside.

"It's not morning," Luke said. He studied the man. "What do you want?"

"To soften you."

A woman screamed in a nearby room. His torturer cursed, and when the woman screamed again, he walked to the door and opened it. Luke heard the man crash to the floor, then the head of a black panther pushed against him. He froze. He could do nothing; his bonds held him tightly to the bed. It was the same creature that had taken the end of his finger and stolen his wife. It sniffed his finger. This was getting worse. Then it turned on his torturer. Luke could see nothing. Glass shattered, and he felt a night breeze brush against him. It had gone.

"Luke?"

He must be delirious; he thought he heard his wife.

"Luke!"

He felt gentle hands loosening the straps that held him firmly attached to the bed. One by one they released. A minute later, someone wetted his lips with water. He sat up and fainted. Seconds later, he recovered.

"Luke, Are you all right?"

He sat up again, more slowly this time. The figures around him came into focus.

"Molly?"

She hugged him.

"I thought..."

He stopped, not wanting to continue.

"I thought I was dead, too," she said. "I'm the last of the original prisoners; we think they're selling us to buyers all over the world. I'm worried they'll sell William."

"William's here?"

Someone brought him to the bed.

Luke held his son and wife in his arms. "Do the police know you're here?"

Luke realised how little Molly knew about his life over the past six months.

"I don't know."

"Luke?" She looked concerned. "We have to escape. Every day, they take women from the room and they never come back."

The thought made Luke sick.

"What about those people you were with last time? The soldiers?" Molly asked.

"They know I'm here. I think they'll search for me."

She examined his hand. "He cut off part of your finger."

"The panther did that after it took you." Luke looked at the bloody man on the floor. "He just opened it up again. At least, this time it got the right person."

"I just want to go home," she said.

She didn't know.

"We don't have a home." Her eyes widened. "It burnt down. The panther."

"The evil thing," she said.

"Except that it just saved my life," Luke said.

"Why did it kill him?" she asked.

"I don't think it's working for them any more. How many of you are there here?" he asked.

"Eight women and children in our room. They may have more somewhere else. The aliens control a local crime lord," she said.

"Daryl Cassard. We know him."

A noise came from the passage outside.

"Something's happening," a woman said from the adjoining room.

Luke walked unsteadily into the next room. The burnt door lay on the floor. Gunshots came from downstairs, and two women rushed back into the room.

"Guards!" one whispered. "They've got guns."

Footsteps approached the room, and his hopes of a rescue vanished.

"The other room," Molly said.

They reentered the room with the torturer's body. Luke walked to the broken window. It looked like the panther had run at it and shattered the glass. Luke remembered how its pads were special; that it could climb vertical walls like normal leopards climb trees. He searched for possible footholds but couldn't see any. They were stuck on the fourth floor; to attempt to climb down the wall was death.

Then he had an idea.

"Help me move the body."

Molly looked at it with disgust.

"He may help us."

She frowned. "Luke, what are you talking about?"

"We have to get rid of the corpse."

She nodded.

Luke pulled the body to the window.

"Luke? You're not going to…"

"Why not? Maybe someone will notice it. Help me."

Together they leant the body out of the shattered window, not caring about the jagged glass, and pushed. It tumbled and crashed into the alley below.

36

Amelia sat in an interview room inside Pentonville Prison in Islington, waiting for the prisoner. Despite warnings, she'd insisted on seeing him alone. She knew he was violent; she'd suffered from it, but her need for information was greater than her concern for safety.

She sat on one side of the table, an empty chair was on the other. The door opened and two police officers led Angel Provost into the room. He stood by the empty chair, his hands handcuffed in front of him.

"Are you sure you don't want us in the room?" one of the officers asked.

"I'm sure."

"He's dangerous," one said.

"I know."

Angel appeared calm but aloof. Reluctantly, the officers left the room.

"Please sit down," she said.

He remained standing.

"What do you want?" he asked.

"To speak to you."

She'd planned what to say but still wasn't sure how best to do this. She'd volunteered to interview him because she felt she stood more chance of reaching him. Jack hated him, and she didn't blame him; he had good reasons. She believed her sensitivity to people would help, but worried she was kidding herself. Psychism was a special ability, but it wasn't a magic ticket to getting whatever you wanted. She waited.

"Do you remember the last time we met?"

She almost immediately regretted saying it.

"I do. Our positions are reversed."

That wasn't where she wanted to go, but the memory of the night she'd spent with her hands tied in the tower in the middle of the mere was still strong. She'd reached him by talking about the panther.

"Where's the panther?"

His shoulders relaxed a little. "On a mission."

"What sort of mission?"

He remained silent.

"When you left the barge on the canal, you said 'she asked me.' Who's she?"

He raised an eyebrow at her. "I think you know."

"The orange witch?"

"That's what you call her."

"What do you call her?"

He stood in silence.

"What did she ask you?" Amelia said.

Again, he didn't answer.

"Where is she?"

"On a mission."

She asked several more questions about the witch, but he refused to answer.

She needed a different approach.

"Is there anything you can tell me about the aliens? I mean, I don't think you're working for them anymore."

"I work for her."

Again she waited. The silence didn't disturb her at all; neither did it appear to bother Angel.

"We want to find the aliens," Amelia said.

"Do you?"

"I do."

He looked at her. "Perhaps, but do the authorities want to arrest them or to work with them?"

It was a concern that had already crossed her mind more than once—she'd even talked to Jack about it—but she didn't want to mention that now. Instead she asked a question.

"What do you mean?"

"What the aliens know is worth a lot of money," Angel said.

"That may be true, but I want to catch them. Help me."

He was thinking, which was an improvement. She'd thought about her questions beforehand and decided the best approach was just to ask them.

"What's the structure of their group? How many of them are there?"

To her surprise, he just started speaking.

"Eva Noone's the leader. In her world, she's an empress. She sits at the centre of the web. She has two sorcerers: Nimori and Walker. After Noone, they're the most dangerous."

"But there are others?"

He shrugged. "Some."

"Do you believe the talk of magic?"

"I didn't, but after what I've seen, I've changed my mind."

"What does Noone want?"

"To open a path between her world and ours."

"Is that so bad?"

She knew it was dangerous, but wanted his response.

"I think you know. She'd return with an army. And worse."

Amelia understood.

"How do we stop her?"

"Let me go. Let the woman you call a witch do her work. They hate and fear her."

"Why?"

"Noone hates her because she killed her husband; they fear her because she's the only person capable of stopping them."

Amelia's eyes widened.

"The orange witch killed her husband?"

She was fascinated and wanted to learn more about the witch and the aliens.

"What about the other aliens?"

"We're killing them."

"We noticed." She thought about what Angel had said about being an empress. "Is she literally an empress?"

"In her world. If she finds a way back there, she could launch an invasion."

This would explain a lot about her imperious behaviour, Amelia thought.

"We saw you suddenly appear in the reception, but no one saw you enter. Where were you before you joined the party?"

She thought he was going to refuse to answer, but he did.

"Upstairs."

She had many questions. She asked the most important.

"What did you see?"

"You wouldn't believe me."

"Try me. I believe things that most people could never imagine."

He looked at her silently for several seconds and nodded. She waited.

"There's something alien there."

"The aliens?"

"Something different. Even Noone's nervous of it."

They all seemed dangerous to Amelia. Neither of them spoke for about a minute, and she considered ending the interview. She'd already learnt a lot.

The door opened, and the prison officers walked into the room.

"We need to take the prisoner back to his cell."

"I need more time—"

"I'm sorry, madam."

They led Angel to the door.

"Anything else?" she asked.

"You have three days left."

The door shut, and he was gone.

37

"That's an order." Alice's features were taut.

Jack controlled his emotion.

Ruth and Amelia remained silent. Although he didn't like the so-called witch, and he certainly wanted her arrested, assassinating her was too much. It was also illegal. Amelia's words were making more sense, too. Perhaps there was political interference.

"Don't be sentimental, Jack. She's a threat to national security, and she was working with Angel Provost, a cold-blooded killer."

She paused for a few seconds, watching his reaction, and then continued.

"Remember, we don't know what she actually is. We can't let her walk free."

He stared at her stonily. Silences didn't bother him.

"Okay, Jack. Your role can be to drive her into a corner; I'll have other people kill her."

This was not the job he was paid to do, even if he wasn't pulling the trigger.

"I agree we must catch her; it's the murder part I don't like."

"This is war. The aliens have occupied part of our country. You were in the special forces, Jack. This is not new to you."

"What about Noone?" he asked.

"That's not your business."

"She's one of them," Amelia said.

"Evidence?"

"We're looking for it," Jack said.

"Well, stop looking for it," Alice said. "MI5 has given her a thorough background check. We're aware that the aliens may attempt to infiltrate the system, but we don't believe they've done so yet. Your only evidence seems to be that an alien told you she's an alien. Not convincing."

"There's Amelia's vision," Jack said.

"You need more than that," Alice replied.

"Eva Noone only appeared on the scene six months ago," Amelia said.

"Records show she was born in Britain," Alice said.

"Fake," Amelia said.

"She's a British citizen and a legitimate parliamentary candidate. Do you think we haven't checked her?"

"She's deceiving you," Amelia said.

"You may be the one who's deceived. Have you thought of that?" Alice said. "You're so keen for us to check for the presence of gills. Well, we have. She doesn't have any."

"She may have had surgery," Amelia said.

Alice glared at her.

Jack wondered if Amelia had been right after all. Perhaps the Security Service was already compromised, but Alice didn't know it.

"You're not paid to think about this," Alice said. "And

stay away from Noone's house."

He exchanged glances with Ruth and Amelia. Everyone had heard that Eva Noone had bought the house from Cassard before he died.

"You understand Luke may be inside that house."

"Luke's missing. There's no evidence that he's inside the house," Alice said.

Jack paused, wondering how to deal with this. "A warrant to search the house will only cause mild discomfort; if we're right, then not searching the house is a security risk."

"That's enough, Jack. It's an order! Don't go near that house. Remember, your job is to locate and assist in the removal of the so-called witch."

"Killing her?" Amelia asked.

"If necessary, yes."

Alice stared at them unrepentantly. "This conversation is finished."

Once they were in their own quarters, they spoke.

"I'm not killing a woman in cold blood," Jack said.

"You can trap her," Ruth said.

"It's the same as killing her. I didn't sign up for that. I had enough in the Navy."

"I don't know what's happened to Alice," Amelia said. "I'm worried that the aliens have infiltrated the Security Service."

"If they have, we'll deal with that when it comes. First, I want to find Luke. Consequences be damned."

They all agreed on that, even if it meant losing their jobs.

"I know someone who can break into houses."

"A thief?" Ruth asked.

He shook his head. "A friend from the Special Boat

Service."

"Breaking in is one thing," Amelia said, "but what about when we're inside? These people are dangerous."

"We'll be armed," Jack said.

"Do you remember how hard it was to fight Nimori last time?"

"We won."

"Only just," Amelia said. "And we had help. Angel told me that Noone is the most dangerous."

"She has a point," Ruth said.

"We shoot fast," Jack said. "But I agree we need to take care. We don't have to rush. We can observe the house. Wait until she's left."

"What about Nimori and Walker?" Amelia asked.

"I think we can risk one of them," Jack said. "We know what they are now. We just shoot."

"I need some sleep first," Amelia said.

Jack was actually impressed by how well the team had coped. It was almost eight in the morning. None of them had slept properly for days.

"We leave at nine-thirty. That'll give me time to organise some help."

A few hours later, they were undercover outside the Knightsbridge mansion. Ruth was in the van with monitoring equipment, Amelia further down the street, Jack sat at a bus stop on a side street, and three ex-military friends waited at other locations around the house.

Jack's ex-SBS friend, Don, was the first to see movement.

"Jack, someone's leaving the house."

Jack walked towards the road at the front.

"Who?"

"A man and a woman."

He'd given Don and the other pictures of Eva Noone and

the two magicians.

"Do you recognise them?"

"The man matches the picture of Nick Nimori. The woman may be Eva Noone. She's wearing one of the famous hats, but the brim's covering her face. Noone was becoming well known for her collection of hats.

Jack turned the corner and saw them get into a car with mirrored windows. The man was definitely Nimori. The woman looked like Noone—the hat was familiar.

"What do you think?" Ruth asked over the radio once the car had gone.

"We go in," Jack said.

"What if Walker's inside?" Amelia asked.

"We shoot him fast."

Minutes later, Jack, Amelia, and Don climbed over the metal fence and then walked along the narrow alley behind Eva Noone's new house. Another team, disguised as workmen, prepared to make a noise at the front of the house. The ground in the alley was covered in overgrown weeds and broken glass. Something was covered by a tarpaulin sheet. Jack pulled it back, not surprised to see a body.

"Cut up pretty bad," Don said.

Amelia examined him. "Those look like gashes from an animal. He may have been dead before he hit the ground."

Jack looked up at the broken fourth-floor window. "I'd like to check that room."

The rusty back door was locked. Don took out his drill and Jack his gun. When the drilling in the road began, Don began work. Five minutes later, they were in. The kitchen was empty apart from the dirty plates and glasses covering the tables and tops.

"Looks like they've been partying," Jack said.

"And that they have a problem hiring help," Amelia

added.

That made sense. They climbed the narrow set of stairs from the kitchen. The first floor was quiet, apart from someone complaining about the drilling in the road. Jack was impressed with the amount of noise the team was making outside. They continued up the next flight of stairs, stopping on the second floor landing. One door was open; two voices came from inside. Jack crept closer. A burst of drilling came from the street, and he risked looking into the room.

Luke was tied to a chair. His mouth was gagged, and his face was bloody. Something flashed behind him. Jack moved back.

"They've got Luke."

Laughter came from the room. They were talking about the election.

"They're speaking English," Amelia said.

He shrugged. "Maybe they're locals."

Amelia recorded the conversation on her phone. Don watched the stairs.

"I want a license for the sole right to import goods from your world." The man had a local accent.

"You'll get it, Mr Taylor, but you must give me what I ask," a man said.

"Naturally," Taylor said.

"One of them's an alien," Amelia whispered.

"Walker?"

She shook her head.

It looked like it was going to plan. If there were only two men in the room, a local criminal and an alien, then, with Don, they already outgunned them.

"What are you going to do with him?" Taylor asked.

Jack assumed they were talking about Luke.

"He knows things that may be useful," the alien said. "One of my associates will probe more deeply later. I don't have time right now."

Don looked from across the landing. "Do you want to go in?"

"Yes."

"How many?" Don asked.

"Two. An alien and a criminal," Jack said.

"We can take them," Don said. "But we kill the alien fast."

Jack walked down the short passage that led into the room. He stopped at the end to look. It was a large room. Luke sat to the right, next to a door. An ornate wooden screen was behind him. On the wall to the left, next to a fireplace, was a mural of an exotic other-worldly scene. Richly coloured curtains blocked the daylight; the room was lit by exotic lamps. In one corner was a leather armchair with a weird-looking blue mannequin of a devilish figure. Taylor stood by the fireplace, a glass of whisky in his hand, facing the alien.

"Will your machine work?" Taylor asked.

"Yes," the man said. "I'll demonstrate it at our celebration party on Friday."

"You're sure your group will win seats?"

"We're working in unseen ways. The country has already changed. This is not the first time we've changed a population."

"I believe you," Taylor said. "What you've shown me is incredible."

Jack walked into the room and shot the alien twice in the chest; he went straight down. So far, so good.

"Taylor, you're under arrest."

Taylor grinned, taking another sip of his drink. Jack

wondered if he was drunk.

A sound came from behind the screen. His stomach dropped as Eva Noone stepped out from behind it. The atmosphere changed.

Don shot Noone twice. She glared at him with pure hatred. "You'll pay for that."

"You're under arrest."

"Careful," Amelia said as Don strode towards her.

Jack looked at her exposed belly, trying to make out the strange tattoo that ran across it. He felt mesmerised by the woman.

"Do you know who I am?" Noone said.

Don didn't seem to care.

She snarled when he grabbed hold of her upper arm. Then he cried out, staggering away from her.

The alien sat up.

This was getting worse. Jack admonished himself for not shooting the man in his head. Jack aimed again, but he felt a strange resistance to shooting. He fought against it, remembering Amelia's words about their ability to control minds. He pulled the trigger but missed. To his right, Amelia pulled Luke's gag away and quickly cut through the rope binding him. Don dropped his gun and held his bleeding hand.

"My sister doesn't like being manhandled," Noone said.

Eva Noone's shoulders were exposed, and with them a small head that grew from her neck. It stared at them with a bloodied mouth. Don's arm began to shrivel.

"Don?" Jack said.

He fell to the floor; his face fixed in a silent scream. Amelia knelt by his side but shook her head in horror.

"My sister's bite's poisonous," Noone said. "I'm afraid it's fatal. You're under arrest for trespass and assault."

Jack noticed that what he'd thought a tattoo was actually

a mouth stretching across her belly. It opened and closed without a sound.

"We must go," Amelia said. "The sickness is coming from her."

"You're not going anywhere," Noone said.

A blood-red mist came from her fingers and rushed towards them, darkening as it got closer. Jack's gun clattered to the floor. He wasn't sure what was happening; he seemed to have lost control of his hand. The shrunken head protruding from her neck looked at him.

"On your knees before the empress," it said.

"She's no empress," Luke said. Then he stopped, gasping for breath.

The blue mannequin on the armchair laughed. Jack stared at it in horror. It was alive. Another man entered the room. He was agitated, pointing towards the stairs. He spoke in the alien language. Jack gasped in relief when the pressure on him relaxed. Whatever the man had said in his alien language had disturbed Noone.

"What's happening?" Jack gasped.

"The orange witch is here," Luke translated.

Eva Noone hissed.

Slowly, they backed towards the door.

The lesser sorcerers moved to stop them, but Noone raised her hand.

"Leave them for now. I want the bigger prize."

The three of them rushed to the door.

"I never forget the scent of a man," the demon said. "I'll enjoy a hunt through London."

Jack shot the demon. It reacted by throwing a flashing object that hit him in the eye. He gasped in pain, seeing flashes of light, then the room darkened. He should have left it; he was finished. Luke and Amelia guided him into the passage. The pain was intense; he didn't want to pass out in this place. Then he noticed a light coming from the stairs.

"The orange witch," Luke said.

Through one eye, Jack watched in disbelief. He hardly recognised her. Lines of fire ran across her face and arms; her intense orange eyes turned to them.

"It's a trap," Amelia said.

The orange witch either couldn't hear or didn't care. She walked past them and then into the room. Jack breathed more easily, as if a weight was lifted from him.

"The witch did something," Amelia said.

Strange sounds came from the room.

"We have to go now!" Amelia said.

"Molly's upstairs with William," Luke said.

"We'll come back for them," Amelia said. "We're no use if we're captured or dead."

"She's right," Jack said. "We'll come back." He was close to passing out, but he forced himself to look at Luke. "I'm sorry, I can't help them now."

"Can you make it?" Amelia asked.

"I have to," he said.

A loud crack came from the room, and then there was silence. They staggered downstairs, and then through the dirty reception room; the front door lay smoking on the floor. He stumbled outside.

"Jack!" Ruth said.

She ran towards him.

He vaguely heard her speaking to his friends and felt hands guiding him. He tried hard to remain conscious. He couldn't afford to mess up by fainting at the last moment. Ruth helped him into the van. He fell forwards and his vision dimmed. The door slammed shut behind him. He blacked out as the van accelerated down the road.

38

Noone and Nimori were gone. It was time to poke the hornet's nest again. With luck, Lucy could destroy the machine that opened and powered the portal. She walked up to the front door of the Knightsbridge mansion, rested her hands on the door and let her fire flow. The door burst into flames. She kicked and it fell inwards, crashing onto the floor.

Fire seeped from cracks in her skin; her eyes were alight. She climbed the sweeping staircase, blending her two magics as she ascended. All she could hear was the roar of her primal magic; she couldn't detect any other magic nearby. Although blending magics sometimes interfered with the senses, she was sure nothing was there. She continued up the stairs.

An alien walked down the stairs. He stopped and stared at her in shock. He had traces of magic. When she reached for her pistol, he turned and sprinted up the sweeping staircase.

She reached the second floor.

Amelia Blake and her team ran out of a room. One of

them was injured. Amelia tried to speak to her, but all Lucy heard was the fire burning in her ears. They were still alive, which probably meant they'd run into some lesser sorcerers. The portal whined. It was time to close it. The room appeared empty apart from a body on the floor next to a painted screen. She pulled the screen away, revealing a crystal machine—the device powering the tunnel to another world.

Something moved in a doorway to an adjoining room, and a figure stepped out. Her stomach hardened. Eva Noone faced her. The woman was alight with magic. A pair of lesser sorcerers stood at her side.

"You didn't expect me, did you?" Noone smiled coldly; all three mouths exposed, and each one with exuding a different magical energy.

"I saw you leave," Lucy said.

Noone laughed. "You're not the only one who can play a simple trick."

Lucy realised her foolishness. She'd been tricked by her own desire to see Noone gone. She wasn't ready for this. The magic radiating from Noone was dark and unpleasant, and was already seeping from the woman's fingers. Lucy picked up an expensive vase from a table and flung it at her. Noone flipped it away with ease, but it slowed the rhythm of a spell. Still, Noone's toxic and sludgy magic snaked towards her. Lucy burnt it, but it took energy.

One of the lesser sorcerers threw a magic-laden punch; the type that could cause multiple organ failure. An advantage of training in magic was that the world appeared to move in slow motion. She slipped inside his punch and touched his chest.

"Stop."

The man's lungs froze. His face turned blue before he hit

the floor. She reached for the crystal machine, which sat on an ornate table, but the second man attacked, knocking her towards the fireplace.

Noone advanced towards her.

Lucy prepared herself. Then blue light flashed towards her. She deflected it with a blast of fire. Something moved to her left.

"Tavth?"

Her situation had become dire. The demon king grinned. He grabbed her, tossing her against the mural on the wall. She hit the wall hard, but something was wrong. She felt a wetness sucking her into it. For several seconds, she didn't understand. Noone and the demon grinned. Why didn't they kill her? They had the chance.

Then she felt the painting pulling her harder. She cursed. This was the portal, and she was being sucked inside. Tavth and Noone threw energetic darts at her. She deflected the first two, but the third grazed her. She screamed in pain, and the force of their magic pushed her deeper into the portal. Still she struggled, but Tavth charged, hitting her like a bull, sending her flying through the portal. It snapped shut behind her.

LUCY STOOD IN A DIM WASTELAND, a dust storm blowing around her. It could have been caused by her sudden entry to this world wherever she was. Her body ached. Feeling tired and hungry, she started walking. She didn't know where she was going. Her only aim was to get out of this terrible dust cloud. The storm seemed to have no end. She prayed that the entire world was not like this. After half an hour, she smelt demons. It was almost a relief, for it meant that something lived here, however unpleasant. Figures loomed through the swirling dust. Demons were mostly not imaginative, and she knew from previous experience that if they smelt her, they'd attack. To prepare, she began a physical transformation that was easier in a universe so far from her own.

"Human, we can smell you," a demon said.

It spoke aloud in a language she didn't know, but she could read its thoughts, making its meaning clear. They were familiar with humans. She ignored its reek and its words. Her skin became copper coloured, and her body stretched. It was painful, even here in a universe where the laws were slightly different. She cried out at the pain of the transformation, and the demons howled with laughter. They misunderstood. Smoke rose from her. The dust storm in which she lay disguised her form. She coiled her body around, checking herself. The transformation was complete.

A copper-coloured dragon stared at four demons. Their eyes widened, and before they could react, she killed the first with an intense blast of fire. Then she stamped on a purple-eyed one. The remaining two demons threatened her with spears, but when she roared, they retreated. They called for help. The dust storm slowed, and she saw more of the wasteland that surrounded her. A few stunted trees grew from the scorched ground but little else. A mountain loomed in the distance. Magic was being practiced there; she felt it tugging at her. But then she was distracted by the growing band of demons. At the moment, they lacked the courage to attack.

Then the body of a demon moved. It should be dead. Its shoulder twitched, and she raised her front claws, ready to cut off its head.

"No," a faint voice cried in the True Language.

"What are you?" she asked. It didn't sound like a demon.

"Nothing."

She was female, but Lucy couldn't discern much more than that except that she had rudimentary magic, but nothing to concern her.

"Nothing doesn't speak."

"I mean, I'm far beneath you, Lady. I'm not worth your time to speak to."

"That may be true," Lucy said, *"but what are you?"*

"A water sprite."

"Like a nymph?"

Lucy remembered the queen of the nymphs.

"Less than a nymph," she said.

"Show yourself."

A tiny water sprite, half the size of her human hand, stepped from beneath the demon.

Lucy was surprised. The tiny creature looked nothing like the sprites she'd seen before.

"They use me for water."

Then she understood its shrivelled appearance.

"What is this world?" Lucy asked.

The sprite appeared confused. *"This is the world."*

"Tell me about the mountain."

"Evil," the sprite said, staring at one of the few plants that grew nearby.

"Drink," Lucy said.

"How did you know?"

"Sometimes I know things."

The sprite bit into the stem and sucked. Her body filled out, making her look younger, but it was still impossible to guess her age.

"The mountain?" Lucy repeated.

The sprite continued drinking.

"I can feel its pull."

"Don't go there," the sprite said. *"The arch demon's palace is inside. It's an evil place full of demons. They've burrowed inside. It's full of tunnels, caves, and vast caverns."*

"There's something else," Lucy said.

"The Gates of Hell."

A portal. Lucy could feel it. That was what it was. She had to go there. She stretched her wings.

"No!"

"What?"

"If you must go, then I must go with you," the sprite said.

"Why?"

"If I remain here," she glanced at the group of demons waiting about thirty yards away, *"they'll kill me."*

"You may die where I'm going."

The sprite shook her head. *"May die is better than will die. You're different from the other life here,"* the sprite continued.

"That's because I'm not from here. If you want to come with me, climb onto my back."

The demons were getting restless; some of them howled.

"Does it ever get light here?" Lucy asked.

The sprite shook her head. *"Not really."*

When more demons howled, the sprite jumped onto Lucy's back, and she spread her wings and lifted into the air. At least this type of demon didn't have wings.

The nearer she flew to the mountain, the stronger the pull of the portal became.

"Do you know a demon called Tavth?"

"Don't say its name," the sprite whispered.

"It pushed me into this world. Tell me about it."

She realised she knew nothing about Tavth, beyond what she'd seen in the north wood, and what the queen had told her. And what the queen had told her could not be trusted without question.

"It's the second in command of the arch demon's army."

Lucy sighed.

As she flew, she saw with the sharp vision of a dragon. Although the wasteland was bleak, life was hidden within it. The struggle for life was hard here. How much more attractive Earth would be to the demons. How much did Noone know about Tavth? Lucy suspected it wasn't much. Wherever this hot arid planet was, it was not the type of place Noone would visit.

The water sprite chattered away, and every so often said something useful about this world. There were more than a dozen demon tribes, and the arch demon ruled most of them. They lacked water, hence her species had suffered. They naturally absorbed moisture from the dry air; the demons then squeezed them dry and often to death.

"Don't fly too close," the sprite warned.

She kept flying. She was now a dragon and didn't care if demons saw her, but she noticed the tiny sprite was agitated.

"Water," the sprite said.

Lucy looked at the hollow in the wasteland below. A handful of stunted trees grew there.

"I smell no water."

"I'm a water sprite. It's hidden, but I can find it."

The sprite might be telling the truth, and she was thirsty; she circled down, landing gently on the ground. The sprite leapt and glided to the ground. Then she ran from place to place. Perhaps it was true; the land was softer here. Finally, the sprite stopped.

"Here."

Lucy sniffed. She was right, after all. The sprite waited, and Lucy realised what she wanted. With a few movements of her front legs, she dug a hole. A pool of water formed at the bottom.

As they rested, Lucy thought about her task. She had to gain entry to the mountain, and then she had to learn how to create a passage to Earth; otherwise, she could end up wandering lost between this universe and hers. She just hoped that neither the demons or Noone had established a permanent tunnel, although she couldn't see why Noone would want a passage to a place like this, nor did Lucy think Noone had the knowledge to build such a tunnel. But perhaps the arch demon did.

The water sprite slept. Looking at her reminded Lucy of the water nymphs. Their queen knew and hated the demons. Lucy decided to attempt to communicate with her. Distant communication was less certain, but even between distant universes, and even between the worlds of the dead and the living, it was sometimes possible.

"Queen of the nymphs."

From a distant place, the queen heard. Lucy sensed surprise.

"You once said you'd help me if I helped you close the turtle portal. I call on your help now."

An image of the blue watery queen formed in her mind.

"How did you enter that place?" the queen asked.

"Tavth," Lucy said. She briefly explained.

The queen hissed her displeasure.

"Leaving is hard."

"I imagine," Lucy said.

"You have one of my creatures with you."

"A water sprite. She says she was captured by demons." The queen was silent, and Lucy continued. *"How did Tavth reach London?"*

"Tavth was trapped in the forest, but when it learnt the alien

humans had the power to open passages to other worlds, it tricked them into using their magic to take it to London."

"I need to stop them using the crystal machine," Lucy said.

"Why?"

Lucy was a little surprised by the question.

"To stop the alien humans opening a way to their world and bringing back an army to mine."

"Tavth's tricked them. That's not what it'll do."

Again, Lucy was caught by surprise. Her skin prickled as she ran through other possibilities.

"What will it do?"

"Tavth's played with the crystal so it'll open a pathway from the demon world to Earth. A demon horde would come to Earth."

"Why?"

"They live in a dry, desolate world. Earth has life for them to feed on."

"I don't completely understand," Lucy said. She'd trodden the hidden paths, but the highways the alien humans and demons used were unknown to her. She was still learning.

"Like me, you've walked the side roads and paths between worlds. Wisdom is found there, in the places no one wants to go, but they have no patience for that. The demons and alien humans seek speed. They create and travel along super highways, seeing nothing but the road."

"I never found a super highway in my journey between worlds," Lucy said.

"Credit to you that you survived the backwaters of that grey world of illusions. Few outsiders do. That gives me hope."

"How do these highways work?"

"Portals powered by devices project one-way paths between universes, like the one Tavth threw you into. The aim is imprecise. If two paths—one incoming, one outgoing—connect, then a highway is formed.

"If the demons connect the Gates of Hell to the portal powered by the crystal machine in London, Tavth's road will become a stable super highway. Until then, it's a random attempt to project paths into distant universes, which often results in death to those who walk the path."

"So Tavth didn't know I'd live."

The queen laughed. "It did not, but it suspected it went to the demon realm. You were the experiment—now it knows."

"So the arch demon needs to control both ends of the tunnel between universes to form a stable super highway." Lucy paused. The possibilities were terrible. "And invade Earth."

"Yes, but there are other worlds, too. Places of power. The demons would attack me."

Lucy immediately understood the queen's concern. She suspected that there were sorcerers on Noone's Palace Moon searching for any pathway she projected towards them.

"If the arch demon suspects Tavth has already projected a pathway to its realm, it'll search for it. These things leave traces of magic. If it finds it, it'll tune the demon portal to the frequency of the crystal machine. Then a direct, two-way road will be established."

"But won't the aliens redirect the pathway to their world?" Lucy asked.

"If they noticed it, perhaps," the queen said, "but their knowledge of portals is less than the demons—and far less than yours. Demons can be subtle; they can hide things.

"For all their power, or perhaps because of it, the human aliens are one-sided. They focus on the details and fail to see the bigger picture.

"Your knowledge of different magics already makes you more formidable than you think. They lack that."

Lucy hoped so, but didn't feel confident.

"Do the alien humans know about this world?" Lucy asked.

"I doubt it."

"Where is this world?"

"It's a sort of limbo. One of the shadows of the bright universes. They lie halfway between the visible ones—like the black keys on the human piano are halfway between the white keys."

"Is Tavth really the deputy leader to the arch demon?"

"Yes," the queen hissed. *"Kill it. Both if you can."*

"How?"

She was surprised when the queen vehemently started speaking. Elementals were notoriously secretive, but the demons threatened the queen's realm. She hated them.

"Trickery, bluff, and speed. If you can, trick them into breaking the natural laws concerning energy portals between realms."

"What are the laws of the portals?"

"That's for you to discover," the queen said.

"You're my weapon against the demons," the queen said. *"If I could help you more, I would."*

Lucy immediately thought about her weapons—Darta and Angel.

"Your blend of soft and hard magic is interesting." the queen said.

"Can't you tell me anything about these laws?"

"Learn to manipulate energy. All relates to that."

Then the queen was gone.

The sprite stared at her.

"Something just happened to you? You're different. I smell water magic."

Lucy wished it were true.

39

Amelia sat in the back of the van and bandaged Jack's eye. He'd regained consciousness. Ruth knelt next to her, helping where she could. Luke was driving to the nearest hospital. He'd already tuned into the MI5 communications channel. Reports were coming in fast; they were being hunted right now.

"If I go to hospital, I'll be arrested," Jack said.

"This is serious," Amelia said. She doubted that even the best surgeon could save the sight in his right eye, but it was worth a try.

"I'll stay with you," Ruth said. "I wasn't in Noone's house, so it's harder for them to arrest me."

Minutes later, they stopped outside the emergency entrance to the nearest hospital.

"What about you?" Ruth asked.

"Pimlico House," Amelia and Luke said at the same time.

"You'll be arrested, too," Jack said. "They'll spot the van and come for you."

"It may be the safest place," Amelia said. "We'll sneak in

via the underground lift. It's hidden. Most of the staff don't even know it exists, and from the first floor up, the building's like a fortress."

"I'll be in touch," Jack said as Ruth helped him towards the hospital.

"He's right about the van," Luke said as they left. "We should dump it."

Five minutes later, they abandoned the van near a Tube station. There was no news about the orange witch. It seemed she'd just vanished. Luke glanced up. Eva Noone stared down at them from an election poster as they walked into the Tube. The caption underneath read, "finally, someone who cares." Amelia frowned. Noone had already made a complaint about an illegal intrusion by MI7 into her home. As they walked through the turnstiles, Amelia noticed Luke was distracted.

"Are you okay?"

"I have to protect Molly and William. The aliens sell slaves."

"Yes," she said. "But I don't want you doing anything risky."

"I need to go back there."

"Luke? What can you do?"

"I can observe the house. If they move them, I'll follow."

"You don't even have transport."

"We have the team motorbike under Pimlico House."

They'd bought a Honda Rebel for emergencies.

"Molly said women were disappearing and not returning. I can't wait," Luke said.

Amelia nodded. She knew in his place she'd do the same. But it was risky. They arrived at Pimlico Tube together. Minutes later, they entered the private underground car park. One section was completely secret—unknown to almost anyone.

Amelia watched Luke ride the bike out of the carpark. She was so tired, she couldn't do anything without a couple of hours' sleep. The car park was dark, but she felt safe. She'd been there many times before. To even get into it, you needed special passcodes. The secret section, which she now walked towards, required finger and eye scans.

Then she stopped.

Her sixth sense told her something was wrong, but she didn't know what. She listened, but everything was quiet. Assuming she was too tired and imagining things, she continued walking. A cat whined, sending shivers up her spine. There should be no animals inside here, but perhaps one had got trapped.

"Here, cat. Are you okay?"

It whined strangely. Then she saw a shadow moving between the cars. When she looked directly at it, it disappeared. She shivered. That was weird. Instead of looking directly at it, she tried looking straight ahead, and then she saw a creature in the corner of her eye. Her skin crawled. It had a cat's body and eyes, but its head was like a monkey's. She backed away, fearful it was one of the things that had killed Toby Upjohn and William's nanny. She slipped out her phone.

"Ruth?" she whispered.

The phone rang, but there was no answer. She called Luke—also no reply. It crouched near the secret section of the car park. She walked back towards the main exit. It screamed. She reached for her pistol. Only one bullet left, and she wasn't sure it would have any effect on something like this, but it gave her a little confidence. She looked over her shoulder; it was following. She walked faster, but it kept pace.

Her phone rang.

"Where are you?"

"Ruth, I'm being followed through the car park under Pimlico House."

"What?"

She quickly explained.

"I'm on my way," Ruth said.

"What about Jack?"

"He's in surgery. They said I can't see him for hours, anyway."

She reached the exit, pressed the button, rushed through the door, slamming it shut behind her. Breathing deeply, she climbed the steps to street level. She'd find another way.

A passerby moved quickly away from her when he saw the pistol in her hand. She was too concerned about the thing following her to care. Another man stopped and stared at her, not seeing the creature cantering along the pavement behind him. His eyes widened when she pointed her pistol in his direction. She wasn't sure why he didn't move. Perhaps he'd frozen in fear.

When the creature rushed past him, she fired, and it seemed to disappear. The passerby came to life and sprinted away from her. She walked in the opposite direction. Then she noticed a third man who was keeping pace with her on the opposite side of the road. He gave her a bad feeling, and when she turned a corner, she ran. Soon she was in an unfamiliar backstreet.

Ruth called again.

Amelia told her about the man following her. "He seems familiar, but he was too far away to see clearly," she said.

"Just as well," Ruth said. "I think I know where you are. I'm on my way." Ruth hung up.

Amelia turned and almost screamed.

"Chief Inspector Gully!"

He was angry, but that was normal. At least her pursuer was gone. Then Gully lunged at her, gripping her arms. Her fear returned. Was this the man following her?

"You're under arrest."

He took her pistol.

"Let go!" she said. "You're hurting me."

The man babbled; she couldn't understand what he was saying. The harder she struggled, the tighter his grip became. He was saying something she couldn't understand, then she realised he was speaking in the alien language. A feeling of terror shot through her, and she started fighting harder against his grip.

"NO!"

She felt dizzy. Gully was launching a psychic attack. She was shocked. "Who are you?"

He slapped her hard, bringing tears to her eyes. She gasped as he squeezed her throat. Her vision was fading.

"Why?" she gasped.

A strange red mask seemed to protrude from the top of his head. Its eyes bulged, then it turned to stare at her. She shook with fear. When its mouth opened in an attempt to speak, Amelia screamed in horror. Then she felt herself losing consciousness. Somewhere in the distance, she heard a shout.

"Not here, not now," she thought as her legs gave way, and she fell to the ground. She felt uncomfortably hot. Then she passed out.

40

Lucy flew closer to the mountain, with the tiny sprite clinging onto her scales.

"Do you know how to enter?" Lucy asked.

"It has four doors. Each is guarded," the sprite said.

"You've been inside?"

"I was sold to a demon who worked in one of the inner chambers."

"Did you see the portal?"

"No. My demon master wasn't high ranked, but I heard about it."

"What would happen if I asked for entry?"

"I don't know. No one has seen a dragon here for thousands of years," the sprite said. "Why not say you're on a diplomatic mission from your island?"

"There are islands here?"

"I was stolen from one."

Lucy thought this over. If she could carry out the bluff for long enough, she could locate the portal. Then she'd just have to reach it, but at least she'd be inside the mountain. As long as she remained outside, she could never return.

"Say you're from the Isles of Poltimore," the sprite said.

"Where are they?"

"In the Western Ocean, but no one here has heard about them."

The bluff appealed to her.

"What's your name?"

"Nell."

"You've just become my attendant. I'll announce myself as Radiant Moon. We're emissaries from the Isles of Poltimore."

She felt the sprite sit higher on her back as they soared towards the mountain. Lucy began her descent to the demon mountain. The largest gates were on the north and south sides; she chose the dusty southern approach, flying low over the ground, trumpeting her arrival, and sending dozens of demons running for cover. When a group of demons rushed her, she blew fire over their heads.

"I'm Radiant Moon of Grand Poltimore, here as an emissary from the Isles of Poltimore in the Western Ocean, seeking a treaty between the Dragon Empire and the arch demon."

She broadcast her message into the minds of all capable of hearing. The demons stopped, confused. She turned to a well in the dusty square before the southern gate.

"My attendant shall fetch water for me while I wait."

Nell happily dived into the well. Minutes later, she returned. She'd trebled her size and poured water onto Lucy's face. She repeated her journey twice more before a large demon appeared at the gate.

"I'm Gart. Duke of the Western Realm. I've never heard of the Isles of Poltimore."

Lucy dripped fire from her mouth.

"You question a dragon?"

She increased the heat in her belly, causing her eyes to brighten as she stared at Gart. She listened while it spoke with its master. The demons thought their speech private, but she was a dragon and could read most thoughts and even the most subtle emotions. They were treacherous, nervous, yet curious. The arch demon wanted to learn more. It wanted to know whether the dragons posed a threat. They would invite her inside. A minute later, she followed the demon into the mountain. The tunnels were wide, designed for armies of demons to pass through, although they narrowed as they went deeper. They stopped in a demon market.

"You can rest here," Gart said.

Lucy roared, helping herself to complete carcasses of animals, to the consternation of the demon traders, which she roasted in her mouth and belly.

"Is this how you treat the emissary of the Dragon Empire? I demand a personal chamber with access to the Gates of Hell."

"What do you know of our gates?"

"I'm a dragon. The gates shine in my mind as clearly as the sun. My queen is interested."

Again, the demon carried out a conversation with his master. This time they whispered, making it harder for Lucy to hear. She heard distant laughter. It was a trap, but her main concern was getting as close as she could to the gates. She had no intention of leaving the way she came.

Gart bowed before her. *"The arch demon has granted your wish, honourable dragon. I will take you to your chamber deep within the mountain."*

Lucy took another carcass from an unhappy demon as she left the market, swallowing it whole. The journey took over an hour, with the passages becoming narrower and narrower. She began to wonder whether she'd fit when Gart turned and assured her that her chamber was a grand place suitable for a dragon.

"It's a trick," Nell whispered.

"I know."

But she felt the energy of the portal as she moved closer to it. Finally, she entered a vast chamber. At one end was a large metal gate. And there was a strange smell. A rivulet ran along one side of the chamber, and several narrow passages led out. All of which were too narrow for a dragon. Energy from the portal radiated from one of them.

"How can I pass through these passages?"

"You asked for a chamber of adequate size with access to the gates. This we have provided." The demon gave an evil grin.

So they believed she was trapped, Lucy thought.

"What's behind the metal gate?"

"The arch demon's throne room. He'll speak to you tomorrow morning."

"Then I'll sleep," Lucy said.

She lay down and closed her eyes. The demon and his assistants left the chamber.

"I'll ensure you're not disturbed," Gart said, slamming and bolting the large door to the chamber behind him.

"Explore, but be careful," Lucy said to Nell.

Nell ran silently down the tunnel to the Gates of Hell. Less than an hour later, an agitated Nell ran from the tunnel.

"A fire dragon guards the gates."

"Tell me what you saw."

"Six giant turtles are chained in a row and tethered to a stone post. It looks as if they're being pulled towards the gate."

"What does the gate look like?"

"A fiery mirror suspended in the air."

"Demons?"

"Two, but the fire dragon is the problem."

"Tell me about it."

"Big with wild magic. It controls the turtles and almost killed me."

Nell kept speaking, and Lucy learnt more about the creature. Reaching the gate should be straightforward, and there was a good chance she could deal with the demons, but she needed a plan for dealing with the fire dragon. If it was what she thought, it was one of the most basic of elementals, and wouldn't respond to reasoning, if it could reason at all.

The next morning, a procession of demons entered her chamber laden with platters of raw meat and fruit. She'd have preferred cooked meat; having to cook it herself cost her energy. She sniffed it. Some platters contained tainted meat. Some were clean. She ate the clean meat and left the rest.

"It's drugged," she said when Nell looked at her questioningly.

An hour later, the demon Gart returned, glancing at the untouched platters of food. *"The arch demon has granted you an audience."*

The demon walked to the great metal gates, and they separated, moving noisily apart, revealing a large coliseum. Hundreds of demons had gathered. They were seated in aisles around the sides. Metal bars separated them from her. In the centre was a large space big enough for dozens of dragons. Outwardly, Lucy remained still. Inwardly, she melded her fire and natural magic. The itching on the top of her head, which she suspected was connected to the third magic, had gone. Perhaps she needed to be in her human form to call it.

Lesser demons removed the dishes of tainted food. A little later, they returned with more food. This time it was safe, and she ate freely.

"Tell me about demons," she whispered to Nell. *"Does their*

magic deplete their strength?"

Nell looked at her, astonished. *"I've never heard of that."*

Perhaps the sprite didn't know. It was hardly something demons would mention. Then she had an idea. She knew the demons planned to trick her. Possibly kill her. The chamber, with its rowdy demon audience, now reminded her of an arena designed for the spilling of blood. She gorged herself on the food. And when she emptied dishes, she demanded more.

"Won't so much food tire you?" Gart asked.

"Yes, but I can rest later."

Gart smiled and ordered more food to be brought.

Lucy felt her body swell. Even some demons in the crowd noticed and howled with laughter. But she continued to eat.

"I'm not sure you should do that," Nell said.

"They don't believe my story about the dragon empire," she said. *"They plan to pit me against an opponent today in this arena."*

"I suspected as much," Nell said. *"All the more reason to remain in shape."*

"Trust me," Lucy said. *"When the trouble starts, I want you to leave me."*

"I cannot."

"You must. It'll be dangerous to be near me. I want you to run back down the tunnel—"

"The fire dragon will kill me."

"Perhaps not. Wait at the other end. If I succeed, I'll join you there."

"How? The tunnels are too small for you."

"Let me worry about that. If I fall this morning, you must take your chances. Even if I lose, I believe the guards will be distracted. You'll have a brief opportunity to jump into the portal."

Nell looked at her, shocked.

"That'll kill me."

"It'll transport you to another place."

"Where?"

"I don't know, and it may be worse than here."

Nell sat on the floor with a grim face as Lucy finished the food. No more appeared. Lucy lifted Nell with her tail and placed her near the tunnel leading to the Gates of Hell.

"Wait till the last moment and then run."

This time she whispered so quietly that only Nell could hear. The tiny sprite nodded but appeared unhappy and confused.

Horns blew from behind the golden throne. The arch demon walked into the throne room, and the demons bowed. Lucy walked towards the throne, exaggerating her size both by expanding her body physically, and by a very gentle reverse invisibility spell. Instead of sending the mental suggestion that she wasn't there, which would have been impossible in such surroundings, she sent the suggestion that she was fatter and more ungainly than she was. This mental suggestion found a fertile home in the mass mind of the demons. They howled hysterically. Even Gart glanced at the arch demon with an amused look in its eye.

The arch demon sat on its throne. It was blue-skinned with flecks of red. Curved horns came from its head. It stared through red eyes. She sensed magic. It would be a powerful opponent. Lucy wondered if the arch demon would challenge her itself. Gart stood beneath the throne. The arch demon addressed the chamber. It spoke in the demon language and seemed to be speaking about her. Silence fell around the chamber. It had accused her of something.

The arch demon turned to Lucy.

"There are no true dragons in this world. How did you come here?"

Not wanting to say anything that might help them, she remained silent.

"Do you have anything to say?" the arch demon asked.

When a demon tried to poke her with a trident, she burnt it to a cinder.

"Enough!" the arch demon roared.

It shouted orders in its language. Lucy listened as it spoke. She caught images of fire. A group of demons wearing blue and red robes chanted, casting a magic spell. The magic didn't seem to be aimed at her. She waited. Then, noticing that some demons in the crowd were looking up, she followed their gaze. A shimmering line had appeared in the air. It gradually increased in size.

She was fascinated. They could magically open portals. They also seemed to use an energy source near the Gates of Hell. Perhaps a device similar to those used by the aliens. When she opened a portal, she used natural magic as the key, and the power of her own body to create the small passage she needed. A fiery portal formed above her.

"Go," she whispered to Nell.

Every demon in the chamber was looking up.

Lucy moved back.

Fire fell from the hole, and the arch demon laughed. Despite their bravado, she sensed the demons were scared of her. She wasn't surprised they didn't want to question her further. Getting information from a reluctant dragon was almost impossible. Trying to kill her made some sense. She prepared herself; her magics mingled. The portal hanging in the air above her widened and a fire dragon flew into the coliseum. The crowd of demons roared.

41

Lucy's copper-coloured scales reflected the light of the fire dragon. Her eyes were like orange embers, and she breathed fire from her mouth, but the fire dragon was made of fire. A true elemental. One that few dragons would recognise as a dragon at all, though it had the outer appearance of one.

It dived, blasting a jet of fire at her. Dragon fire was seldom pure fire, but fire with magic within. She countered its magic, and it turned in the air as she shot fire back. It absorbed her blast without a sound. Again it dived at her; this time it spat fire balls, more like bombs, that exploded on her scales. The heat was intense, even for her. For minutes, it circled and dived, each time pushing her against the wall. She was in a defensive posture. To attack meant moving from the tunnel entrance, which she didn't want to do. She bided her time, taking the blasts as they came. They were now hurting her, yet her attacks on it seemed to have little effect, although she noticed it kept its distance.

Then it dived again. Lucy waited for it to turn and become a better target. But it didn't. It flew directly at her.

Too late, she lifted into the air, but it hit her hard, knocking her against the rock wall. She was engulfed in a fireball with the dragon, and its claws ripped scales from her body. It bit hard, burning her flesh.

Feeling the tunnel entrance against her back and her energy fading, she stopped fighting the fire dragon. Instead, she absorbed its fire, pulling on its energy. She was wracked with pain as her body expanded. The fire dragon's attack became frenetic as it sensed victory.

When her body had expanded to its limits, Lucy executed her plan. Transformation cost a lot of energy, but now she had so much energy that it threatened to kill her. Sticking her claws into the dragon, she started to change back into human form. She shrank rapidly, and as she did, the vortex of magic whirling around her protected her from the violence of the dragon. The food she'd eaten had gone, her previously brimming internal fire had cooled, and as she continued to suck energy from the fire dragon, it dimmed, too.

The demons wailed as their champion screamed in pain. It pulled away, landing about twenty yards away where it stood, confused. A whirling magic masked her human form. Feeling weak, she slipped into the tunnel wearing only her specially designed shorts and T-shirt. Running barefoot was okay, but she decided that in the future, she'd design special boots, too. Behind her, she heard the dragon thrashing at the sides of the coliseum.

Nell drew back when she approached.

"It's me," Lucy gasped.

She knew that Nell now saw a human.

"You're not a dragon?"

"I'm half dragon."

She rested for a few minutes but could afford no more

time. Slowly, some of her energy returned. She edged towards the end of the tunnel. Six giant snapping turtles were chained in a line facing the portal, which now appeared as a bright mirror. Those strange creatures were the power source. A demon frantically worked beneath the portal. The second guarded the entrance to the chamber. The arch demon would soon want to return the dragon to this chamber. Lucy imagined it played a part in controlling the turtles. But she guessed the demons would have to wait until the fire dragon calmed down. And, with luck, the arch demon would have no idea what had happened to the copper-coloured dragon that had disappeared in a blaze of magic. Hopefully, it'd think she was dead, but it'd become suspicious when it found no trace of her remains. If it did manage to return the fire dragon to this chamber, she was dead.

She crept towards them. Exhausted from the fight and the transformation back into human form, she knew it would be hard to use her depleted primal fire. Instead, she relied on the softer natural magic to camouflage herself, trying to blend into the dark and smoky chamber. The demons didn't notice her or the water sprite that sat on her shoulder, but the sixth turtle turned its head to watch her.

Turtles were cold creatures, and she kept her distance. With one snap, any one of them could crush her body and eat her. But she needed to speak to them. Standing hidden by the darkness and by her spell of invisibility, she thought about the best way to approach them.

The fifth turtle also watched her.

Lucy studied the energy that tethered the turtles. It was formed like a rope with many strands, but each strand was made of magical energy. The strands reminded her of the energy snakes that had emerged from the portal and attacked her in the western woods.

"*I can release you,*" she whispered so quietly that the demons couldn't hear.

She hoped her claim was true.

All six turtles listened, but only the fifth and sixth watched her.

"*You don't look like much,*" the sixth turtle said.

"*I can untie your bonds.*"

"*How do we know this is not another of the arch demon's tricks?*"

Lucy shared the memory of her battle with the fire dragon. The six turtles tensed. They hated the creature.

"*The arch demon will send it back here,*" she said. "*At least, let me try.*"

"*Try, but expect nothing in return.*"

"*I expect passage for myself and my friend to Earth. After that, you can go where you want.*"

The lead turtle spat at the demon attempting to work on the portal. The demon rushed at the turtle with a raised club, but the moment it stepped too close, the turtle's neck extended, and it swallowed the demon whole. Lucy could tell from its expression before it had died that it hadn't expected that from the turtles. The demon by the door wailed.

"*We don't bargain with humans,*" the first turtle said.

Lucy guessed that would change when the fire dragon returned. As would their freedom to kill demons with impunity. Working with her hands and natural magic combined, she separated one strand. She knew the turtles noticed. She continued her work unbothered by the other demon that now crept along the edges of the wall, keeping as far away from the snapping turtles as he could, to see the fate of his friend.

Once she was confident she could release the turtles, she stopped her work.

"Continue," the first turtle said.

"I require something in return."

Someone banged on the door.

"Open the door!" It was Gart.

The demon staring at the boot beneath the lead turtle's head, which was all that remained of its companion, slowly edged its way back to the door.

"You must decide quickly if you want your freedom," Lucy said.

She was beginning to wonder whether they'd agree, and she studied the portal itself. She could step through. Her natural magic was the key, and the energy of her body would push it open, but she'd then have months or years travelling through a hostile and magical land. With the power the turtles possessed, she could catapult herself back to Earth. She decided to wait.

"What do you want?" the lead turtle asked.

"Passage for myself and a sprite, and the knowledge of how to manipulate the energy of the portals."

"Are you capable of understanding?"

Nell stood on her shoulder and shouted insults at the turtles.

"That's my problem."

Lucy hid beneath the sixth turtle as more demons entered the room. She created a vision, showing them the oceans of Earth. Within the seas, she showed them the fish. They all listened now.

"The fish are dying," the sixth turtle said. *"Humans have killed them."*

"You have the power to stop the fishing," Lucy said.

"True."

Looking at the line of turtles, she showed them advancing through the succession of portals until they reached Earth.

"You offer this world?"

"I offer the oceans," she said.

Her stomach dropped as she offered what she had no right to offer, but these semi-magical creatures needed something attractive.

"We accept," the snapping turtles said.

A demon found her. It screamed something and charged at her. When she leapt closer to the sixth turtle, it bit the demon's head off. The demons were surprised by the turtle's action and took care to keep their distance from the giant creatures. They'd seen her but now chose to edge towards the portal itself, which was whining. One of the middle turtles whipped its stubby tail at a passing demon, cutting it badly.

"You do know how to release us?" the first turtle asked.

"I will soon."

The demons gathered at the front, making some sort of adjustments to the portal.

"Faster," the lead turtle said. *"They're trying to loop the path back to the coliseum."*

"I thought that was where it pointed anyway," she said.

"We changed it to keep that evil thing away from us. Now it points towards your oceans."

A little of her primal magic had returned, and she burnt one of the threads. The line of turtles jolted forward. She climbed onto the back of the sixth turtle, then pulled apart two more threads of magic, but the final one was taut. She couldn't move it.

"Burn it," the sixth turtle said.

The demons seemed to sense a change. They were searching for her again, but she'd blended herself in with the colours of the turtle's shell using her invisibility spell.

"Quickly!" Nell said.

"I know."

She attempted to fire the thread with the little energy she had. Finally, it burst into flames. The turtles clicked their mouths open and shut in anticipation. The tether snapped, and they shot through the Gates of Hell, the first in a series of portals spanning many worlds. She heard it snap shut behind them.

They flew through time and space, colours rushing together around them. Nell sat on her lap and pointed at a dark shape on the side of the turtle's shell. Something from the cavern had attached itself to the shell, but she couldn't see it clearly. Then they passed through another portal. It was a grey version of hell with demons toiling by distant fires. Then it was gone, as they hurtled into a third portal. This was a brighter world with sun and forest, but then it, too, vanished when they rushed into a fourth portal. Soon, portals flashed open and closed as they flew through them. As they flew, the turtles gave her instructions.

"Won't you be dragged to her crystal machine?" Lucy asked, voicing one of the concerns she had.

"No longer. Ages ago, we argued and were captured because we'd become divided. That will never happen again. When united, we don't obey the rudimentary portal mechanics of humanoids and demons. We're energy. We command the portals of the multiverse."

"Can you create portals?" she asked.

She wasn't sure that all the portals they'd passed through had been there before. She heard the turtles laugh.

"You're learning fast," the sixth turtle said.

"Show me."

The turtles spoke amongst themselves. Finally, the first turtle answered her.

"We'll show you how to construct the most basic portal. And then our debt to you is ended."

Lucy readily agreed, and the sixth turtle taught her more about the types of portals, and passages that connected them to other, more distant, portals. She already knew how to detect and open existing portals, now she learnt how to create simple portals where none had previously existed.

Hours seemed to pass as she listened to the turtle, then she sensed they were close. Worrying about reappearing in Noone's inner chambers, she focussed her mind on Angel. Visualisation was part of inter-universal travel. And she needed her assassin as soon as possible.

"You're more than you think," the lead turtle said, regarding her.

The turtles then turned towards the Thames, and the chain connecting them began to fragment. With her own magic alight, she let go, flying through one of the more fluid planes of Earth. Something attached itself to her; she was sure it was the dark shape she'd seen on the side of the shell. In the distance, she heard the turtles dive into the Thames.

Lucy fell onto a hard concrete floor. Bruised, she sat up. Wild-eyed men stared at her in shock. Riding the turtles had needed more magical energy than she'd realised. With the pressure gone, her inner fire had nothing to contain it, and it blazed, falling through cracks in her skin. A man pushed his way through the crowd of men that stared at her. She looked around, still feeling disoriented. The room smelt of sweat.

"Angel."

The Orange Witch

"An impressive entrance," he said, an eyebrow raised.
Then she noticed the grey walls and barred window.
"Where am I?"
"The gym."
She was confused.
"In Pentonville Prison."

42

Lucy stood in the prison gym, barely able to control the fire within. She shook as flames escaped through cracks in her skin. The prisoners still stared in shock. She felt the water sprite cry, and then she was gone. Lucy hoped she'd not evaporated her by mistake, but there was nothing she could do as she desperately tried to bring her magic under control.

"What day is it?"

"Friday," Angel said.

"I need to get out of here."

A prisoner laughed nervously. Slowly, she controlled the fire in her belly, and the flames flickered out. Although the fire had gone, her eyes still glowed.

"What's the blue thing?" Angel asked.

Her stomach dropped when she saw it, but she now understood what had attached itself to the turtles and then to her.

"A demon."

"It seems to be making friends."

She wondered if she should kill it. Perhaps she could,

but that would drain energy, making her more vulnerable—something she couldn't risk. Her mission was more important than a criminal gang recruiting a simple-minded demon. It was grinning at the coarse language of the convicts. She had no idea if it understood a single word.

"And the other thing?"

She followed Angel's gaze and was relieved to see Nell standing on a man's hand in the corner. The tiny sprite was happily chattering away to a small group of prisoners.

"She's a friend—a water sprite."

Angel accepted her answers at face value, not pushing to know more.

"Angel, I need your help."

He smiled. "I know that for you it may seem like a mundane issue, but I'm locked in prison. They'll never release me."

"I wasn't thinking of asking anyone's permission."

She glanced around the gym. Nobody was exercising. About one third of the men were in close conversation with the demon, and another third seemed to be mesmerised by Nell. The remainder stared at her.

Angel crossed his arms. "Can you walk through walls?"

Lucy thought about what the sixth turtle had taught her. Portals had uses other than being doors to other worlds. A short hop should be okay.

She shook her head. "Walking through walls is advanced magic. But I can hop through them."

She paused and looked him in the eyes.

"Getting out isn't the problem—stopping the aliens is."

He looked at her impassively.

"We need to finish this. The aliens must die. They're too dangerous; they threaten our world."

She paused.

"The chance of any of us living through this is small. I've told Darta, and she's accepted it. But you're free to decide. It's your choice."

"You make a tempting offer," Angel said.

She smiled sadly. She didn't want any of this. The chance of them living to see tomorrow was small. But she still needed his help. She had to stop the empress.

"Will you help me escape even if I choose not to follow you?" Angel asked.

For once, she couldn't read him, but she'd already thought about this question.

"Yes, if that's what you want."

He looked at her intently for several seconds. She knew he read her for the truth. Then he nodded.

"Let's do it."

She patted the stone wall. "What's on the other side?"

"Freedom."

"Before we go," she said.

She walked over to the tiny sprite who was now sitting on a dumbbell, telling her audience a story. Nell winked at Lucy and continued her story. Although the men didn't know it, the sprite spoke partly in the True Language, although she was picking up human speech fast.

"Are you okay here?" Lucy asked. *"I can help you go somewhere else, if you want."*

"This is perfect. I have so many people to tell my stories to. And their stories are interesting, too."

Lucy could imagine.

"Then I'll say goodbye."

Nell leapt from the dumbbell and hugged her ankle.

"Behold! A magician of great power!"

The prisoners looked at Lucy with widened eyes. Then Nell hopped back onto the dumbbell.

"Screws," a prisoner said.

"It's really time to go," Angel said.

Lucy rejoined him in the corner. The door swung open, and four prison officers marched in. She almost laughed at their expressions when they saw the blue demon. But that was no longer her concern.

"Angel."

She drew a door in the air, blending her magic into it. It glowed in burnt orange.

"Come."

She took Angel's arm and stepped through the portal, feeling the breeze against her face. The prison gym had vanished. They stood on an Islington street; a startled passerby cried out before rushing away.

"This way," Angel said.

43

Luke was pleased he seldom drank; otherwise, he'd be lying on the floor drunk. Instead, he paced the living room of Ruth's third-floor flat in Pimlico House, fraught with worry.

The situation was impossible. He was trapped. Ruth had distracted security, allowing him to re-enter. They didn't know he was there, but he was unsure what to do next. He'd even considered surrendering to the police, but Eva Noone seemed to have an excessive influence over them; she'd already reported him for breaking into her house and assault. And Molly and William were still prisoners.

He ran his hands through his hair. He'd been so close to rescuing them. After spending hours observing Noone's house, Ruth had eventually persuaded him to delegate the job to one of Jack's friends in MI5, who was now outside the house. Luke had only agreed when he'd heard about Amelia, but now he worried he'd made a mistake. The list of disasters was endless. Jack, who had lost his eye, was under arrest in hospital. Amelia was unconscious in her flat downstairs; she was also under arrest. Ruth had found her lying on a street near Pimlico House. They still didn't know what had happened. The police were searching for him, and the aliens were trying to kill them. He suspected that parts of the government were working for the aliens, whether they knew it or not.

He looked up when Ruth entered.

"How is she?"

"Still unconscious."

Ruth had fought hard to have her recover at home. A doctor was to visit every afternoon, and a nurse to come every morning to check her condition. The guards downstairs were there to ensure Amelia didn't leave. The doctors had no idea what had happened. One specialist said she'd probably fainted and hit her head, another that she might have had a stroke. Tests were still underway. Chief Inspector Gully argued for her to be admitted to hospital; the doctors agreed with him, but Ruth had proven extremely stubborn.

The phone rang. No one called on the replica antique house phone apart from Alice. Luke raised an eyebrow.

"What does she want?" he muttered.

Alice had started as a good director, but had changed, becoming very hard to work with. He suspected political pressure, or worse.

"Hello," Ruth said, flicking the loudspeaker on.

"How's Amelia?" Alice said.

"Still in a coma."

"I want to move her to hospital."

Luke frowned and shook his head.

"We've spoken about that," Ruth said. "She's safer here. She has a nurse, and the doctor comes every day."

"That's not a request; I'm telling you she's moving."

Ruth frowned.

Luke wasn't sure Alice had the right to issue commands like that.

"Placing her in a hospital leaves her vulnerable to alien interference," Ruth said. "To murder."

"You're becoming emotional. I want you to remain rational. She's better off in hospital. I'll arrange for her removal this afternoon."

Alice hung up.

Ruth shook her head. "I don't know what's wrong with her; the danger's very real."

"The aliens have got to her," Luke said. "And to members of the government." His mind slipped back to his family. "I have to get Molly and William back; time's slipping away."

The phone rang again.

"Hello, Alice," Ruth said.

"Bad news."

Luke and Ruth exchanged glances.

"MI7 has been disbanded. Chief Inspector Gully will arrive at Pimlico House shortly. You'll surrender your weapons to him, and he'll return Amelia Blake to the hospital where she'll be properly taken care of. He assures me there's no threat of alien interference in the UK."

"And you believe him?" Ruth asked.

"Chief Inspector Gully has been tirelessly researching the question of alien infiltration. They're a problem, but they've not penetrated our institutions. Ms Hardy, you'll no longer involve yourself in any operation against suspected aliens. And you must vacate Pimlico House by four o'clock this afternoon. Do you understand?"

"I understand."

She put the phone down. Ruth's face told Luke all he needed to know about her thoughts.

"Jack will be allowed out of prison soon," she said.

"How do you know?"

"I asked the police. They'll place an electronic tag on him later today. Then he'll be released on condition he doesn't leave the hotel room they'll arrange for him."

"Which he will do?" Luke said.

"Of course."

The phone rang a third time. Again, Ruth answered. This time it was security on the ground floor.

"Chief Inspector Gully demands you come down now and surrender your firearms."

Ruth hung up.

"They know nothing about our acquisition of the bullet-proof clothing," she said, fingering her fashionable and very functional jacket.

Someone knocked loudly at the door.

"What's wrong with them?" Luke said.

Ruth walked to the door. "Perhaps you should hide."

Luke opened the door to the adjoining room and stepped inside. It was one of their personal security guards; the one assigned to Amelia's room.

"What?" Ruth asked. "You were told not to leave your post unless there was an emergency."

"I wanted to speak to you directly."

"What's wrong?"

Luke was concerned that Amelia's condition had deteriorated.

"Ms Blake just entered the building."

"That's impossible," Ruth said. "She's in bed in a coma."

"I know," the guard said. "The new Ms Blake borrowed a spare key from the guard downstairs."

"And you just let her in?"

Luke watched the embarrassed man through the half-open door.

"I don't know what happened. The new Ms Blake approached me, and then I think I fell asleep. Voices are coming from inside. Someone is with her."

"You fell asleep?" Ruth repeated.

Luke knew this guard well, and he decided to risk exposure. He walked into the room, checking his pistol.

"Dr Lee?" the surprised guard said.

"Don't tell anyone you've seen me. Not yet," Luke said. An alien had tricked her way in. Amelia was in severe danger.

44

Her intuition had alerted and called her here. Lucy wasn't yet sure why. Looking at Pimlico House from the outside, she was drawn to the second floor. Amelia Blake's face flashed in her mind's eye; she was in trouble.

Entering a building was no longer hard. She had several choices. Mental suggestion wouldn't work with her enemy, but with most people, it worked like a charm. She assumed the aura of Amelia Blake; after having literally spent time in Amelia's mind, it too, was straightforward. Minutes later, she was speaking to an amazed security guard. Adding charm to the mix worked well. It was one of the simplest types of magic—one that many people possessed without even realising it was magic—and soon the grinning man was giving her a spare key. The man guarding the door upstairs was stubborn, but a good man. Unfortunately, she had no choice but to stun him with a small blast of primal magic.

As he slumped against the wall, she entered the flat. Her skin tingled in shock. Something was with Amelia Blake. Taking a deep breath, she slowly opened the bedroom door.

Her eyes widened. Amelia lay unconscious on her bed, surrounded by light. An angel stood by her bed.

"Hello," Lucy said.

The angel smiled. *"I knew you'd come."*

Now she understood the cause and intensity of her intuition.

"You have a connection with Amelia, don't you?"

"You're perceptive," the angel said.

She turned her attention to Amelia.

"How can I help?"

"I think you know."

Lucy stepped closer and studied the dark net of magic covering Amelia. This was no ordinary coma. She breathed deeply as she traced each thread. There were many, and all were invisible to normal eyes. She shifted her vision, seeing the web of magic connecting all life, and with the light the angel gave, she saw it even more clearly. Something unpleasant had attached itself to Amelia Blake. It was stealing her life.

The angel was right. She instinctively knew what to do, and without fuss, she began her work. Fire tempered by her magics burst from her fingertips. She felt the tingling sensation return to the top of her head, too. Carefully, she followed each alien thread, cutting the weakest ones first, scared that cutting the stronger ones would provoke a reaction from whatever had attached itself to her.

Despite her care, Lucy saw distant shadowy faces, including Noone's, searching for her. But one of the presences was much closer. The face of a man stared at her with intense hatred. She recognised him from somewhere. She continued to work. The face became a head which attempted to bite her, then she shuddered in recognition. It was a man she'd killed.

The ghost of Frank Olney had attached itself to Amelia. This didn't make sense. Surely she would have noticed it before? The angel urged her on, and, ignoring his cries, she continued to cut through the dark strands, burning away the flapping and evil-smelling bonds Olney had grown in and around her. Eventually, the broken bonds fizzled on the floor, fading into nothingness. She suspected Olney had more than one host, perhaps in London, and had decided to possess Amelia, too. She had no time to think about this, but it was likely that her enemy knew what had happened, even if they didn't yet understand how. Amelia opened her eyes and gasped as the angel lent healing energy to that which Lucy gave.

"I'll have to be careful," Lucy said. "I may lose my reputation if I keep doing things like this."

Again, Lucy felt the pull of magic on the top of her head. Like someone was pulling a single strand of hair directly upwards. It was the third magic reaching down, but the feeling only lasted for a fraction of a second and then was gone.

"Thank you," Amelia said. She looked at the angel. "Both of you."

The angel smiled, then faded from sight, but the light remained for several seconds.

"You called an angel," Lucy said.

"I think it was an unconscious decision."

Lucy nodded. "But you've done this before."

"How do you know?"

"I just do. Can you sit up?"

She helped Amelia up.

"I hope you feel strong."

"I feel much better. My energy's returning."

Lucy looked at the window.

"It's not over, is it?" Amelia said.

"The pressure's building." She felt Noone probing the room. "How did Olney's ghost attach itself to you?"

"I'm not sure," Amelia said. "But it happened after Chief Inspector Gully attacked me."

"I need to meet this chief inspector."

Amelia stood unsteadily. She still wore her hospital gown.

"Do I have time—"

"Yes," Lucy said, immediately understanding.

Amelia quickly dressed while Lucy listened to the hidden energies swirling through Pimlico. The house was surrounded by dark forces. Something tapped on the window.

"What was that?" Amelia asked.

"Nothing to worry about, yet."

A loud hammering came from the front door. They exchanged glances.

"Answer it," Lucy said.

45

Luke knocked again and the door opened.

"Amelia?" He wasn't sure if this was the real or fake one; she looked pale and anxious.

"Are you okay?"

"Come in. Just you and Ruth."

Luke shook his head. "Someone's entered your flat."

She seemed strangely subdued. Worried for her safety, Luke drew his gun and walked into the flat. "Wait here," he whispered to the security guard. He still wasn't sure that this was the real Amelia. He went quickly from room to room. A minute later, he returned to the door, feeling confused. "There's no one here."

The guard frowned. "I heard voices."

"I may have been speaking aloud," Amelia said.

The guard left, and Luke and Ruth joined Amelia on the sofa and armchair facing her bookshelves.

"Luke, what's wrong?" Amelia asked.

"A woman impersonating you entered this building. She took a key from downstairs, did something to the guard, and entered your flat."

"I think I can answer that," Amelia said, "but first, I need to tell you about Gully."

"What about him?" Luke asked. The change of topic seemed strange.

"He attacked me."

"What?" he said.

He exchanged a glance with Ruth. He wondered if Amelia was suffering from concussion and still confused. Or perhaps this wasn't the real Amelia. He quickly sorted through questions that could help him find out.

"What did he do?"

"He tried to strangle me."

"Amelia?" Luke asked.

He supposed it was possible; Gully was certainly odd. Amelia seemed distracted and kept glancing into the corners of the room. The phone rang, and Amelia flipped the loudspeaker on. It was the ground floor security guard.

"Chief Inspector Gully has demanded access to your flat. He's on his way up with four other police officers."

"We can't let him in," Luke said. "Not if he's attacked Amelia. He'll arrest us, too."

"We've not finished our job," Ruth said.

"Let him in," a voice said.

Luke looked around the room. Someone else was there.

"Who's here?"

He reached for his pistol, but Amelia rested her hand on his arm.

"It's time to talk," she said.

"Amelia?" Luke said, feeling confused.

"Please. She won't hurt you; she saved my life."

"What's happening?"

"There," Ruth said.

Shocked, Luke stared back at the two burning orange

eyes watching him from the couch opposite. Slowly, the form of the orange witch appeared in the shadows.

"Why are you here?" he asked.

"I sensed a great need."

He wasn't sure what to say.

"She helped me," Amelia said. "Without her, I'd be dead."

A loud knock came from the door. "Police! Open the door!"

"Let Gully in. I want to meet him," the witch said.

"Why?" Luke asked.

"Something about him is strange; something alien."

"He spoke in the alien language," Amelia blurted out.

"Why didn't you tell us?" Luke asked.

"I don't know," Amelia said. "I think I'm still in shock."

"Let him in," the orange witch said quietly, "but no one else."

"Why should we listen to you?" Luke asked. "Because I'm the only person who can help you. Do you want to get your wife and child back or sit in jail playing their game?"

Luke sat up straight. She was right. Something was wrong with Gully. Perhaps it was time to find out. He stood as the police knocked again.

"This house is surrounded by forces of darkness," the witch said.

"A bit melodramatic," Luke said, although he didn't completely disagree.

She shrugged. "It's the truth. The enemy knows I've cut Amelia's bonds. They're assembling their forces. Gully is one part of that."

"What's wrong with Gully?" Ruth asked.

"I have my suspicions, but we're about to find out for sure," the witch said.

Something scratched at the window, and Ruth jumped, spilling water from her glass.

"What was that?" Ruth asked.

Luke shivered, wondering if it was literally true that they were surrounded by the forces of darkness. He walked to the window and held his breath as he quickly pulled back the curtain. Nothing was there.

"Police. Open the door!"

"I need him alone," the witch said.

As they knocked again, the witch faded. Luke screwed up his eyes, trying to focus on her. Her indistinct form grinned at him.

"Forget me for now," she whispered.

He was sure she'd whispered in his mind.

Luke drew his pistol and opened the door, pointing it at the men.

"Gully, come in!"

"You're under arrest," Gully said.

Luke fired into the passageway, making the police officers leap back.

"Inside," he repeated, pointing his pistol at Gully's head. "Now!"

"You'll go to prison for this," Gully said.

He stepped into the room, and Luke slammed the door shut behind him, quickly locking it. He took Gully's gun.

"Sit," Luke said, pointing at the couch.

Gully walked to the couch. The police outside were now frantically banging on the door. Gully was right about him going to prison, but saving his family was more important.

"Sit."

Gully sat on the couch.

"You're all going to prison," Gully said.

A pair of orange eyes appeared in the shadows, then the

contours of the witch's body reappeared next to the couch. Gully drew back, staring at her in shock.

"You."

The man was afraid.

"What did you call?" Gully asked Amelia, his voice became shrill. "It's not human."

"Are you?" Luke asked.

Chief Inspector Gully didn't appear to hear him. When the witch touched him, he screamed and fell back, staring at her in fear.

"He's possessed," the witch said.

Luke wanted to question the witch. This was quickly moving into an area where he felt very uncomfortable. Then something tapped at the window, and this time Luke saw dark shadows moving on the other side. There was something there.

Ruth stared at the window in shock. "Will they break in?" she asked.

The witch shrugged. "Perhaps." She stood over the prone man. "Hold him."

Luke realised he was committed. Nothing he could do now would make it worse. And Gully's fear pointed to something strange. He held the man's wrists. Amelia and Ruth each held an ankle.

The witch spoke in a language he didn't know. Gully's eyes were wide, and he was breathing rapidly. He shook, and Luke tightened his hold. Then she chanted in what sounded like another language completely. The light around her altered. A red swelling protruded from the side of Gully's skull. Facial features appeared, forming a twisted mask. Luke shuddered, recognising the dead alien sorcerer. It mouthed a silent scream. Luke, Ruth, and Amelia clutched Gully as he bounced on the couch.

The light bent around the orange witch, and Gully's form darkened. Gully spat and screamed obscenities. The witch remained locked in concentration. The window shattered, and four red-eyed monkey-faced cats cantered over the carpet. This was the first time Luke had clearly seen the things that had stolen his child; he reached for his pistol.

"Keep hold!" the witch rasped as the chief inspector's body leapt into the air.

Luke wasn't sure he could keep a grip on the man, who was now bouncing up to two feet from the couch. He was being moved by some unseen force, but the witch's tone convinced him to keep trying. The creatures crept towards the witch, hissing, but they hesitated, too. He wondered if they feared her.

The banging on the door continued.

Nothing seemed to perturb the witch. When the creatures leapt at her, she calmly turned round, without a second's disturbance in her spell, and tapped each one with a fiery finger, before returning to her work.

The creatures screamed and hissed. Like balloons blown up and then let go without a knot, the air rushed from them, and they flew through the shattered window. Reduced to the size of oranges, they disappeared into the night.

Gully's body was now levitating two feet above the couch. All three of them were struggling to hold it. Only the witch seemed in control, and still she chanted. Luke felt relief; it seemed to end. Gully sank back onto the couch. Fine threads of light pulsed from the witch's fingers. Then Gully screamed. Ruth and Amelia stepped back, and Luke trembled in genuine fear. Olney's pale, ghostly body detached itself from Gully and stood, suspended in the air. It stared at the witch in terror.

"No!"

She'd now stopped chanting and faced the apparition. Luke shuddered, but the spectre's pleading seemed to have no effect on her.

"NO!" Olney screamed.

The ghost looked down with bulging eyes. Luke blinked, unsure what he was seeing. An unworldly hand appeared to rise from below and grasp the apparition. The ghost gave a blood-curdling scream and vanished.

Luke wasn't sure what he'd seen, but his view of the world had altered yet again. This was beyond magic; something bigger was happening. There was no other way to see it. And the witch had spoken the truth. Chief Inspector Gully had been possessed by an alien ghost. Gully moaned. He'd rolled off the couch and now lay on the floor babbling like a baby.

"It's finished," the witch said. She looked tired and worn.

Amelia offered her a glass of water, which she drank in one. She then walked towards the door.

"Where are you going?" Luke asked. He wanted to ask more questions.

She looked back. "To Noone's house. She's hosting a celebration party tonight."

"What will you do?" he asked, worried about Molly and William.

"Kill her, if I can."

Her expression was serious. Luke cared nothing for Eva Noone. In fact, he'd be happy to see her dead, but he did care that the witch may be putting Molly and William at risk. He'd already seen one alien owned house burn down.

"My wife and son are being held upstairs."

She looked at him quietly for several seconds; Luke had the feeling she was reading him like a book.

"Get them out tonight. It may be your last chance."

Luke felt desperate. He'd be arrested if he went anywhere near Noone's house. "MI7 has been disbanded. The police are looking for us." He glanced at the door. The police had started kicking it down.

"If you want to rescue your wife and son, you'll be there. Just don't get in my way."

Luke felt invigorated. Perhaps it was the magic in the room. The witch was right; he would be there. She reached for the door. But there was the problem of the police.

"They won't just let you go."

"I won't ask them."

She opened the door, and four large police officers rushed in, pushing her back. When they grabbed her, she touched each one on his chest; one by one, they fell to the ground.

"You've killed them?" Luke said.

The witch looked genuinely surprised.

"I've stunned them. They'll wake up in a few minutes, but they may not be in a good mood. I suggest you leave immediately." Then she slipped through the door and was gone.

46

Lucy glanced up at the tree in front of Noone's house in Knightsbridge. A pair of orange eyes watched her from one of the branches.

"Wait till I call."

She heard the panther purr in her mind.

Walking up the steps to the front door, she smiled at the doorman. Unperturbed by his lack of response, she continued to charm him as he looked at her fake ticket.

Charm was one of the most enjoyable types of magic, and she waited while her magic worked its way into the man. His energy was dense, and warmth was alien to him. He began to brush off her charm, but she sensed cracks in his armour, and through those cracks she poured love. Nothing sentimental or romantic. Simply the fulfilment of need, of which this deprived man had many. For a moment, she became a healer. Confused, he blinked away a tear, and she entered the lower reception.

Entry to the private reception upstairs would be harder. She glanced at the barrier at the base of the sweeping staircase. Angel was in position as part of the security team. She hoped he was her second ticket. Her magic burnt slowly inside her, waiting to ignite, but she didn't want to use it until she faced the enemy. Playing with magic now would expose her to her enemy too soon.

She walked to the bar. It had moved and was now located over what had previously been the hole overlooking the pool. She ordered two portions of chicken and a bottle of wine.

"Hungry?" a man asked.

At least it was a different man from before. And a different type.

"Very."

It was a good idea to stock up on energy. She didn't know what she was walking into, but upstairs was where the power was. Three or more sorcerers would be there. The thought filled her with dread. She hoped they'd at least got rid of the demon.

The man asked more questions; he was trying to ascertain who she was.

"Are you a journalist?"

"Am I so obvious?" he asked.

She nodded as she scanned the room for people she knew. There were no magic practitioners, but there was more security by the kitchen doors, as Angel had told her. Then she saw the team from MI7; she was pleased they were there.

Her food arrived.

"What do you do?" the journalist asked.

"I travel the multiverse and vanquish evil."

He raised his eyebrows. "You mean metaverse?"

She grinned at his expression.

"What do you think of Eva Noone?" he asked. "Some people see her as a future prime minister."

Lucy shook her head while polishing off the first portion of chicken.

"I think she's on the way out."

"Oh, why's that?" the man asked, suddenly interested in the possibility of learning something new.

She downed her drink in one and proceeded to finish the second plate.

"Aliens aren't suited to the rough and tumble of British politics."

The man laughed. "You don't believe that rumour, do you?"

"It's the truth. Stick around tonight, and you'll have the biggest story of the century."

She left the startled reporter by the bar and walked towards the table occupied by the three intelligence officers. Jack Ross, the military man who still distrusted her, had a bandaged eye. Only the woman she'd given the dog to wasn't there. They were staring at Angel and didn't see her approach. Jack stood. He was about to confront Angel; Lucy could feel his animosity.

"He's working for me," she said. She wanted nothing to interfere with her plans tonight.

They turned to face her.

"Sit down. I have information that may interest you."

Jack returned to his seat, and she sat on a spare stool.

"I hope you're here to rescue the prisoners," Lucy said.

"That's the plan," Luke said.

"Wait for me to make my move."

"What are you going to do?" Jack asked.

"Pay a visit to Noone and her crew."

"You mean try to kill her," Jack said.

"Killing her is best, but if I could banish her from this universe, that would do."

His eyes widened. "You're honest, at least about the first part. It may not be so easy."

"Nothing about it is easy." Lucy had run out of options. She had to act, whatever the consequences. To do nothing was worse.

"She's deadly," Amelia said, "but I've seen some of the things you can do."

Lucy took the food proffered by Amelia.

"I have no choice."

"You can walk away," Jack said.

Lucy noticed that neither Luke nor Amelia seemed pleased by his suggestion.

"I'm prepared to die fighting, although I'd prefer not to. The stakes are high. Britain has grown comfortable. No one here, even those few who are aware of the aliens, could imagine the nightmare of alien, or worse, demon controlled areas. I've seen worlds controlled by both. They're not pretty. If I don't stop this tonight, two enemy forces will battle for Britain. And then the world. The aliens already have agents in France and Belgium, and a demon's been seen in California. The alien device is ready. They're just making adjustments."

"How do you know?" Luke asked.

"I can directly sense the manipulation of magic. Magic is the key to unlocking the portal, and they've been playing with it each day since I've returned. They only stopped an hour ago. I believe they're ready."

"If magic is the key, why do they need a machine?" Luke asked.

"It assists them. Power is also necessary to open and use a portal. Unlocking a door is not enough; you need to open it as well. And after you've pushed it open, you need to make a path."

"Can't they just push?" Luke asked.

"Pushing requires power. I can push a portal open with my personal power, but that's not what they're attempting. The crystal machine will open the portal and power something like a wormhole to another universe. Without it, they'd be forced to find paths through the world of illusions that lies between universes. It's hard, dangerous, and requires a type of magic they disdain. I'm not even sure they're aware that it's possible." She paused. "If they do manage to form such a wormhole, then expect a horde of demons or an alien military incursion into London. Perhaps both."

"Demons?" Luke asked.

"It's a long story," Lucy said. "I believe you dealt with one the last time."

Luke grimaced. "It was hard to get rid of."

Lucy hoped she was impressing the importance of what she was doing. At least long enough to allow her to act.

"I should call the police," Jack said.

"To arrest me or the aliens?" Lucy asked.

"She's right," Amelia said. "That won't help."

"Yes," Luke agreed. "They'd arrest us, too, before we could rescue Molly and William."

Jack said nothing.

"Wait for me to go upstairs, then take the back stairs."

"The kitchen's guarded," Jack said.

She shrugged. "Two unarmed guards on this side; an armed guard inside."

"How do you know that?" Jack asked.

"Angel's part of the security team."

Jack looked equal parts shocked and impressed. "How did you fix that?"

"A little bit of charm, plus some help from contacts Angel made in Pentonville."

"And Angel will let you upstairs," Amelia said.

"He'll escort me," Lucy said. "If I kill Noone, I promise you they'll be distracted."

A look of something close to respect passed over Jack's face.

"But can you do it?" Luke asked.

She shrugged.

"When will you go upstairs?" Luke asked.

Lucy felt the magic building above her.

"Now."

She stood.

"You understand that the police will arrive, and they won't just allow you to leave," Jack said.

She laughed. "I'll probably be dead by then."

Lucy walked directly to the main staircase. Angel saw her coming and whispered something to one of the security guards. The man nodded and left the staircase, leaving only Angel and one other man.

"Ticket," Angel said.

Lucy gave a second fake ticket.

"This way."

"Don said no more people upstairs," the other security guard said.

Lucy wondered whether Don was the man Angel had just sent away.

"I was told by Eva Noone personally to take this woman upstairs. Don's getting a replacement for me."

Lucy sent a mental suggestion that all was well. The guard nodded, and Angel led her upstairs.

"We have to get you in before Don gets back. He's not the type to be influenced easily."

"Are you armed?" Lucy asked as they walked up to the second floor.

Angel nodded.

"Anyone else?"

"Not on the second floor. Not with the prime minister there."

They walked past more security. The men nodded at Angel.

"I've brought some rope," Angel whispered.

Lucy raised her eyebrows questioningly.

"My escape plan."

She hoped it could be so.

Then they walked into Eva Noone's private reception room. Lucy remembered every detail of the room. The portal, disguised as a mural of a desert world, was still on the wall to her left. It was open. The crystal machine sat on a table in the middle of the room.

Luckily, the room was crowded, and the guests were drunk. Raucous laughter came from the newly elected politicians celebrating their win. All attention was focussed on Eva Noone and the prime minister, making it easy for Lucy and Angel to slip into the room unnoticed. Noone introduced the machine and portal, talking of future trade and riches.

For a few seconds, the odds against her success almost overwhelmed Lucy; she questioned her ability to succeed. In an attempt to push her fears away, she studied the occupants of the room. Then she noticed something odd. The demon lord, Tavth, sat rigidly in an armchair next to the portal. Something was wrong. Lucy pretended to be in deep discussion with Angel, but really she listened to the conversations around her. Eva Noone was now discussing the mural painted on the wall to mask the portal. It was a desert scene from Dnasis—the alien planet. Lucy recognised the elegant towers topped with elongated pyramids that were characteristic of the alien architecture.

Alistair Walker stood to the side, looking at the mural. He wore his crimson cloak. His power worried her almost as much as Noone. Lucy kept her magic silent, fearful they'd notice her.

"I can't see Nimori," she whispered.

"There," Angel whispered.

She followed his gaze. Nick Nimori rested on a couch by the window with his head in his hands. He looked ill. The black magic creatures had been his, and their sudden demise had hurt him.

"Any more magic?" Angel asked.

"Five lesser sorcerers," she whispered.

Angel frowned. "Not good."

"No."

Eva Noone smiled at her guests.

Lucy had to admit, the woman had magnetic charm, but it was manufactured. Noone had great skill in sending mental suggestions, which she was doing right now. At least, that meant the sickening magic coming from the mouth in her belly had stopped. Instead, brighter colours seemed to wash around her, sensed but unseen by the guests.

"This is the greatest opportunity in history," Noone said.

Even Lucy was being drawn into the sweet sticky web Noone had spun around herself.

"It's a desert world."

That much was true.

"A gallon of seawater, even polluted river water, would be worth a bucket of rare minerals—such things are as common as dirt on our planet, and even more on our moon."

The lie snapped Lucy out of the sweet trance, but Noone's listeners fell deeper under her influence. She pinched Angel. His eyes widened, and he nodded at her; it was affecting him, too. The lie Noone told was enormous. It was true that they'd destroyed their environment; they didn't care. Their attitude was to use and move. They could do so because their technology was advanced beyond human imagining. Manufacturing water from the elements was child's play. They even recycled the moisture given off from the people living in the ubiquitous sealed cities of the planet. The aliens had no need of water.

Lucy exchanged a smile with Ethan Cole, who, this morning, had been re-elected as prime minister, as he passed her on the way to the table laden with food and drinks.

"What do you think of all this?" the Prime Minister asked.

"Too good to be true," she said.

He nodded. "Perhaps, but it's worth considering."

Noone excitedly raised her voice, and Cole returned to listen, apparently forgetting whatever he'd wanted from the table.

"He's caught in her web," Lucy said.

She studied the crystal machine, and, for the first time, she let her mind touch the machine directly.

She almost dropped her glass in shock. The machine was not what she'd expected.

"What?" Angel asked.

"The crystal machine is sentient."

47

Lucy spoke in the True Language, and the crystal responded in its simple manner. She felt as if she was stroking a stray dog. It was surprised and hummed in happiness within her mind.

"What do you want?" she asked.

She let the crystal life form absorb the question, expecting more a sense of yearning than a reply. She intuitively sensed that this was the first time it had ever been asked that question. Perhaps any question. The answer she received was an increased tugging on its tether. It wanted freedom; perhaps it was looking for its home. She'd not noticed the tether before. It was hard to see—quite similar in kind to the tether that had held the snapping turtles in place for so long, but this one was simpler. Alistair Walker's energy signature was on it. It seemed that he was their portal expert.

If the crystal life wanted freedom, perhaps she could give it. She'd have to unravel the threads Walker had used to tie it in place. Whether this was a good idea, she wasn't so sure. Carefully, she thought through the possible implications of releasing it. It would close the portal, which was good. But unless the timing was right, it could trap the aliens on Earth, which was not her wish. Not unless they were dead. The crystal machine sensed the direction of her thoughts and became excited. Lucy was shocked when it lit up in what she could only describe as joy.

Gasps came from the guests. Eva Noone stared at the machine in shock and whispered something to Alistair Walker. The politicians and wealthy benefactors gathered round the machine, curious.

"Perhaps it's a time for a demonstration," Noone said. "Time to show you the portal in action."

Lucy's stomach sank. This wasn't a positive development. If Noone actually knew how to control the machine, which she wasn't yet sure, then the room could suddenly be filled with imperial soldiers from her world or demons from hell.

"The blue alien will return to his realm."

Lucy remembered the stationary demon. Tavth hadn't moved since she'd entered the room. Noone spoke quietly to Walker, who grinned and started adjusting the machine.

"It's ready," Walker said.

Curious, Lucy entered the crystal's mind.

"Where are you pointed to?"

She received an image of fire.

The aliens were lying. They planned to kill the demon.

"What's wrong with it?" someone asked.

"It's been too long away from its world and has become sick. The sooner we send it back, the better. These creatures should never exist in either of our worlds."

Noone blended truth with lies.

"Stand!" Noone commanded.

Stiffly, the demon stood. Alistair Walker was also mentally compelling it to move its legs. It resisted with each step. Lucy had no love for the demon, but she was curious to know what they'd done to it. She gently brushed its mind. Tavth's eyes turned to her, but its head faced the portal. Being part dragon, Lucy could use the True Language on a deeper level than almost anyone.

"What have they done to you?" she asked.

"Ice and poison," Tavth replied.

"What?" Noone said.

She'd heard the demon, but not Lucy.

"She wants to send you to a fiery star," Lucy said.

She felt the demon stiffen.

"You wouldn't want to return to the arch demon's realm, anyway," she said. *"It wouldn't welcome you."*

It was a guess, but from what she knew of demons, it was probably true. One of the lesser sorcerers smirked from beside the portal.

"I'll make a deal with you," Lucy said.

"Why?" the demon asked.

"What a strange question from a demon," Noone said, mistakenly thinking the question was for her. *"Because I want to send you back, of course."*

"I know how to change the destination," Lucy said. *"You'll sense it when you're closer."*

"I sense fire," Tavth said.

Walker and Noone laughed. They continued to compel the demon to step closer to the portal.

"For one favour, I can switch your destination to one of the shadow realms."

She showed Tavth one of the worlds she'd passed through when she'd returned.

"What do I have to do?" Tavth asked.

"Die," Noone said, enjoying her imagined wit.

"I want you to take the smirking sorcerer by the portal with you."

"With pleasure."

The demon seemed to smile.

"I'll change the destination; once you sense it too, stop resisting Noone's magic. Allow yourself to be sucked in."

"And you?"

Noone shook her head. *"I've had enough of this stupid conversation."* She increased her power.

"I want to kill them," Lucy whispered.

"Do it!" the demon said.

Lucy mentally stroked the crystal life form, and it glowed brightly, switching the path to one of the distant shadow worlds.

"Now!"

Tavth seized the surprised man, and together they flew through the portal.

Two less problems, Lucy thought.

48

Noone exchanged a look with Walker, who shrugged. The shocked guests backed away from them, and the prime minister stared nervously at Eva Noone. Lucy suspected he was already regretting his involvement with her.

She's overplaying her hand.

Then the lump on Noone's shoulder moved.

Lucy's stomach sank. It was about to begin. Fire bubbled from her uncontrollably. Her eyes already glowed, and sparks came from her fingertips. They would see her in seconds.

"Get ready," she whispered to Angel.

The small head burst from Eva Noone's suit. It stared at Lucy and screamed. Nick Nimori rushed to Noone's side. She was now flanked by her two most powerful sorcerers. Frightened, the guests backed up to the wall, leaving her and Angel in the open.

Noone's eyes widened. "I thought you were dead."

"Security!" Ethan Cole shouted.

Men ran into the room, joining his two personal bodyguards. Noone nodded at her security team, which now consisted of four lesser sorcerers. They attacked the prime minister's bodyguards with a combination of martial arts and magic. Seconds later, the men and women lay dead on the floor. Lucy knew that if Noone won, she'd attempt to manipulate the guests' memories. The lesser sorcerers formed a line in front of their mistress. A glowing net began to form in their hands.

Lucy's stomach sank.

She felt despair as she faced the phalanx of seven sorcerers. So much magic could rip her apart. And so much evil.

But Angel had told her that unless groups of attackers were trained to fight together, they could easily get in each other's way. She hoped Noone had skimped on training. Lucy decided to take it one step at a time. Each sorcerer she killed would be one less for MI7 and the armed police to deal with. Her goal was to survive long enough to make a difference. At least she had Angel. He stood next to her with a face of stone. He was lethal, too.

"Take her!" Noone ordered.

The first line of sorcerers stepped forward. Lucy had fought this type before and was familiar with the ethereal net they held. They stared at her and foolishly ignored Angel. He shot the middle two dead, and they dropped into the net, their bodies becoming entangled inside it. The sorcerer to her left slapped then stabbed Angel with a magic-laden hand. Angel fell to the floor and didn't move. Lucy didn't know if he was alive or not. The sight of his body unmoving on the floor turned her cold.

She now faced two lesser sorcerers.

Blood dripped from the man's hand. The woman kicked

her dead comrades away and pulled the net free. Lucy felt cold to both. The woman ran at her first, hissing with hatred. Lucy dropped down on one leg, scooping up Angel's pistol. The man punched her head whilst also making a weak attempt to mentally influence her. His attempt to influence her failed, but his punch knocked her back. She hit the woman in her stomach. The sorceress fell into her own net.

The man tried to mentally influence her again, but it still didn't work. With her jaw still throbbing, she shot him dead. Lucy didn't worry about the groaning woman enmeshed in her own net. She pointed the gun at the three sorcerers of power and fired. She fired until she ran out of bullets. Noone, Walker, and Nimori, stared at her with stony faces. Their power of suggestion was strong, making her miss their faces. She only hit their armoured bodies. She tossed the gun away.

"Are you ready?" Lucy asked.

Noone looked at her in hatred, then turned to the crowd of onlookers. "This witch has murdered innocent people." They looked at the bodies littering the floor. Then she pointed at Lucy. "Kill her!"

Lucy felt the magical suggestion take root in the minds of the politicians and guests. She understood that if the guests killed her, Noone would have little problem manipulating their memories later. The guests looked at her, first in horror, and then in anger.

"What should we do?" a man asked.

"Rip her apart!" Noone shouted.

Before the crowd could react, Lucy clapped her hands, sending a telepathic shock that momentarily rid them of their illusion.

"Look!" She pointed at the small head peering from Noone's suit.

Their shock had a new target.

Lucy was surprised by the confusion on Noone's face. The magic was elementary, but, perhaps for Noone, it was novel. Noone seemed to forget the people watching, and from her three mouths, she vomited a black vapour that fell to the floor where it turned into a churning liquid. Nimori and Walker lent her power, and the liquid rose in the form of a wave. It rushed towards her.

Lucy grabbed the magical netting containing the struggling sorceress and pulled hard; she slid into the path of the wave. She screamed, using the last of her strength to create a barrier, but the toxic sludge flowed over it, drenching the woman, who began to dissolve. At least, her final act prevented the stuff from reaching Lucy. Walker impatiently waited for the woman to disintegrate and the black smoke to disperse.

When the woman's body had finally disappeared, Alistair Walker stepped forward, quickly pulling a whip from his cloak. He lashed Lucy's body, which she protected, but she left her head exposed. The second lash came fast, and the whip wrapped around her neck, stinging, and choking her fire. It was alive with magic. Walker pulled her towards him. She gasped, hardly able to breathe. Tears came to her eyes as she struggled against it. Eva Noone cackled as Lucy fell to her knees. She was losing consciousness, and despite her magical strength, she couldn't rid herself of this thing. When she gasped for breath, the tip of the whip darted into her mouth, stabbing the nerves in her gums. The pain was intense, making her see stars.

At the same time, Nimori kicked her repeatedly in her side. Each kick was laden with power, and with each kick, he cursed her with foul language. She'd never known how much he'd hated her. She suspected he may have broken her arm, too. All she could see was a faint light from the crystal machine.

Her mind went blank, and as the light began to disappear, she sensed Darta's concern.

"Help me!"

The window shattered, and the fire-breathing panther attacked Nimori, her razor-sharp claws slicing through his neck, decapitating the startled man. The speed of it even surprised Lucy. Darta left his headless corpse, turning fast to place herself between Lucy and the two sorcerers.

Lucy gasped, ripping the whip from her neck.

"NO!" Noone screamed.

She no longer bothered with even a pretence of normality. Both her heads were fully exposed, and all three mouths chanted together, sucking the air from the middle of the room. Walker quickly stepped back as a whirlwind formed around Noone. Lucy was forced to use her remaining energy to root herself in place. The wind rushed around Noone, and then reached outwards, hitting Darta hard, flinging her into the wall. Several politicians were thrown to the floor, and one of the guests flew through the broken window and into the night. Lucy felt the intense pain the panther felt, then nothing.

"Darta?"

There was no response. She lay in a crumpled heap by the window and didn't move. Noone glared with hatred at Lucy. She returned the hatred, rushing at Noone, but Walker came from her side, tripping her. She fell to the floor, but quickly rolled away from his magic-laden kick. She stood and slipped in close to Walker, touching his heart with her hand.

"Stop."

She felt energy surge around his chest. He looked at her incredulously.

"Don't you know who I am?"

Lucy's hand became a fiery blade, and she stabbed at his liver, but he slapped her hand down. Her blade merely cutting his belly. Walker struck her with a magic-laden punch that knocked her into the wall behind her. She struggled to breathe. She'd hoped to burn him, but his magic was alight. He'd already sealed the cut. All that remained from her attack was a wisp of smoke rising from his belly.

"You're dead," Walker said. "You're not a match for either of us."

He spoke in such a matter-of-fact way, believing it a foregone conclusion. But she couldn't allow herself to think it. She stood exhausted by the wall, desperately calling for a magic that didn't want to come. The dead lay everywhere. Neither Darta nor Angel moved. Downstairs, someone was banging on the front door. The remaining guests huddled in a corner in fear.

"You've killed those better than yourself," Walker said, glancing at Nimori's headless body.

Lucy would have cursed him if she'd had the strength, but she had to retain every last bit for the final attack. At least, her arm still seemed to move. The two dark sorcerers summoned their magic, and Lucy felt the small hairs on her arms rise. Eva Noone loomed larger, glowing with black light. Then the room darkened. Lucy shuddered, wondering if it was even possible to defeat them. The thought of Angel and Darta lying there, possibly dead, ensured she wouldn't give up. She cared about nothing except the present moment. Her mind was empty—Darta had taught her how to prepare mentally.

Then something changed.

The emptiness within her mind had created space. The third magic briefly touched her, tugging at the top of her head.

Noone attacked.

The mouth in her belly vomited dark red centipede-like creatures that slid down Noone's legs, then came straight for her. They were black-magic creatures, not fully living, ensouled with Noone's spirit. It was a dark magic.

Lucy screamed in shock and agony as they swarmed up her legs, biting and attempting to burrow into her flesh. One tried to crawl inside her mouth. Forgetting the third magic, she blended her two magics, but she was too weak, and her magic drove the disgusting things into a feeding frenzy. She was being eaten alive. Then it was over; her magic was gone. She was empty.

"Help me!" she prayed.

As she stood alone, in pain and facing her death, the third magic descended. Pure power rushed through her. The evil creatures dropped to the floor, where they lay burning around her. Eva Noone staggered back; the death of her creations had hurt her.

Alistair Walker quickly stepped forward and struck Lucy across her face. Then he screamed. In shock, she realised he couldn't let go. Of its own volition, the third magic flowed through her body and into his, burning him from the inside. For all his strength, he lacked her training; he lacked her tempered soul. Desperately, he pulled away, but couldn't move. She struck him hard, and he fell to the floor, but his hand remained stuck to her face. She flung it away in disgust. Despite the distance between them, the third magic still coursed through her body and from her into him. For Lucy, the third magic was white light. Its intensity hurt her, and she felt faint. For a few seconds, she wondered if she was dying. Then its power diminished and her vision returned.

She watched in horror as black holes punctured Walker's skin, and dark puss poured from them, bubbling and steaming around him. He struggled to stand, but his feet fell away from his body. More dark puss flowed from the ends of his legs. His body shrivelled as he tried to crawl away. Then his hips separated from his torso, which he pulled towards Noone. Noone had moved back to the mural of her world, staring at her sorcerer in shock.

"Help me!" he screamed.

His body disintegrated, and his head rolled towards Noone, sending out a handful of coloured flames. It reminded Lucy of the most feeble of fireworks.

Then the third magic was gone.

Noone stared at her.

Lucy faced her enemy, sensing uncertainty. She had little left except her wits and a touch of natural magic. Shakily, she rested her hand on the crystal machine to steady herself and felt its excitement. Faint light shone from it and flowed into the open portal.

"What did you do?" Noone asked in a hoarse voice.

"I called the third magic."

"Impossible."

"What do you think killed Walker?"

The empress growled, and her eyes narrowed as she studied Lucy carefully. "You've got nothing left."

The empress had good instincts, but Lucy was fairly sure that Noone had depleted herself, too. Losing the creatures she'd created from her own spirit had weakened her. Knowing the empress wanted the crystal machine undamaged, Lucy kept it between them.

"It was luck," Noone said.

"No, it wasn't luck," Lucy said.

She felt the magic attack coming, but the change in Noone's long fingers made her blink. They now extended several feet towards her. Leaping back, Lucy struck down a wasp-like strand of magic that flew from Noone's forefinger. She was surprised when no more stinging wasps appeared, but remained alert to a second magical attack. It didn't come. Perhaps it was the empress who had nothing left. Noone pulled a dagger from her clothes. Lucy shifted position as Eva Noone moved closer. Then Noone charged, stepping directly between the portal and the glowing crystal machine.

At last, Lucy thought.

The crystal machine tugged excitedly at its tether while Lucy pulled loose the last bond, unleashing it.

"Good journey."

The machine shattered, but the crystal flew towards the portal, hitting Eva Noone directly in her belly. The chanting stopped, and Noone's eyes widened in terror. She screamed as she and the bright crystal flew through the open portal. Lucy ran to the portal, looking at the path her enemy had taken. Then she slammed it shut and locked it, leaving only the scorched mural on the wall.

Lucy touched Angel, sending a little healing energy into him. He opened his eyes.

"Help Darta," he said, struggling to sit up.

Lucy rushed to Darta. The panther was still breathing, and she poured what healing magic she had left into the animal.

"We have to go," Angel said. "Now."

The guests stared at the scene in horror, but she knew they'd recover soon. She needed to get away.

"Help me move Darta."

They struggled to get the panther on her feet. She was heavy. But eventually, she stood unsteadily. As the three of them stumbled out of the room, Lucy heard men running up the stairs. Angel pointed upstairs. She nodded, but Jack Ross reached the landing first, pointing a pistol at Angel's head. "You're under arrest."

He'd not noticed her; his hatred for Angel was so great. Before his men could reach him, Lucy struck Jack with the lightest strand of magic. It was the most she could manage, but it was enough for him to lose his grip on the gun. Angel punched him and took the pistol. Weakened, and perhaps disoriented from the loss of his eye, Jack staggered back and fell against the bannisters.

"Goodbye, Jack."

"The police are here, Angel. You won't escape."

"This way," Angel whispered.

Lucy, Angel, and Darta supported each other as they struggled up the next flight of stairs. More footsteps came from below, and Angel fired down the stairs to keep them away. She heard the Prime Minister shouting orders.

"Keep going," Angel said.

When they reached the fourth floor, she thought she was going to faint.

"Here."

He stopped at one of the rooms on the left and stepped over the remains of the door that Darta had burnt. The room was in disarray. It was where the hostages had been held.

Angel led her to the window. Lucy doubted that any of them could climb down in the state they were in. And she certainly couldn't open a portal; she was close to passing out, and Darta was weak. Angel attached his rope to a piece of furniture and threw the other end out of the window.

"It should help. I'll hold it, too."

She noticed he was still bleeding from where the sorcerer had stabbed him.

"Let me help," she said, hoping she was still able.

"It's nothing."

He was lying. She tried to seal the wound with her magic, but nothing came.

"I'm sorry."

He shook his head and pushed her towards the open window. She could hear footsteps rushing towards the room they were in. Angel fired through the doorway, then helped her out. She started sliding down the rope; Darta, usually adept at climbing vertical surfaces because of her special pads, slid down after her.

"Angel..."

She was too weak to finish her sentence.

"Too late," he said.

Shots came from the room.

Lucy and Darta continued to slide down. They were almost at the bottom when Darta fell on top of her. They hit the ground hard.

Lucy didn't know how she found the strength to stand, but she did, and with Darta by her side, she limped down the narrow space between the houses. Someone shouted from the window above, but she'd already reached the fence at the end.

Darta growled.

Lucy found it hard to focus and was seeing stars. Two figures faced them from the other side of the metal fence. The man pointed a pistol at her.

"Luke," she said hoarsely.

She could do no more. Lucy grasped the metal railings, trying not to faint.

Luke looked at the bloody woman and panther in shock. Once the authorities realised what was happening, MI7 had been reformed. They had orders to shoot the panther and arrest the witch. He breathed deeply, feeling conflicted. Without this woman, the rescue would've failed. She'd helped save Molly and William. With the aliens occupied, the rescue had been easy.

"Luke?" Ruth asked.

"I can't do it," he said.

He put his pistol away, stood on the red stool he'd brought to help him climb over the fence if he needed to, and extended his hand towards the witch.

She took it.

"Luke?" Ruth said. "You're going to arrest her, right?"

He helped her over.

Ruth's eyes widened when the panther leapt. It caught a paw on the fence and lunged headfirst toward her. She fell backwards and rolled on the ground. Its bright orange eyes were inches from hers.

"You softened her fall," the witch said weakly.

Ruth stood and brushed herself down. She looked between the woman and the panther in confusion.

"We can't just let them go," Ruth whispered.

"Are you going to shoot the panther?"

Ruth shook her head. "But the courts can decide if she's innocent."

"She's on our side," Luke said.

He heard shouts from the front of the house. The police would arrive any minute.

"Go," Luke said.

"We'll meet again," the witch said.

Luke watched the witch and panther walk into the night.

"We'll be in trouble," Ruth said.

Luke shrugged. He didn't care; he had Molly and William. His family was together; he wanted no more.

EPILOGUE

Luke stood in a bleak northern graveyard. He kept glancing towards the twisting road that led to the old stone church. Nothing moved. The road was the only way to get here unless you hiked across the moors. Ruth petted her golden retriever, Jack and Amelia stared into the open grave, and the local vicar stood in silence.

It was an exposed location; the only vegetation, apart from wild flowers and lichen, was a dead tree that stood about ten yards from the grave. It looked like it'd been blasted by lightning.

They waited for the final mourner.

Hidden from sight, behind gravestones and by the church, were police snipers. Uniformed police waited inside the church.

Luke looked at the coffin. For some reason, the witch had insisted that it not be nailed shut. Although it seemed beyond belief, he prayed she wouldn't attempt some form of necromancy. If she showed up at all. So much of what had happened over the past six months was beyond belief but true. Luke wondered how many other unimagined truths existed in the world.

"I still can't believe you let her go," Jack said.

"She helped save the life of my wife and child." Luke wasn't normally emotional, but he felt his eyes moisten. "Her panther saved my life, too." He still couldn't believe he had his family back; it was a happiness beyond anything he'd hoped for.

"She saved my life, too," Amelia added.

Jack nodded. "True, but she's killed men in cold blood. The law should decide her guilt. If she turns up, then maybe it still will."

Once, Luke would have agreed with Jack; he no longer did. People were complex, and so was the world. He wasn't sure justice would be served by arresting her. He also knew that Jack's feelings were deeply coloured by her connection with Angel. Although, since Angel's death, Jack's attitude towards the witch had softened a little.

No one knew why she'd insisted on this desolate place for the funeral. It could have been that, unknown to any of them, Angel had some link with the area. Luke suspected she wanted to be able to see if it was a trap, which it was. The chance to arrest or kill her was too tempting for the authorities.

"Do you think she'll come?" Jack asked.

Luke shrugged. "I hope not. It seems wrong to arrest her."

"We won't be able to stop them if she does," Jack said.

"I know."

"When is she coming?" the vicar asked. He'd already made his irritation known about the police in and around his church.

They ignored him.

Luke then noticed an orange light to his left. A line had appeared on the tree. Mist seemed to be seeping from it. He exchanged glances with Amelia, who'd noticed it, too.

The orange witch walked from the mist. Her red hair seemed to brighten when the sun briefly shone through the clouds, and her eyes glowed as brightly as those of the black panther that padded by her side.

"She's here," Luke said.

The vicar started. He backed away, staring at the woman with wide eyes. "I want no evil in my church."

The witch glanced around the graveyard.

"I said five people."

"You don't think the authorities would ever agree to that?" Jack said.

She smiled. "No." Then she pointed at the coffin. "Open it."

"This is highly irregular," the vicar said.

She shrugged. "I need to see the body. Perhaps I can bring him back to life."

Luke's mouth fell open. "You can't be—" he started.

She grinned. "I'm joking. But I still need to see the body."

Luke and Jack removed the lid. The vicar stepped forward.

"I really must object."

He froze when the panther growled. Darta then jumped into the grave and put her head inside the coffin to smell Angel's body. She mewled softly before returning to the witch's side.

"We both had to see for ourselves," the witch said. "You can bury him now."

Luke and Jack drove nails into the coffin, then the vicar began the ceremony.

"William Angel Provost was a sinner. He murdered men, women, and children. Yet he sought to atone for his sins."

Luke watched the witch, unable to read her expression.

"He sacrificed his life in order to complete his mission, and he gave his life to save this woman."

The vicar looked at her uncertainly.

"Or whatever you are."

The vicar said a prayer. "May he rest in peace."

When the service was done, Luke turned to the witch. "Who are you?"

She gave him an indecipherable look. "That's a long story, and I have little time."

She glanced at the police, who were standing openly by the gravestones, before turning to Luke.

"She's sorry for taking your finger," the witch said.

Luke became aware that he'd been rubbing the stump.

"You can speak to the panther?"

"I can speak to all animals."

"I don't know why you came today," Luke said, "but this may not be good for you."

"I came to pay my respects to an imperfect man who, at the end of his life, tried to make amends."

"And failed," Jack said.

"He was deeply flawed." She glanced again at the police now walking towards her. "I knew about them, but hoped they'd wait until the funeral was finished."

"But not a second longer," Jack said. He turned to the vicar. "Keep talking."

"I've finished."

"Recite a prayer!" Jack could be blunt.

"Please," Ruth said.

The vicar's face reddened, but he continued.

Jack raised his hand, and the police hesitated.

"Where did Eva Noone go?" Luke asked.

"I'm not sure," the witch said, "but not to her home world."

"And the demon?" Jack asked.

"To some sort of limbo."

"So you don't know where she went," Luke persisted.

"She won't come back, if that's what you mean. I've closed the way. At least you don't have her to worry about."

"But other stuff came through, right?" Jack asked.

"A handful of lesser sorcerers. I suggest you kill them."

Luke guessed that MI7 may have more work after all, but hopefully of a less intense kind.

"But they have magic," Luke said.

"As I told Angel, bullets are faster than magic, and the remaining aliens lack the power of those who are dead or gone."

"What else is here?" Luke asked.

"Three lizards in one of the northern forests, but if you leave them, they'll probably leave you alone. In fact, I recommend not entering any of the alien forests, especially the northern one."

"Something's been reported in the English Channel," Ruth said.

"The snapping turtles. Don't go near them; they're dangerous, but I expect that after a few hundred years, they'll get bored with this world and travel to another."

"A few hundred years?" Ruth said. "That's not normal."

"There's nothing normal about them," the witch said.

The vicar finished the prayer and walked quickly towards the church.

"You never told us your name," Luke said.

"Lucy is the one I use most." She glanced at the police. "I must go."

Lucy walked towards the tree, which was still surrounded by mist. Luke was surprised to see that it wasn't actually dead; it had several shoots on its branches, and a tiny red fruit grew from one of them.

"What about the sickness?" he asked.

"Now Noone's gone and her followers dead or dispersed, it'll fade. It's already lessening," Lucy said.

The police moved closer. One of them had a loud hailer.

"You're under arrest."

"I just want to walk to the tree," Lucy said.

"Stop, or I'll order my men to fire."

Lucy stopped next to the tree.

"Did your magic take Olney's ghost?" Luke asked. He wasn't sure what he'd seen that day, but he couldn't stop thinking about it.

"Some things are beyond magic." Her face was serious. Then she picked the tiny red fruit from the tree and gave it to Ruth. "Plant it on the grave." She smiled at Ruth's reaction. "It's not the forbidden fruit, but it's special."

"What is it?" Ruth asked.

"An alien graft to help cure an alien sickness. When you visit Angel's grave, you'll see." She paused as the golden retriever nuzzled her hand. "Oh, and the alien trees have started to talk to the native ones."

Ruth's eyes widened.

"I'd wanted to study them," Lucy said, "but I didn't have the time. The trees in the north are waking up." Lucy grinned at Ruth's surprised expression and then glanced again at the approaching police.

"You'd better step back," a police officer said through the loud hailer.

"You're going through the portal, aren't you?" Luke asked. The orange light shone in the mist.

"Prisons don't appeal to me."

"Where will you go?" Amelia asked.

Lucy rubbed the panther's fur. "She's a huntress. And we have a trail to follow."

"Why do you do this?" Luke asked. "You don't have to."

"I let loose evil into the multiverse. And if I don't do it, who will?"

No one had an answer for that.

The police were now only fifteen yards away.

"Goodbye."

Lucy's eyes glowed, and then, with the panther at her heels, she stepped into the mist. Light flickered from within, and the mist evaporated, leaving only the old tree with new life growing from its branches. The orange witch had vanished.

The police ran to the tree.

"Where's she gone?" a police sergeant asked, as he walked around it.

"Somewhere in the multiverse," Luke said.

The police officer gave him a sour look, and he ordered his men to spread out and search the graveyard.

Luke shook his head; they'd never find her. The four friends and their dog returned to Angel's grave, where Ruth pushed the red fruit into the soft ground.

"I wonder what will grow."

PLEASE LEAVE A REVIEW

If you enjoyed The Orange Witch, please leave a review. Reviews can help a writer's work be read by more readers and help promote their career, so allowing more books to be written. Thank you!

BOOKS BY NED MARCUS

Blue Prometheus Series

- Young Aina #0
- Blue Prometheus #1
- The Darkling Odyssey #2
- Fire Rising #3

Orange Storm Series (duology)

- Orange Storm #1
- The Orange Witch #2

SHORT STORIES

Ned Marcus also writes novelettes, and short fantasy and science fiction stories.

Visit nedmarcus.com for details.

KEEP IN TOUCH!

Visit nedmarcus.com to sign up to the Ned Marcus newsletter and receive free copies of the novelette Young Aina and the short story The Huntress of Prometheus—prequels to the Blue Prometheus series.

ABOUT THE AUTHOR

Ned Marcus is an author of fantasy and science fiction. He writes novels and short stories. He lives in East Asia.

nedmarcus.com

ACKNOWLEDGMENTS

Thank you to my editor, Parisa Zolfaghari, and to the members of Taipei Fantasy and SF Writers' Group for their help with this novel.

www.ingramcontent.com/pod-product-compliance
Lightning Source LLC
LaVergne TN
LVHW040039080526
838202LV00045B/3406